NO LONGER THE PROPERTY OF
BALDWIN PUBLIC LIBRARY

The Further Adventures of
Menachem-Mendl
(NEW YORK — WARSAW — VIENNA — YEHUPETZ)

Library of Modern Jewish Literature

Other titles in the Library of Modern Jewish Literature

The Further Adventures of
Menachem-Mendl

(NEW YORK — WARSAW — VIENNA — YEHUPETZ)

Sholem Aleichem

Translated from the Yiddish by **Aliza Shevrin**

SYRACUSE UNIVERSITY PRESS

BALDWIN PUBLIC LIBRARY

Copyright © 2001 by Aliza Shevrin

All Rights Reserved

First Edition 2001

01 02 03 04 05 06   6 5 4 3 2 1

The paper used in this publication meets the minimum requirements of American National Standard for Information Sciences—Permanence of Paper for Printed Library Materials, ANSI Z39.48-1984.∞™

Library of Congress Cataloging-in-Publication Data

Sholem Aleichem, 1859–1916.
   [Short stories. English. Selections]
   The further adventures of Menachem-Mendl : New York—Warsaw—Vienna—Yehupetz
/Sholem Aleichem ; translated by Aliza Shevrin.
      p. cm. — (Library of modern Jewish literature)
   ISBN 0-8156-0677-X (alk. Paper)
   1. Sholem Aleichem, 1859–1916—Translations into English. I. Shevrin, Aliza. II. Title. III. Series.
PJ5129.R2 A27 2001
839'.133—dc21   00-055701

Manufactured in the United States of America

To the memory of Avram Lis,
DIRECTOR OF BET SHOLEM ALEICHEM, TEL AVIV, ISRAEL,
Distinguished Yiddish Scholar and Archivist,

and to
my youngest granddaughter, Hannah Page Shevrin

Aliza Shevrin has translated and published five novels by Sholem Aleichem, including *Marienbad, In the Storm, The Nightingale,* and *The Bloody Hoax,* as well as three collections of his children's short stories. She has also translated and published short stories and a novel by I. B. Singer. Ms. Shevrin lives in Ann Arbor, Michigan, where she teaches Yiddish and lectures about her work.

Introduction and Acknowledgments

Tevye and Menachem-Mendl are two of Sholem Aleichem's greatest and most beloved characters, their very names evoking laughter, sighs and memories in innumerable readings and dramatizations. They are also synonymous in Yiddish literature with the Jewish shtetl, their devotion to family, their eternal striving by whatever imaginative means to survive in a hostile world and, above all, their absolute love of God and the Jewish people.

Sholem Aleichem's epistolary novel, *Menachem-Mendl*, was written in 1892, appeared sporadically over the next eighteen years in the journal *Haynt* (Today), was published in 1909, and is included in the twenty-eight volumes of *Ale Verk fun Sholem Aleichem* (Collected Works of Sholem Aleichem). The first volume was translated into English by Sholem Aleichem's late granddaughter, Tamara Kahana, and published in 1969 by G. P. Putnam's Sons as *The Adventures of Menachem-Mendl*. Beloved by readers and critics alike, Menachem-Mendl came to represent the definitive *luftmensch,* the man "living on air," the Jewish Everyman, the product of the two-thousand-year struggle of the Jews to survive by their wits and spirit under adverse and at times impossible conditions. The first volume consists of Menachem-Mendl's many failed hare-brained schemes as a jack-of-all-trades and speculator on the fringes of the stock exchange, all of which are described in hilarious detail in letters to his wife, Sheyne-Sheyndl, in Kasrilevka, Sholem Aleichem's generic name for any poor Jewish town. Sheyne-Sheyndl's letters to him tell of her struggle with the crushing poverty and ever-present persecution of life in the shtetl as well as of her great desire to have her husband home. The book ends when, after failing time and again, Menachem-Mendl finally abandons his long-suffering wife and flees to America to seek a livelihood.

Most readers thought this was the last of Menachem-Mendl. But during one of my visits to Bet Sholem Aleichem, the archives and library in Tel Aviv, the late respected director, Avram Lis, generously gave me a *second* volume of letters between Menachem-Mendl and Sheyne-Sheyndl, written in 1913 and previously untranslated into English and unpublished in the

United States. It consists of twenty-eight letters from Menachem-Mendl and seventeen from his wife.

In this book Menachem-Mendl has returned to Warsaw after a disastrous stay in America and has a new job as a writer on a Warsaw newspaper. His assignment is to offer opinions on world events, politics, people, wars and Jewish problems; he will write about these matters in his letters to his wife, but, unknown to her, they will be printed in the newspaper. Sheyne-Sheyndl's letters to him will not. Still the same impetuous, justice-loving Menachem-Mendl, he is no longer a desperate-to-survive businessman and marginal broker but a journalist and man of politics.

Through Menachem-Mendl's letters we share the perspective of the unworldly, small-town Jew who transforms accounts of international intrigue and politics into basic shtetl language. These events stimulate harebrained schemes involving kings, toppled emperors, and international millionaires in addition to grand plans to find a homeland for the Jews. Menachem-Mendl is sent to cover the Zionist Congress in Vienna, and from there we get a full description of events, including the movement to adopt Hebrew as Israel's official language. The many delegates mentioned by Menachem-Mendl in his account of the Congress were noted Zionist leaders, as well as former presidents of various organizations such as the World Zionist Organization, educators, philanthropists, writers and politicians.

There is a great deal of Sholem Aleichem in Menachem-Mendl. Sholem Aleichem also wheeled and dealed on the Kiev stock exchange, at which he was a failure, losing a great deal of money, before turning exclusively to writing. Maria Waife Goldberg, Sholem Aleichem's daughter, writes in *My Father, Sholem Aleichem,* her excellent biography of him, "the world of Menachem-Mendl was so much like the world my father lived in for the first eighteen of his thirty years of literary creativity . . . but he found such a life (on the *birzha,* the stock exchange) exasperating, mortifying." Sholem Aleichem also attended a Zionist Congress and shared Menachem-Mendl's Zionist passion and love for the Yiddish language.

Sheyne-Sheyndl is the flywheel balancing her husband's flight into one fantasy after another, reminding him in her letters of how hard everyday life is for herself, her family, and the residents of Kasrilevka, who live in the path of the swiftly encroaching cataclysm. Her letters are peppered with quotes from her mother's wise (and sometimes cracked) aphorisms as she struggles to make sense of Menachem-Mendl's schemes while urging him to be sensible and return home.

I have made every attempt to convey the difference between Sheyne-Sheyndl's down-to-earth practicality and lack of education and worldliness and Menachem-Mendl's newly acquired worldly preoccupations through the kind of language they employ in their letters. Hers is blunt, elementary, full of curses upon her many enemies' heads, and highly idiomatic. (Pity the poor translator!) His are full of political terms, some probably newly learned, hinting at an intimate relationship with every crowned head of Europe and Asia as well as knowledge of their political motives and strategies. He throws together Russian, Hebrew, and idiomatic Yiddish peppered with biblical allusions to make his points and to make the reader believe he really *can* change the events of history. (Again, pity the poor translator!) He is also aware that the letters are for the benefit of the newspaper readers, and he elevates the level of his language accordingly. The historian or economist attempting to follow the events and business dealings described by him will be thoroughly confused, as in all probability Menachem-Mendl was.

As for that poor translator mentioned above, I must say that there is indeed great pleasure as well as frustration in tracking down these obscure words and phrases and their application, more, I believe, than in any other book I have translated. A very few, words and phrases, in spite of much effort, I could not find and do apologize for their omission. I am grateful to my learned and helpful consultants in Yiddish, Hebrew, and Russian. I give thanks to Sara Kuperschmidt; Rivka Rubinfeld, my daily walking companion of over fifteen years; Anya Abramzon; Elina Zilberberg; Prof. Herbert Paper; and Prof. Gavriel Shapiro. My daughter-in-law, Caroline, was instrumental in helping me manage the new-fangled disk. Throughout my years as a translator of Sholem Aleichem, his granddaughter, Bel Kaufman, and her husband, Sidney Gluck, have been generous, supportive friends and I thank them. Most special and essential was the ongoing, page-by-page collaboration of my husband, Howie, who also translated the novel's poems. His literary gifts and linguistic ear have always been my inspiration. He has always acted as my in-house editor and indispensible "second set of ears." I love the rest of him too.

Ann Arbor, Michigan   Aliza Shevrin
February 1999

The Further Adventures of
Menachem-Mendl
(NEW YORK — WARSAW — VIENNA — YEHUPETZ)

1. Menachem-Mendl from Warsaw to His Wife, Sheyne-Sheyndl, in Kasrilevka

To my dear, wise, and modest wife, Sheyne-Sheyndl, may God grant her many years!

FIRST OF ALL, let me tell you that I am, blessed be His name, in good health and spirits, and may the Blessed One grant that we hear from one another only good news of comfort and salvation for us and for all of Israel—Amen.

SECOND OF ALL, let me tell you that I am in Warsaw. How did I end up in Warsaw? Listen. It's hard to believe.

From the last letter I sent you with money from America, you already know how I had to suffer the torments of hell, my life made wretched in that free land of Columbus, wasting my time bowing to their idols, breaking my back, eating a crust of bread maybe once in three days, changing a shirt maybe once in three weeks so as not to come to anyone for help, God forbid—until the Creator, blessed be He, came to my aid. And after long and bitter suffering, I finally managed to a find a way to make a bit of a living, a respectable and honest living as befits me: namely, I became a newspaper writer and occupied myself with writing. And as I wrote you in my previous letter, if remember, I was highly successful at it and prospered. Naturally, I started small and climbed higher and higher, which is the way it's done in America. At first I sold newspapers on the streets for a kopek (there it is called a "penny"), until I realized this was not for me. I would never become a Rockefeller or a Vanderblit selling newspapers on the street. So I thought it over and decided to read through those newspapers. What were they writing about that made the crowds snap them up like hotcakes? And I soon figured out that it wasn't such a difficult trade, this writing. Hadn't I once been a bit of a writer myself, if you remember, when I was in Russia? So I made it my business to drop into their offices to see how it was done and I was astounded!

First of all I got to know the redactors (there they call them "editors") and the writers and I discussed every detail of their work with them. What shall I tell you, my dear wife? All you need is luck, nothing more! So I began to think, would it bother God if things were the other way around? Let *them* hawk papers on the street and *Menachem-Mendl* will sit in their place writing! And on the sly, with one eye, as it were, I observed how they put together this stuff—and I realized that I had been a big fool. I had thought that everything they printed in their papers they had actually written *themselves*. It isn't that way at all. What a joke! You would really find this amazing! A fellow sits at a large table (there it is called a "desk"), piled high with newspapers from all over the world, snipping away with a pair of scissors like a cloak-cutter and opposite him sits a boy with fat lips, also with scissors in hand, cutting up a novel. I could swear it was familiar, one of those trashy Shomer romances. The boy with the fat lips reads the book while chewing something and snips away, here a page, there a page—and by morning, you have a story! "Eh-eh-eh-" I thought to myself, "Now that I know how you do it, I can do this trick better than you!" And I went off to the market and bought up a whole load of story books of all kinds and threw myself into the work in true American style: restitching old rags, coming up with one new story out of two or three old ones, all garbled and tangled together under a shocking headline—and it worked like a charm!

It won't surprise you to learn that in short order I was working for three papers at once, of course under a different name at each one. What does God do? The Jewish writers in America declare a strike! Since Columbus discovered America and since the beginning of the world, no one anywhere had ever heard of Jewish writers declaring a strike! Just my luck—with God's help Menachem-Mendl becomes a bit of a writer, begins to make an honest living and can send home a few dollars and they suddenly get the urge to declare a strike! When I visited my three editorial offices, one after the other, the bosses told me, "What difference does it make to you, Reb Menachem-Mendl, strike-shmike? What business do you have with those rascals, the strikers? Do your work. You can even come out ahead from this nonsense." Sounds good, eh? My door opened and in came two young men, also workers like myself, but real rabble-rousers, and announced to me in these words, "We've been sent to you, Mister Menachem-Mendl, from the new writers' union and ask that you please be so kind as to lay down scissor and paste and not dare to write so much as a word for the duration of our strike! And if," they said, "you don't listen and do try to write, our writers' guild will consider you a strikebreaker, and a strikebreaker has his bones broken! That's the way it is here in America." Hearing those words, I said to them in their language, "Alright!" In our language it would be, "I hear you."

In short, why should I go on at length, my dear wife, I saw this was a dead end. I had to say good-bye to the pen. But time doesn't stand still, one week follows another, my purse was running low, the few dollars were dwindling away, where would this end? And just for spite, I was really falling in love with this writing trade. I couldn't get interested in any other work. I suffered plenty! And then I heard from home the cry, "Amnesty! Amnesty!" What does this mean? All Jews would get equal rights under the law—and if that's the case, who needs America? Would it be such a bad idea, I was thinking, for me to do an about-face and go back home across the ocean? Once they begin talking about amnesty, it's a different story and a different government! In short, I bid farewell to Columbus and his land of liberty, let them live and be well till the Messiah comes—what kind of freedom is it that when a Jew wants to make a living, they send someone to tell him he's a strikebreaker and they'll break his bones? I bought myself passage and back I came, with the intention of going directly home to Kasrilevka.

But till I survived the crossing and lived to reach the Polish border, and with a passport not worth the paper it was printed on, I went through hell. In the meantime, nothing at all came of the amnesty. They just promised to forgive the three-hundred-ruble fine for god-knows-what violations and it's most probable that they won't even do that either—so there you have Jewish luck and Jewish salvation and consolation! If that's the case, what will I do at home when two more packs of trouble await me there? One brother of mine, Nekhemiah, blessed be his memory, as you know, died, who knows how long ago and they forgot to remove his name from the register. My other sibling was mistakenly put down as a male although she is really a female, my sister Sossi, who that idiot of a rabbiner had written down as *Yossi*. Now they're most likely trying to find "him" and for those two I'll probably have to pay twice the three-hundred-ruble fine. That's all I need! In short, my dear wife, you yourself will tell me that I did the right thing by not coming home and did better going directly to Warsaw. And when you reach the end of this letter, you will realize that we have an almighty God and He works wonders. But one thing I ask of you. Don't get upset with me, don't jump to conclusions and hear me out to the end.

I arrived in Warsaw cleaned out, without a penny to my name! The city, God bless it, is large, full of people, lively, busy, everyone rushing, everyone doing business, almost like in America, forgive the comparison.

Still I was the only one wandering the city without any work and with an empty stomach besides. And to make matters worse, my heart was pulling me to my writing trade to which I've become so deeply attached that I can't live without it! What to do! But I was among Jews who are, after all, children of Israel, so I began to inquire about where the biggest Jewish newspaper might be located. They looked at me strangely: What's a "newspaper"? I explained to them that newspaper is the word for gazette. So they said, "You could have just said gazette." I then said, "It's not my fault, I just came from America, and in their funny language a gazette is a newspaper." They said, "A peculiar language!" I said, "Peculiar or not, better tell me where to find your biggest newspaper—tphoo! I mean, your biggest gazette?" And they directed me to a certain address. "There you'll find the editorial offices of the very biggest gazette." When I arrived, I looked around. This is the biggest gazette? The exact opposite of America, down to the last detail! In America a publishing house is a tower of twelve floors, with gilt letters and everything up-to-date! And here, a nothing, a courtyard like any other courtyard. A building like any other building. I went into the main editorial office—full of Jews. I asked, "Which one of you is the editor—tphoo! I mean the redactor?" They looked me over and answered, "What do you want? Do you want to buy a gazette or do you want to place an ad?" I said, "I don't want a gazette and I don't need to place an ad. I need to speak to the redactor." They exchanged puzzled glances, probably thinking, what can this little Jew want with the redactor? But they replied in a quite friendly way, "Sit, the redactor will be here soon."

I sat myself down on pins and needles because who knows if I could work anything out? And who knows what kind of a person the redactor was. I imagined that this must be some real big shot like those American big shots with fat bellies, automobiles, always with an "alright." You won't believe it. It turned out that I was approached by this little man with a goatee who took me in with one glance and said to me, "What is it you want?" I was thinking, what does *he* want? And I replied to him, "What does it matter to you what I want?" He became a bit angry and said to me, "Look, mister, what do you want? We don't have time to waste here." "Just like in America," I said. "There they never have any time either. 'Hurry up,' they say in their language. I want nothing, I just want to see the editor—tphoo! the redactor." He smiled and said, still a little gruffly, "I'm the redactor. What's on your mind? Who are you?" "Who am I?" I said, "A Jew from Kasrilevka is what I am. Actually, I'm really a Mazepevker but in Kasrilevka I'm accepted as one of theirs. For a time I did business in Yehupetz, but now I'm coming from America and, you may not know my name, it's

Menachem-Mendl." As soon as I uttered those words, the angry face of the redactor suddenly changed and he spoke to me in a different tone, "Really? You're really *the* Menachem-Mendl? Welcome, Reb Menachem-Mendl. How are you? And how are things going for you? What are you doing here? Why are you standing? Why aren't you sitting? But wait, listen. Come into my office." "Eh!" he commanded in Polish, "Bring tea! Two glasses of tea! With food!"

Why should I go on at length, my dear wife? This was only the beginning of the wonders that followed! Before I even had a chance to tell him everything I had suffered in America, before I had a chance to tell him that I needed a position, perhaps with a salary, he stopped me and said to me in these words, and I am writing it word for word so you will know what a mighty God we have, "Listen carefully, Reb Menachem-Mendl," he said to me, stroking his goatee, his head nodding knowingly, his thoughts racing, "Listen carefully, pay attention to what I say. I'll make you a deal, a nice deal that will be good for you and for me and for all of us. You need to make a living, you want to work? I will give you work. Here you have a desk, ink and a pen and paper, sit down and write . . ."

God almighty, I was thinking, there is a heaven after all! And I replied to him, "What do you want me to write for you—stories?" He became a little gruff again and began to wave his hands and shuffle his feet. "No-no! Not stories! Stories we have more than enough! Just write those letters to your wife once a week, maybe twice a week, as you've been doing. Your name is well known (Do you hear those words?), your letters have a reputation (How do you like *those* words?). You write your letters, he said, and before you send them off, I will have them printed exactly as you write them in my newspaper—do you understand what I am saying?" These were the redactor's very words as he took me in with his gaze and I was thinking: for everything there is a time. For Menachem-Mendl's letters too there is also a time. But I was still somewhat reluctant and said to him, "Very well, you want to print my letters, so print them. But won't you want me to revise them. . . ?" He didn't let me finish and said to me, "No! On the contrary! Exactly as you always write to your Sheyne-Sheyndl. I want you to write about whatever your heart desires: about politics, about wars, about decrees, about troubles, about business, about the world, about people, whatever you hear or see, what you read and what you know. Remember, you mustn't hold back, just as if you were at home. And I," he said to me, now more congenially, rubbing his hands together, "I will, God willing, pay you for this." "Really?" I say. "Really," he said, "I will see to it that you have what to eat and drink, a suit to wear and cigarettes to smoke and spending money in your pocket so you can enjoy a coffee with a friend along with everything else a human being requires. And as it is getting close to Passover and your Sheyne-Sheyndl is probably looking forward to a little cash, I will have them send her on account a hundreder for now."

At this point, my dear wife, my head was spinning! I thought I was dreaming. It had to be a dream! But it was no dream. I saw with my very own eyes how he sent off a hundreder to you. May I as quickly see only good things for you and for our children, amen, God of all the universe! And as I don't have time now—I have just now rolled up my sleeves and set to work—I am making this short. God willing, in my next letter I will write you everything at length. In the meantime, may God grant us all health and success. Kiss the children for me and send my best and most friendly regards to your parents and to the whole family, each and every one!

From me your husband Menachem-Mendl

ALMOST FORGOT! I arranged with the redactor that he would only print the letters I write to you, but not your letters to me. I gave him to understand you have a short temper and sometimes come out with a harsh word. He promised me he wouldn't. You can write me whatever you please and not worry because except for me no one will read them. I just beg you, my dear wife, not to be too upset. You yourself can see that God doesn't want me to be a Kasrilevker. He knows how much I long to return to Kasrilevka. After I saw America and had a chance to see those people, your Kasrilevka has become to me dearer by 99 percent, as God is my witness.

As above.

2. Menachem-Mendl from Warsaw to His Wife Sheyne-Sheyndl in Kasrilevka

To my dear, wise and modest wife, Sheyne-Sheyndl, may God grant her many years!

FIRST OF ALL, let me tell you that I am, blessed be His name, in good health and spirits, and may the Blessed One grant that we hear from one another only good news of comfort and salvation for us and for all of Israel—Amen.

SECOND OF ALL, let me tell you, my dear wife, I say to the devil with that golden land of America with her Columbus and her freedom and her "alright" and her high towers reaching to the clouds and her "business." With God's help, it is going much better for me here than in America. May it not get worse. Here you get up in the morning, say your prayers, grab a bite, take your cane, and go right to your office at the newspaper. You are greeted with a "Good morning" from all sides: "Good morning to you, Reb Menachem-Mendl!" "A good morning, a good year." And you go right to your desk, you sit down to your work, and bury yourself in politics. You will ask how one can bury oneself in politics? I will explain it carefully so you will understand exactly how this can be done.

First of all you ask for tea and the goy serves you tea and cigarettes like royalty. The newspapers are already waiting for you, piled so high that in Kasrilevka you would have enough to read for a year. Not that you are obliged to read everything. Only the gist, what is interesting and important. And what is important today if not war? War—that's the main thing. As soon as a Jew opens his eyes, he wants to know what's new with the war. What are the dispatches from Constantinople, Sofia, Belgrade and Albania? How can I tell you about this? I have in these last few weeks read so much about the war the Slovenes are waging against the Turks, that at night I dream of nothing else but blue pants, red skullcaps, half-moons, Adrianople, Scutari, Khalemonja, and other wild names that even a goy when sober would never be able to pronounce. You realize, of course, that no one is as confused about politics and how wars are fought as your Menachem-Mendl. I do know the Turk cut off his own hands. Had he asked me, the Turk, I would never have allowed him to defeat himself! I would have advised him, that Uncle Ishmael, to try first to work things out peacefully. A few months back he was in a position to work it out easily. I am as certain as today is the first day of Passover all over the world that the war would never have come to Adrianople, despite the boast of those four Slovenian kings—the Bulgarian, the Serb, the Greek, and even that beggar from Montenegro who makes such a fuss—that they would celebrate the holiday there. It was a miracle that those high and mighty powers finally stepped in and openly warned that big shot from Montenegro to stop dreaming of glory and to retreat from Albania or else . . . He would already know what "or else" meant because of the ships and cannons those high and mighty powers paraded before him as "peace makers."

Those ships may be German, French, and English, but they are really sent by "us," I mean by that "our" Russia, but "we" ourselves haven't sent out a single ship, because "we" don't have any ships in those places and as your mother would say, "If you don't have any fingers, you can't make a fist." But it doesn't matter, "we" have the best intentions. It turns out that when that Montenegran big shot saw those ships with ready cannons, he wasn't terribly impressed by the warning and drew strength from his ancient heritage. In the meantime he snuck into Scutari and took over the little city, but it won't make any difference—they'll soon ask him to kindly leave. As it happens, those high and mighty powers are well respected, and if not for that the Slovenian crowd would long ago have taken over Khalemanja (let a goy try to pronounce that name!) and would long ago have been in Istanbul. And I will tell you, my dear wife, the honest truth. I really worry that the Bulgarian, God forbid, might in the end sneak into Istanbul, and because he doesn't dare stop, will go further and further. So what will happen then? What if those high and mighty powers really want Istanbul for themselves? In the first place, they will certainly want it. Why shouldn't they want it? And in the second place, what will "we" say if it comes to the Dardanelles? How can "we" do without the Dardanelles? Will "we" keep quiet? That's another story. That can lead to a real war among the big powers themselves: "we" and the French and the English on one side and the Germans and Franz Josef and the Italians on the other. In the midst of all that mayhem the Slovenes would get what Pharoah got in Egypt, but the Turk would get it too, woe unto his red yarmulke. His biggest problem, I tell you again, is that there is no one to give him the right advice. Do you know what he needs? He needs a broker. If a good broker were to intercede for him, it would be altogether different. It was the same with Mother Russia and Franz Josef. If those two "brokers," the prime minister of Russia, Witte on one side and Roosenvelt on the other, hadn't mixed in, who knows what would have happened? How much those brokers made off with in that business I won't tell you. I wasn't there. They surely didn't lose anything; of that I am absolutely certain. I was once a broker on the stock exchange, may it never happen again. On the stock exchange it's a given that merchants sometimes fail but a broker never loses a kopek.

Now that I've cleared up these political matters for you, my dear wife, let me tell you how I spend my day at my new job. After I've finished with politics, that is, tired my eyes out reading newspapers and smoked my fill of cigarettes, I take my cane and go off to my coffee house for a coffee and a chat with a friend. My coffee house is on the Nalevkes at Khoskl Kotik's. Why at Khoskl Kotik's? To spite the Polack! The Polacks have placed a ban on the Jews, they call it a boycott, which means you can't buy from Jews or sell to Jews—no dealings with a Jew. So if it's a boycott, why don't I also follow along? There's a real problem with the local Jews: they don't have brains! Just because the Polack doesn't want anything to do with Jews, just because he spits in the Jew's face and boycotts him on all sides, the local Jew has to go out of his way to rush to the Polish shops, to the Polish coffee houses, to the Polish theaters, to the Polish lawyers, to the Polish doctors. They are not to be believed! Well, as for the upper class, the aristocrats that call themselves "Moses's Polacks"—I'm not talking about them. For them it's a source of honor and pride to be worthy of leading their daughters to the altar in a Polish church. That those Jews will sacrifice themselves for the rich Pole, speak no other language but Polish, support the *Dva Groshe* organization, hate a Jew and help to boycott Jews—is no surprise. They are known here quite well and they aren't considered Jews. In fact they are neither Jews nor Polacks, but some strange in-between. I am talking about the Jews with the long gabardines and with the little hats who pray in the little Chasidic shuls and go long distances to visit their rebbi. Where are their brains and hasn't it occurred to them to answer the enemy and his Polish boycott with a Jewish boycott? It seems it doesn't require any great talent or money, but only to have your head screwed on right and one drop of honor in your heart.

There is a city not far from Warsaw called Lodz, a city with a good number of Jews, long life to them. Out of spite, the local Jewish bakers decide before Passover to hire, not Jews, but goyim, to bake their matzos. Well, I ask you, my dear wife, why does our mighty God destroy two cities, Sodom and Gemorrah, but forgets entirely about Lodz! I know you're not allowed to say it, but when you see Jews themselves boycotting Jews everywhere, it breaks your heart! We spend hours and hours talking together, Khaskl Kotik and I, over a coffee, talking about our fellow Jews and what they could have accomplished right here in Warsaw with this boycott if they just had a bit more backbone.

Mostly the talk is about politics. These days, you must know, there is no writing done except about politics! For good reason I thank God daily for leading me to this very trade that is so necessary these days, that is admired and that people pay money for—a timely trade, this writing. I pray to God I will be able to accomplish a little something through politics for the world and a little for myself as well. These are times, my dear wife, when everybody is out for himself! And add to that that I've just arrived from a country exactly like this one, from America! My head is swimming with all kinds of plans and projects. One project of mine is so grand and ambitious that if, with God's help, it succeeds, I can become so famous that I will be known throughout the world! But as I don't have any time now—I must rush off to the office to read dispatches—I am making this short. I hope in the next letter to write everything in greater detail. In the meantime, may God grant us all health and success. Kiss the children for me, send regards to your mother and all the family from me in the most friendly way.

From me your husband Menachem-Mendl

ALMOST FORGOT: About what we were just discussing, that Jews help boycott Jews and employ goyim instead of their own, listen my dear wife, to this story that happened right here in Warsaw. Before Passover this year some rich Jews from Radomishla came to town to spend some money. What were they up to? They were marrying off a daughter. They needed to have sumptuous silk and velvet garments sewn for a trousseau. Whom did they commission so they could earn a few thousand? Jewish seamstresses? Heaven protect us! Since when does a Jew give another Jew work especially after coming all the way to Warsaw from Radomishla? Did you ever hear of anything like that? Now I am sitting here and beating my brains out trying to figure out who these rich folks from Radomishla can be who have become so spoiled, so spendthrift, and are so well known everywhere that they write about them in the newspapers? I am afraid they are those same Radomishla crowd with whom I once did business on the stock exchange. God help me, I brokered the sale of several factories for them. If that's so, it's really bad. If those are the wealthy Radomishlers I am thinking of, then not only are they millionaires, they are also very pious Chasidim. And once you have a Radomishler and a millionaire and a Chasid and especially a very pious one into the bargain, then you have big problems.

As above.

3. Menachem-Mendl from Warsaw to His Wife Shayne-Sheyndl in Kasrilevka

To my dear, wise, and modest wife, Sheyne-Sheyndl, may God grant her many years!

FIRST OF ALL, let me tell you that I am, blessed be His name, in good health and spirits, and may the Blessed One grant that we hear from one another only good news of comfort and salvation for us and for all of Israel—Amen.

SECOND OF ALL, let me tell you, that the aggravation I am having from the Turk is too much to bear! I can't eat, I can't sleep, I go around in a dither. They have beset our poor Uncle Ishmael. They want to drive him crazy! Remember how I wrote you how the whole world was standing by watching and waiting to see what would happen once Scutari was taken? Who do you think finally took it? Who else but King Nikolai of Montenegro. The time for the Messiah is upon us, I tell you! May God not punish me for these words, but have you ever heard of a king who insists on putting the Turkish sultan's feet to the fire? This despite the pleading of ministers and kings who begged him as one would the devil himself, at first amicably, "Why do you need Scutari? What earthly good will it do you?" Better take the few millions as payoff while the taking is good, because those high and mighty powers will not allow a nothing kingdom like Montenegro to have dreams of glory about swallowing up big cities. When they realized a friendly approach wasn't doing the trick, they took a hard line, sent diplomatic protests and placed a naval blockade, as I wrote you, of several fine ships with cannons along the shores of Albania.

In short, he softened some, the king of Montenegro, and began to bargain. The price went up, the price went down, and the dispatches began flying back and forth. They were offering twenty million but he wanted twenty-four! Then there was a rumor that they would not give even twenty million or fifteen, they wanted to knock down the price. Then out of the blue the news arrived that Scutari had fallen and that the king of Montenegro had entered with all his princes in grand style! Very likely you think he is some kind of hero, or has a big army or a lot of money. But listen to this! More is the pity, and it is not something to noise around, but he is, in fact, a penniless pauper! His people are perishing, they say, three times a day from hunger except for supper, the soldiers are without soles on their boots, have no bullets in their guns, and, just between you and me, if not for "us" occasionally fattening him up a little on the side with some bread to eat, clothes to wear, fuel for heat, and bullets for their guns, he would strike a wretched figure among the other rulers!

And once the Balkans declared war against the Turk, Nikolai, who had made an alliance with them, was the first to attack the Turks one unlucky night. Not to say anything bad about anyone, but those high and mighty powers had openly warned him not to be so impetuous. But Nikolai is not the kind of goy who scares easily. While the sharpest minds were sitting in London and those high and mighty powers were firing off diplomatic notes, he was pushing forward, pushing forward until he was finally in the saddle!

No doubt this is a slap in the face to old Franz Josef! Surely the old man won't remain silent and will take out after the Serbs. Why the Serbs? Because if not for the Serbs, Nikolai would never have laid his eyes on Scutari! Though even the local wags mutter under their breaths, and I'm afraid it's true, that it's not the Serbs he has to thank, but the Turks themselves, meaning the Turkish commander of Scutari, Reb Saud Pasha. It's likely that this Saud Pasha felt insulted or something else must have happened so that it was none other than Saud Pasha who surrendered Scutari to Nikolai, giving up every last inch. Having struck a bargain with Nikolai, this Saud Pasha commanded his Turkish soldiers to turn east so the enemy could shoot at them from the west—one, two, three and it was over! Anyone can be a hero with that kind of shooting! I could conquer the whole world like that. Let the world stand still for a moment facing east, I will shoot them from the west, and the world is mine.

That wasn't very nice on Saud Pasha's part, you see, and certainly not honest. The Slovenes are screaming bloody murder, raising hell, insisting that it was *their* brothers and *their* heroism that conquered the famous city, but all that is neither here nor there. As your mother would say, "Blow your nose and your face gets smeared . . ." Reb Saud Pasha defended himself by saying the story wasn't so. True, he said, the Montenegrans didn't show any great heroism. It was he who helped them out, opening the gates of the city out of kindness. But he said he was not guilty. The guilty parties were the elders of the city who, he said, forced him against his will to surrender to the enemy. What could he do, he said, when the elders themselves were willing? But whatever the story is, this way or that, old Franz Josef will not remain silent and the fall of Scutari will simply not be tolerated. And since he will declare war, "we" will probably not be silent either because we are for the Slovenes and we will have to come out, against our will, to oppose an old friend, Franz Josef. Will we have any other choice?

As I wrote you in previous letters, it appears that Franz Josef is not very frightened of "us" because he isn't the only one in the game. They are, you see, a group of three. On his side are the Austrians and the Italian, Victor Emmanuel, actually a son-in-law of Nikolai. "We" are on the side of the father-in-law, Nikolai, so how can the son-in-law be against "us"? Don't bother asking. In wartime it doesn't matter whether it's a father-in-law or a son-in-law. It can be your own brother and even a father. War is war. But if those three, Franz Josef, Victor Emmanuel, and Reb Wilhelm with the mustache decide to attack "us," one's blood runs cold just thinking about it. But you needn't be afraid, my dear wife, we are also, God forbid, not alone in the game. As I wrote you, we are also a group of three. On our side we have, thank God, the French, who are our avowed trusted ally, may I earn a tenth of what we owe them—and it is likely that in addition to the French "we" still have the English too, do you understand? "We" have taken precautions both by land and by sea. Did you think our diplomats are idiots? In short, it's possible that a war can break out and there will be no end of trouble!

All this would be doing the Turk a great favor because by becoming so embroiled with each other, they would forget about him. But how will it all end? Is this what we have struggled so long for, to destroy one another with our own hands? What are we, wild beasts or human beings? But I tell you, it won't come to that so quickly. Old Franz Josef, long life to him, will not allow it as long as he's alive. Nikolai has pushed himself into Scutari and that's certainly not good. For whom? Again the Turk. Misfortune always strikes the sickest person. Job's trials! Everyone who can, takes from the Turk. The first blow was delivered by old Reb Franz Josef himself, long life to him, who lopped off Bosnia and Herzogovina for himself. Then came the Italian who took Tripoli. Next the Balkan gang: this one—Adrianopol, that one—Crete, the other—Albania. Who knows what someone else will take tomorrow? There's even talk that the English are smiling on Egypt, the German is sharpening his teeth for Israel, the French have long since laid their hands on Tunisia. Well, are "we" supposed to stand by and remain silent? Is our Minister Sezonov a naïve child?

In the meantime Uncle Ishmael remains without good advice and why? Only because there aren't, as I already told you, any go-betweens, any brokers. A broker is what he needs, a real broker who has the right ideas and knows how to put a deal together. For example, I have a scheme in mind, and not just one but several, which if God helps me bring them off, the Turk could have the world at his feet. These schemes of mine are keeping me awake. They keep me floating on air. It's as clear as crystal that if I could have a little talk with the Turk or have a little correspondence, he would be helped. But one thing is killing me. Except for Yiddish I don't understand any other language. So I tore off to my friend, Khoskl Kotik. He is my confidant. I tell him everything. "Your mind seems very far off these days, Reb Menachem-Mendl," he says. I say to him, "How can it not seem far off when it is full of so many far-off things?" And I set everything out for him like on a platter, first shaking hands on it so that not a bird would hear of this, just he and I and God! I figure, God willing, that if this project is carried out, he should also have a share in it, what do I care? Maybe even equal to my share. Why not? From a partnership's income you don't get poor. That I learned on the stock exchange, heaven help me. On the contrary, I figure that this business will need to draw in more than one partner. It's alright, there will be enough for everyone. May the One above grant that I work it all out, because this matter is a bit complicated! I wish I could explain it all to you, my dear wife, chew it and digest it for you as I enjoy doing. But as I don't have any time I am making it short. I hope in my next letter to write everything in greater detail. In the meantime, may God grant us all health and success. Be well and kiss the children for me, send regards to your mother and all the family from me in a friendly way.

From me your husband Menachem-Mendl

ALMOST FORGOT: Remember, my dear wife, how the bosses of the American Yiddish newspapers ridiculed the writers' strike? "What do writers own," they sneered, "except their five fingers?" The Belgians, seeing what the American writers were up to, also went on strike. What a strike! A half million people as one person went out on strike. And it's likely that the Belgians got more than the Yiddish writers in America. What a world it's become. No matter what happens—a strike! A strike or a boycott. And a boycott for a boycott. You boycott me, I'll boycott you. That really appeals to me because there is no other solution. I say that with Warsaw in mind. If Warsaw Jews would listen to me, they would do what I do. I don't speak any other language but Yiddish. I don't read any other newspapers but Yiddish newspapers. I don't go to any other theaters but Yiddish theaters. I don't smoke any other cigarettes but Jewish ones (as for food and drink, that goes without saying.) I don't take a cab unless the driver understands my language. I'd rather go by foot, just like that Polack who last week hired a carriage in Warsaw to drive out to a village, and on the way the Polack realized the driver was a Jew. He spat three times and jumped out of the carriage half way there and walked back seven viorsts on foot—what else? If we're talking boycott, let's talk boycott!

But how long do we have to beat it into the heads of our Warsaw Jews before they realize what their own best interests are? Khoskl Kotik is right, I'm sorry to say. He says, "You don't know these Warsaw Jews, Reb Menachem-Mendl. You have a better chance of the Turk accepting your project than you have of seeing the Warsaw Jews giving up their fawning over the Pole." But what do you expect, my dear wife, when even our local rabbis, these so-called holy men, are so different from the ones at home. Can you imagine that Polish firms, the same ones that are boycotting Jews, decided just before Passover to pay these rabbis for the kosher seal for *their* Passover merchandise? That makes the Jew unkosher and the groshen kosher. When I heard about this I was beside myself and tore right off to Khoskl Kotik, "In God's name, Reb Khoskl, why are you silent? It's worse here than in Sodom!" He smiled, Khoskl Kotik, cool as a cucumber, as is his manner, "Simmer down, Reb Menchem-Mendl," he says, "Wait a while, you'll hear much worse, much worse . . ." A strange Jew this Khoskl Kotik!

As above.

4. Sheyne-Sheyndl from Kasrilevka to Her Husband, Menachem-Mendl, in Warsaw

To my dear, honored, renowned, generous, and wise husband, Menachem-Mendl, may his light shine forever.

FIRST OF ALL, let me tell you that we are, thank God, in the best of health. Pray God we hear the same from you, never worse.

SECOND OF ALL, I am writing you, my dear husband, that we had a winter here—may such a winter never return! My father, who hadn't been feeling well for a long time, began to complain that something was growing inside him and that he couldn't eat. The doctors began to stuff him with pills, told him it would pass, but as time went by he ate less and less, while they, the doctors, kept feeding him more pills and pocketing more and more money, may it all go for their own sicknesses, until he finally stopped eating altogether and slowly died of hunger, faded like a light, quiet as a dove, without a whimper, without a sound, just shut his eyes and—gone! As Mama says, "Lived a simple life, died a saintly death." His virtue should stand us in good stead in the *next* world because he suffered enough in *this* world.

You cannot imagine, Mendl, how my poor mother tore her hair! May our enemies say what they will, they cannot say that my father, of blessed memory, didn't have a good life with her—may those enemies suffer Pharaoh's plagues! If only they had seen how my mother beat her head against the wall, wailing that they should bury her together with him as he lay on the earth! And where were they, those know-it-alls, when she fainted three times at his grave—they could barely revive her. And do you think she can be consoled even now? Does she eat? Does she sleep? Day and night, either she is weeping or praying. "It is written," she says, "that a wife without a husband is like a shattered pot that no one needs and should be tossed out." Her only comfort was that you were coming home soon, and as it turns out . . . well, I have to be stronger than iron to endure it. Just try to imagine my situation. I thought angels were playing games with me when I received your beloved letter with the dollars saying you were leaving, with God's help, that fine land of America which should have burned up before you ever got there. The whole town was already congratulating me, "May God love you and your guest!" Not to mention the children who were in seventh heaven. No small thing, soon-soon they would be seeing their father whom they hardly remembered! Who would imagine such a stroke of bad luck, that Warsaw would draw him away like a magnet and not let him go! As if those golden Yehupetz ventures weren't enough, they still leave a bad taste in my mouth, God had to send him a new trade—scribbling! And to boot, there are fools in this world who are willing to pay him money, throw hundreders around—who would have believed it? For everything there is a time. As my mother, long life to her, says, "When Purim comes, even Yukl-Moishe the beadle gets rich." What she means by this you yourself can figure out. And if not, I will tell you what she means. She means: may it last and may the same not happen with your writing, God forbid, as happened with your Yehupetz lumber, land, and factory deals that were always brewing and brewing, but it was the cat that came along and licked out the sour cream and not you.

You can say, Mendl, that I am just a woman, but I simply cannot imagine that there are people, empty-headed people, who have nothing better to do than read your letters and still lick their fingers with pleasure at a time when people are nine cubits deep in poverty. If they would see with my eyes how Jews are being driven, worse than cattle, from the villages to the towns and from the towns to the cities, they wouldn't have in mind such nonsense. Can you imagine that Kasrilevka has become the big city, gathering up all those who are being driven out from everywhere else? Do you have any idea what they will do here? What they will live on? We pray to God that the goyim won't pick on Kasrilevka itself and drive us all out of here, God forbid, the way they have driven Jews from everywhere else. And for what reason? Because we're Jews! As my mother, long life to her, says, "Don't ask God questions because they've already been asked and He doesn't answer." I tell you, Mendl, she really is a wise woman, my mother. Not because she's my mother but because she makes such wise observations.

For example, we were sitting and eating during Passover when she suddenly put down her spoon and said to me, "Just look, Sheyndl, what sort your Mendl is. God sent him such good fortune that a Broder merchant is crazy enough about his writing to pay him real money. So how come your clever husband doesn't think to grab a piece of paper and get a signature on it? Suppose the merchant from Brod wakes up after a good night's sleep and changes his mind?" So tell me, Mendl, doesn't she have a point? I received the money, Mendl, you sent me from Warsaw, but as my mother says, "To have luck you also need luck. If God finally does look kindly on my daughter and she sometimes does get a few groshens from her blessed goldspinner, it turns out she can't benefit from it."

Listen to the fine thing that happened with your money, Mendl. It turns out that the ones paying for your scribbling are only doing it half-heartedly. They're sending me the money by mail in an envelope, without so much as a letter enclosed, just the hundreder, a whole hundreder, a freshly printed, spanking new bill hot off the press, as if to say, "Here, choke on it!" And when does this miracle happen? Right before Passover! This is exactly the opposite of what happened with the dollars sent from your fine America. I suffered enough until I lived to see a few rubles from them. It's a good thing that Shimshon, the miller, is a distant relative of mine, may he have as many boils on his face as the rubles he's cheated me out of. I thought that a dollar equalled two rubles *plus* something, and it turns out he gave me two rubles *minus* something—may he suffer for it!

Well, I took it, your hundreder, and ran down to the market to change it—fat chance! I went to this one, to that one, to a third—they looked at me, "Are you making fun of us, or what?" One actually had tears in his eyes, "Eh! If I had change of a hundreder, te-te-te—would I hang around here?" And another one, Motl Zvinerodker, you remember him, a real fresh mouth, a real Zvinerodker, stood there joking with me, "Tell me the truth, how many more hundreders like this one do you have sewn in your underclothes?" Smart-aleck! I can see he's green with envy! Everyone, the whole town is jealous of my hundreder. But what good is this hundreder when there's no place to change it! It's just before Passover and I need, need, need!

I promised poor Moishe-Hershele new boots last Passover, and the other children also need things. And here I am with a worthless hundreder! But with a bit of luck, at least my credit has become good here. "Buy," they say to me, "Buy as much as you want, Sheyne-Sheyndl, we trust you. After all, your Menachem-Mendl is, *kayn eyn horeh*, a good provider." What do you say to that? Now you've become a good provider to them, may they suffer my toothaches! But tell me, where were they when you were struggling—may it not happen again—in that fine America, may it sink into the earth, and I was strapped for a groshen? Now they give me credit, may God give them chills and cramps. As my mother says, "What God doles out by the spoonful, people heap on by the bushel."

Because of all that credit, my dear husband, we had a Pesach—may it be so for all our loved ones! To begin with, we had all of the best—matzo and eggs and poultry and goose fat and horseradish and wine for the Four Goblets. And you should have seen how our Moyshe-Hershele, God bless his little heart, conducted a seder—with all the trimmings, like a regular adult! All the tears that we both shed, my mother and I, could fill an ocean. My mother remembered that just a year ago at this time Papa, of blessed memory, was presiding over the seder. The pain he was suffering then should be visited on all our enemies. Still, it was better than being dead. As my mother says, "It is written, better to be alive *above* the ground than dead *in* the ground . . ."

And do you want to know why I was crying? I was crying about my bitter luck, that I was born to be left all alone here with my children while my poor husband is always wandering, roaming from country to country, never laying his head down in the same place twice. As my mother says, "It is written that a bird has a nest, a cow has a stall, a dog has a yard, but a person, alas, cannot find any refuge . . ." She sends her warmest regards to you, Mendl, and has one request: if possible, since Papa, blessed be his memory, didn't leave any sons, only daughters, would you be so kind to say Kaddish for him?

Be well and make lots of money so you can more quickly be delivered from Warsaw as you were delivered from that bleak, cursed America, may it burn down right after Passover, and may that wish be fulfilled as my wish that you have only good luck and the best of fortune, from your truly devoted wife.

Sheyne-Sheyndl

ALMOST FORGOT! We had a scare here in Kasrilevka just before Passover! Do you remember Yoylik, Reuven the tavern-keeper's eldest son? He is now also a tavern-keeper. To spite his father, he opened a tavern right across the street from his. So just before Passover Yoylik got into a fight with *his* eldest son, Kopl they call him,—a young scoundrel! Well, if you have a bad child, you get angry and punish him. You put him over your knee and give him what for! But not Yoylik. He throws Kopl into the cellar and locks the door from the outside. Kopl begins to scream bloody murder. You could hear him all the way to Warsaw. You'd think he was being slaughtered! A goya goes by and hears a person screaming and takes it upon herself to run out into the marketplace and let out an alarm that Jews have laid their hands on a young gentile boy and are slaughtering him for Passover! Well, what can I say, Mendl, the sky split open! Before you could say *Sh'ma Yisroel*, the marketplace was full of goyim, men, women, and children. Jewish children began to wail in terror! Jewish women were hurried to the rooftops! The older folks ordered Yoylik to open the cellar but he wouldn't hear of it. "I don't care what happens to him, he'll have to stay there till the first seder!" They pleaded with him, "Fiend! Open up!" Does a wall listen? So they ran off to Reuven, the boy's grandfather. He came rushing over and orders Yoylik, "Open the cellar, Yoylik, and let the child out!" The daughter-in-law, Yoylik's wife, Ettl-Beyle, decided to put in her two cents worth, "Who are you to tell Yoylik what to do with his children?" Reuven doesn't pay her the slightest attention and again calls out to Yoylik, "I'm telling you again, you oaf, open the cellar and let the child out! Do you want a pogrom on your head?" Only then, when he heard that magic word "pogrom," did Yoylik take fright, open the cellar, and let the brat go free. Then it all quieted down. May all my angriest, fiercest, bitterest dreams fall on their heads—that clan!

5. Menachem-Mendl from Warsaw to His Wife, Sheyne-Sheyndl, in Kasrilevka

To my dear, wise, and modest wife, Sheyne-Sheyndl, may God grant her many years!

FIRST OF ALL, let me tell you that I am, blessed be His name, in good health and spirits, and may the Blessed One grant that we hear from one another only good news of comfort and salvation for us and for all of Israel-Amen!

SECOND OF ALL, my dear wife, with God's help I will not do badly at all in my present position, not badly at all! The reason: everyone admits that when it comes to politics, I have, if I say so myself, a sixth sense. I said right away that the commander of Scutari, that same Saud Pasha, would accept no money for the job he did in handing over the town to the Montenegran king. That would have been too coarse. And incidentally, they say he is himself powerful enough. They bought him off with payment in kind. Here's the evidence—it's said that this Saud Pasha has crowned himself king of Albania. The real ruler of that little country remains as before, the Turk, but he, this Saud Pasha, considers himself more like the king's minister—not a bad a deal for a fez! And even though, just between ourselves, this little town named Scutari, is no bigger than Kasrilevka, still and all you should see how the poor Old Man, Franz Josef, is carrying on over it! May I be wrong but I'm afraid the old man will, God forbid, give up his throne as he's often threatened to do. And that would be a terrible shame! You have no idea what a gem of an emperor he is. A true friend of Israel! Jews think the world of him, love him with all their hearts! "Our dear little Franz Josefl," they call him. A few years ago this same emperor drove through Galicia, stopping in Lemberg. You should hear what went on there! The Jews carried him high on their shoulders, dancing in the streets with Torahs! A Lemberg Jew himself told me that Franz Josefl ate a Jewish meal with fish at his own home. I wouldn't have believed it but he swore a solemn oath and the tears actually stood in his eyes! You might ask, since this Scutari is so small, no larger than Kasrilevka, why should Franz Josef eat his heart out and sacrifice himself over it?

Let me clear the matter up. You understand that this has nothing to do with money, honor, or even conquest, but with something entirely different. We are talking about *neighbors*. A country has to know who its neighbors are. A bad neighbor is worse than a plague, as we say every morning when we pray, "Save us from every evil neighbor." But in order for you to better understand, my dear wife, let me illustrate with an example. Take your mother, may she have many long years, and her neighbor, Ziml, the paper bag cutter, who lives in the house right next to yours and is your neighbor. So long as Beyle-Leah was living in the paper bag cutter Ziml's ruin of a house, things weren't too bad. But then Ziml decided to throw Beyle-Leah out and bring in that dark-haired Charneh, who is at sword's point with your mother. Do you think that made her happy? That's exactly the way it is with Franz Josef and the king of Montenegro. So long as Albania was Albania and Scutari belonged to the Turk, Franz Josef could sleep in peace. But now that this Mikita from Montenegro has snuck into Scutari, most probably the Albanians will stick with the Slavs, and it becomes very likely that all the Slavs will throw in their lot with the Turk, on whom I have long kept an eye. Franz Josef's kingdom would then be in big trouble because, keep in mind, his own nation is made up mostly of Slavs, Czechs, Russkies, Croats, and Slovenes. And what about the Polacks—are they stray dogs? And where are the Bosniaks and the Herzogoviniaks? In short, it's a patchwork country: striped, dotted every which way. Were all the Slavs to get together they would pull down his little schoolhouse and he would be left without a place or position. Now do you understand why he needed like a hole in the head that the Slovenian king of Montenegro take over Turkish Albania?

But what can one do when he has moved into Scutari quite openly like into his own father's vineyard and there's no way of smoking him out? It's likely that his son, Danilka they call him, himself no babe-in-the-woods, has already proclaimed and sworn before the whole world that from this day forth Scutari is the capitol of Montenegro—and try to stop him! Certainly Franz Josef is working madly behind the scenes, carrying on and complaining, "How could this happen? Who ever heard of such a thing?"—firing off dispatches to kings everywhere, urging them to denounce that Mikita of Montenegro so he will on the instant clear out of Scutari or else all hell will break loose!

The kings are saying, "What can we do? He is already ensconced there—drag him off like a reluctant cantor clutching the pulpit?" Do you understand what's going on? Probably, my little silly, this was all done with the approval of the Turk. Uncle Ishmael was delighted that Scutari and Montenegro on one side, and his general Saud Pasha on the other had worked out a deal. And this Saud Pasha really did it very cleverly. Besides reaping for himself honor and riches—after all, he was now the king's minister—he also made his entire family prosperous. They write that he has already appointed two uncles as governors in two Albanian cities, I forget their names-who can remember them? Well, and after the uncles, how long before the nephews and the cousins, also no fools, want something? Ah, you ask, what does the Turk get out of it? No more, no less than nothing, unless he consoles himself thinking, "Fight each other, children, knock your heads together, tear each other's hair out, as long as you leave me alone."

It's the high and mighty powers that surprise me. How could they allow this? Where were those sharp minds who sit and wag their tongues in London? I'm afraid that those sharp minds have dull brains, and not so much dull as cold and uncaring. Otherwise how can they sit by in these times? Where are their eyes? Now they must be scratching their bald heads saying that they hadn't forseen such alliances. How could enemies who were ready to bite one anothers' noses off wind up making deals?

As God is my witness, my dear wife, if I didn't foresee it all! Not only that Mikita-Nikolai, the king of Montenegro, but that all the Slavs, rather than squander millions or spill their blood, would make a deal with the Turk and work it out among themselves. With good will everything works out better and with the Turk anything can be managed. He is a business-man, you understand, a descendant of Ishmael, and the Ishmaelites, as we know from the Bible, were always businessmen. You remember Khoskl Kotik, whom I wrote you about, he'll vouch for what I'm telling you. I can't count how many times I told him, "Reb Khoskl," I said, "throw away this foolishness of yours (he is in the same profession as I am, writing, but he doesn't write about politics, just books), let's take advantage of the war and we'll make out a lot better!" He looked at me as if I were crazy. "What business do we have with war? We are Jews busy with our writing." I said to him, "Maybe we don't really have any business with war but if we set our minds to it, we could have a strong influence." And I laid it out for him like on a platter. I gave him to understand that the war was not going too well. From this war, may I be wrong, no good will come for anyone, but the Turk will suffer most of all, those *shlimmazels*. And why? Only because the Turk lacks an experienced broker. If only I had come from America a little sooner! If only I had thrown myself into my new profession, politics, a lit-tle earlier! Had I come here two or three months ago, well-well-well! Be-lieve me, my dear wife, I am not crazy. You know me from way back. I am not a braggart like others who would show off for you. I would never make empty boasts as others would that if I, Menachem Mendl, were to get in-volved in the war, the world would be a different world and the map would look entirely different. No! The world will remain the same world and the map will remain the same map. So what do I have in mind? Your husband could by now own, do you hear, three tall buildings in the heart of Warsaw! But don't think that my chances are all gone, that the cow is lost with its tether. Be patient and in time, with God's help, you will hear from me about such deeds that your Kasrilevkers have never dreamt of! As I have already written you my head is bursting with schemes, but *one* scheme is *so* clever that I cannot write about it because someone might find out about it, God forbid, and claim it as his own. These things have happened more than once, on the stock exchange and in politics. People everywhere are greedy for money. When Witte, "our" prime minister, traveled that time to the American Roosenvelt to make arrangements between Uncle Pini of Japan and Mumeh Reyze, our Russia, he was also stingy with his words, a gold coin per word . . . so that's one thing.

And second, there is another problem—language! It's this language business that's killing me! Except for our Yiddish I don't know a single other language—I wasn't taught any. Oy, if only instead of biblical studies I had learned French and even a bit of Turkish, I would by now be far, far ahead! I'm looking now for someone who knows French and Turkish. He would earn a good share of the profits, maybe even fifty-fifty. This might all work out well for everyone, as I've already written you. But someone like that you can't find in Warsaw no matter how hard you look. You can find someone who speaks a little French. But Turkish—not a one! I hope to God I will be able to find someone. I need to look among the Zionists who do business on behalf of Zionism—they would know where to find such people. But now I must get back to work. And as I have no time—we are busy here, all the people at the newspaper—we are expanding—I will make this short. Pray God in my next letter I will write everything in greater detail. In the meantime, may God grant us all health and success. Kiss the children for me, send regards to your mother, whom I honor, and to all the family, each and every one, in the most friendly way.

From me your husband, Menachem-Mendl

ALMOST FORGOT: Do you remember what I wrote you Khoskl Kotik told me about the Warsaw Jews? "You will achieve your great project with the Turk, Reb Mendl," he said, "long before your Warsaw Jews renounce their Polish language." Do you want to hear something really good about what our Jews are capable of? There is a club here of sales clerks, Jewish sales clerks. They get together at night after the shops are closed to talk, read a page in the newspaper, play a little cards—that's what they call a club. And every club, you must know, has its minutes, its by-laws and its managers, as it's supposed to be. One night the sales clerks have a meeting and they declare, "Fellow members! In what language should we Jewish sales clerks speak at our Jewish club?" They break out laughing. "In Polish, of course?" "And why of course? Why not in Russian?" "Because Russian is not Polish and Polish is not Russian!" In short, Polish-Russian, Russian-Polish, back and forth—until one of them speaks out, "Jews! Why don't we speak in Yiddish? Aren't we all Jews?" There was an uproar, "Yiddish? Zhargon? Feh! Forget it!"

And right then and there they established a rule and it was noted in the minutes, "Insofar as we, a Jewish organization of sales clerks from Warsaw, have met in our club on such-and-such a date, and could not agree in which language we should speak, therefore it has been agreed by all and a rule has been established that in our club anyone can speak in whichever language he wishes—Polish, Russian, German, *but not Yiddish.* And if anyone breaks this rule and speaks, God forbid, in Yiddish, we will do to him what the Polacks do—we will boycott him. That means he can talk from today till tomorrow and no one will answer him. This rule is now vaild and in effect . . ."

ALMOST FORGOT AGAIN: At this very moment we received the news that Mikita has suddenly decided to retreat from Scutari. You can imagine, my dear wife, what excitement this has caused here.

As above.

6. Sheyne-Sheyndl from Kasrilevka to Her Husband, Menachem-Mendl, in Warsaw

To my dear, honored, renowned, generous, and wise husband, Menachem-Mendl, may his light shine forever.

FIRST OF ALL, let me tell you that we are, thank God, in the best of health. Pray God we hear the same from you, never worse.

SECOND OF ALL, I am writing you, my dear husband, that I received from your people yet another hundreder, not all in one bill but in small bills and again without so much as a written word, though you'd think even two words would do, if only for appearance' sake—but not even that. Are they really that busy? As my mother says, "Do they sleep in their clothes?" Or maybe my family background isn't as good as theirs? I don't know which. If we sat down and figured it out, my background is as good as theirs.

What's more, Mendl, I am writing you that I asked some of the young people here about the business you're in now, this scribbling, and they were very impressed. They say that gazettes are today the best business and that the people you're writing for are making money hand over fist, are up to here in wealth, because gazettes they say, are today more necessary than anything, even eating. We would sooner give up our morning glass of tea than the gazette. That we must have! Especially, they say, when the Friday gazette comes out and you know that in it will be a letter from your husband, then it's time for a celebration! If that's the case, Mendl, if you have, as my mother says, fallen into a honey-pot, why don't you try to lick more up for yourself? Why should you always have the habit of relying on someone else's generosity? You yourself say that America, may it burn to ashes, so unhinged you that you don't dare trust anyone at all. Then how come you allow yourself to be milked like a goat before a holiday? Would I write for them? A death certificate I would write for them, that's what I would do! What kind of scribbling is this you do, earning just enough, how does my mother say, "for a pinch of snuff." What's wrong? Can't they remember to throw in an extra hundreder once in a while? Why should you let them spit in your kasha? If you asked me, this is what I would tell you, Mendl—it's simple arithmetic. First they have to cover your expenses. You aren't obliged to throw away your family on account of them. You have a wife, may she live till a hundred and twenty, and children, may they be well. Food and drink and a suit and a cigar to smoke, a stamp in case you need to send a letter home and other such things—all that must be on their account, why should it be otherwise?

To me a hundreder—that, it's understood, they must send the first of the month or even twice a month. And why not every week? And it wouldn't be beneath them to give you a hundreder a week too. Don't worry, it would come in handy, if not now then later if, God help us, you ever come to blows with them. And what about all that money pouring in from the gazette? In all fairness I think that they should divide their money with you, fifty-fifty. Why should they get it all? That's how I figured it out. But you probably understand better because you are, after all, smarter. How does my mother say, "He's not as bright as he is handsome, and not as handsome as he is good, and not as good as he is clever." My mother, when she comes out with a saying, you have to smack your lips. Don't you agree?

What's more, when you write me, Mendl, that because of the Turk you don't eat, you don't drink, you don't sleep, really, this is very foolish of you! Why should you eat your heart out over these things? Where do you come to Drinople, Sivestople? Mikita Shmikita? As far as I'm concerned, let them tear each other to bits, so long as the gazette has something to write about and you can earn your money. When you write me about your big projects, I'm afraid, my dear husband, they will come to the same end, heaven forbid, as your other great schemes in Yehupetz, may it never happen. They're paying you to write—write. What more do you need? And who is this Kotik whom you've cozied up to so quickly, and can't be without for a day? To which Kotiks is he related? Is he married? See to it he doesn't lead you astray or trick you—you're an easy mark!

What you write me, Mendl, that the Polacks are boycotting Jews, that I can understand. That's why they're Polacks. But when Jews themselves boycott Jews—that's too much. I hope, Mendl, that between deciding what and what not to do, they don't end up boycotting *you!* I don't know why, but I hate Warsaw and I hate the Warsaw Jews. I hate the Warsaw Jews because they have that silly accent and talk with an *aye* and a *vye* and I hate Warsaw because it's a city of thieves. My father, of loving memory, was once in Warsaw, it was long ago, before I was born. He used to tell how they swiped a purse right out of his pocket in broad daylight! Luckily it was empty. Our Kasrilevka shopkeepers, mostly notions sellers, often go to Warsaw and they also say it's a nasty city. Oh, the city is pretty, but the people are nasty. To them it's a good deed to take visitors for all they're worth. All our merchants have lost money there many times. But the cloth merchants go broke in Lodz. That's the same place you write me should sink into the earth like Sodom. You have my blessing on that. I won't argue with you about it. If you ask me, the same should happen to Warsaw, but not while you're there. You are so busy, Mendl, with your politics and your kings and your king's ministers that your home can't even creep into the corner of your mind. You don't ask about your wife, your children, never mind your family. How can you be bothered asking about your family when it's obvious that you yourself are about to become a king's minister? And why can't you sometimes just write to me, my dear writer, about how you are living and where you are living, what you eat and where you sleep? It seems I have a right to know, don't you think? What am I, a wife, till a hundred and twenty, or a mistress, God forbid? May your Warsaw Polacks who boycott Jews never live to see that day, may they be boycotted by God, as I wish you all good things and eternal success from your truly faithful wife

Sheyne-Sheyndl

Good, I remembered! Tell me, Mendl, what's the meaning of *"Ikkeh,"* or *"Mitte,"* or *"Shmitteh,"* that Jews are signing up for? Many, many Jews have already signed up and are waiting for their group to be called. I asked some neighbors about it, but you know our Kasrilevka smart-alecks. Just let something come up and right away they're making fun of you. You have, they say to me, a husband like Menachem-Mendl, so how come you don't know about this? What have you done to them? As my mother says, "It's a fact that when a dove goes to ask advice of a fox, she ends up sacrificing her children's children." How deep that is! Since my father, may he rest in peace, died, she hasn't shut her Yiddish Bible.

7. Menachem-Mendl from Warsaw to His Wife, Sheyne-Sheyndl, in Kasrilevka

To my dear, wise, and modest wife, Sheyne-Sheyndl, may God grant her many years!

FIRST OF ALL, let me tell you that I am, blessed be His name, in good health and spirits, and may the Blessed One grant that we hear from one another only good news of comfort and salvation for us and for all of Israel—Amen.

SECOND OF ALL, you should know, my dear wife, that he is clever, that king of Montenegro, for backing down just in time. It's nothing to joke about when a person is playing in luck! At first, it seemed, he was biding his time, letting the whole world know he was saying no with a capital N, that he wasn't going to withdraw from the city he conquered, unless they carried him out in a shroud. Then he realized that Franz Josef had moved a few hundred thousand troops closer to the border and that Victor Emmanuel, although one of his own, a son-in-law, had also prepared himself with thirty thousand soldiers, and that we, his "friends" in St. Petersburg weren't sitting idly by, twiddling our thumbs. We immediately let him know that he was wasting his time, that he couldn't depend on us—and not being a fool, he understood and immediately became soft as butter and began singing a different tune.

It didn't please him, he said in his first dispatch to the English, that a great strong power (he was referring to Franz Josef) should use force on him, a poor, weak Montenegran king. After all, it is written, he said, what is man and what is his life? How do you like those words? Wasn't I right when I wrote you that they have respect for the high and mighty powers? The same thing happened with the prime minister of Albania. Girding their loins, the old Franz Josef and the Italian Victor Emmanuel let it be known that it wasn't on account of one Albanian city that they were moving toward the border. Scutari, they said, was their last concern and the king of Montenegro, they said, wasn't even on their minds. He would, they said, clean out the city in any case, and if he didn't do it peacefully, he would do it with force. The main headache was Albania itself. They had to teach the Albanians a lesson so they would tear away from the Turk. What does this mean, this tearing away from the Turk? The Albanians should have done it long ago. So what's the problem? They aren't the only ones. There are older and better countries that should have done the same. Albania must be a country on its own, as I already explained in an earlier letter, on account of their neighbors and because Austria and Italy must have a way open to the Adriatic Sea.

And for that very reason a plan was worked out between Franz Josef and Victor Emmanuel that they themselves would tear Albania away from the Turk and divide it between themselves, half for me, half for you. Hearing this news and seeing that it didn't look too good for him, the self-proclaimed king of Albania, Saud Pasha, thought it over and denied every last thing. He said he never had in mind to proclaim himself king, nor prime minister or even third in command. That, he said, his enemies had thought up. On the contrary, there never was a more passionate Turkish patriot than himself, Reb Saud Pasha. He was, as always, a loyal servant of the sultan and a devoted soldier of his Albanian fatherland for which he was prepared to go through fire and water! If you're talking patriotism, it's clear we end up thinking this proclamation is somehow nice and fine and good and peace-loving—no more war, no more mobilization and there's an end to it.

But the problem is, my dear wife, that I don't feel easy about it. And as long as *I* don't feel easy, it's a bad sign! I have in these matters, you must understand, a sixth sense. I have a certain gut feeling. May it never happen again, but that's how it was when I was working on the stock exchange and all the speculators and all the brokers would sit calmly at their white marble tables drinking coffee and eating ice cream, I among them. And suddenly I would get this feeling in my gut and I would take off for the street. Ask me why and I don't have the slightest idea. And I proved right! In less than half an hour a dispatch had arrived from St. Petersburg with the news that the stock market had crashed, all hell had broken loose. Naturally in no time at all our speculators and brokers with their orders and their stocks jumped in and made out like bandits, I among them.

The same exact thing is now happening with the war—something is eating at me about it. I hope I am wrong but this retreat by the king of Montenegro doesn't sit well with me. I hope it's not the same as in 1812 when we were at war with Napoleon. We also retreated from Moscow. I am afraid, you understand, that if the king leaves the city, the city itself might go up in smoke. He might burn it to the ground. Do you think I care that much for the city? So we'll have one fewer city! What bothers me is something else. Who knows what kind of tricks that speculator Mikita Nikolai might yet come up with? And who knows what that Saud Pasha can yearn after? Suddenly we hear this rumor that Montenegro and Serbia might become one country! Can you guess what that smells of? I hope I'm wrong but I guarantee that before this letter arrives in Kasrilevka, the wheel will turn and there will, God forbid, be shooting somewhere in the Balkans. You don't know what a powder keg it is and you don't know this king of Montenegro.

I am sticking with my belief, hear me out, that he is a real speculator and that he is playing on the stock exchange. May we become as prosperous—I'm talking about our Jews. He is a dyed-in-the-wool speculator! I see it clearly from all his actions. I am, in all modesty, an expert at finagling. I myself was once, curse the day, a speculator and know the art of making something out of nothing. First you bid low, expecting stocks to fall through the floor. You buy up as much as you can for the end of the month. Then you turn around and bid high, expecting prices to rise in order to sell them and rake in a profit. Now for the second month you sell everything you have and throw in something extra. And when you finally have to pay up, you once again put in a low bid. Oh, we know these games!

I just read a dispatch reporting that the king of Montenegro was figuring that having given up the city, he could give up his claim to the country. What kind of wild prank is he playing! Khoskl Kotik loves to contradict me, "How do you know," he says, "what's going on in the king of Montenegro's heart? Maybe he just wants to retire in his old age. Money he has. His children taken care of. What else does he need?" What do you say to that reasoning? No! You can't convince me and no one will change my mind, come hell or high water. I have no doubt he's a speculator and speculates on the stock exchange, maybe together with his son-in-law, Victor Emmanuel! How else do you explain it? Every war, my little silly, is no more than a speculation, a speculation among kings who speculate with their soldiers. Of course not for money in their own pockets but for the benefit of their countries and their people. And speculation in a war is, like all speculations, a matter of luck, a wild card. Whoever wins, takes the pot. He gains a country and wealth and all kinds of goods and honor without end. Whoever loses, that one is left utterly destitute because in addition to losing the war, he loses a chunk of land, his soldiers, and his stock on the market falls through the floor. He loses his credit in the eyes of the world and on top of all that he still has to pay his enemy through the nose for all their expenses—it's called reparations.

In short, war is a speculation. What then is the difference between speculation and war? The difference is simply that with speculation both sides, the seller and the buyer, have an agreement, while with warring speculators it usually happens that one side agrees but the other—absolutely not. But there's no way out. One country comes to the other and says, "Let's speculate." The other country answers, "I don't want to." The first one says, "You don't want to? But I *insist*." One word leads to another—pitch-potch, they're at war! That's what happened over Tripoli, in Africa. The Italian king, Victor Emmanuel, went to the Turkish sultan and said to him, "Listen to me, red yarmulke! How's about making a speculation together?" The Turk then asked him, "First tell me what kind of speculation you have in mind?" Emmanuel says to him, "Inasmuch as my country is getting a bit overcrowded, and my workers are emigrating to your Tripoli year after year, and as my people will soon, God willing, outnumber your Turks, my Italian businesmen are demanding that your country, Tripoli become part of my kingdom. If you agree, all will be well. If not, you'll make it worse because I will take it from you by force and you'll have to pay reparations in addition. Have you digested that?" The sultan became furious, raised a big fuss, and sent off a fiery note to the great powers:

"Help, save us! Bandits have attacked us in broad daylight!" The great powers heard his cry and answered his note, not heatedly, but measuredly, as befits great powers. On the one hand, they found it really was a crime and they would certainly have their brokers—that means their diplomats—apply all possible pressure to settle this conflict in an honorable manner. But on the other hand, they must allow that the other's complaints had some basis because what could he do if his country was overcrowded and his workers had, after all, settled in a new country? Ordinarily they would not allow such an injustice to take place, the world is not lawless. But as he, the sultan, was also not a nobody, and his nation ranked among the great powers, it was therefore their conclusion that His Highness should accept this challenge and go against the enemy with sword and gunpowder and in so doing uphold his own honor and the honor of his country and of his people. The result of this I believe I've already written you about: Tripoli now belongs to Italy and reparations will be paid by the Turk for years and years.

The same thing will now happen in the Balkans. The speculation—I mean the war—in the Balkans is almost over and both sides are working out a peace treaty with all kinds of conditions. One asks who was the winner? The winners were the Balkan kings and now the brokers—meaning the diplomats—must decide how to divide the conquered territories and how to arrange the reparations. Wait and see what a *kasha* they will cook up! Then the real fun will begin! In any case, the Turk will have to pay and they'll probably cut off a piece of his land—of that there is no question. But what will happen afterwards? How will the Balkan kings divide the dividends—I mean the reparations—and the conquered cities? Each one will surely want the best part. Each will maintain and will be correct in saying that the speculation—I mean the war—cost him more soldiers and therefore he deserves a larger share since they had previously agreed that the division would be according to the number of soldiers killed. What do you think will happen? Scornful insults, arguments and fights, scandals, and new speculations—I mean new wars—among these very parties that will end up with an appeal to the higher powers to mediate between the sides, which in the long run will benefit the Turk! What's the sense of it? The sense of it is plain and simple. When both sides appeal to the higher powers to mediate, the higher powers will do what my rebbe did with the two boys who got into a fight in *cheder* over an egg. Both boys claimed the egg was the same egg his mother had given him for lunch. One word led to another and you know how boys are—they started beating each other up, bloodied each other's nose! The rebbe came between them and made a compromise: he peeled the egg, called over his own son, the two of them made a blessing over the egg and ate it up while he took the boys to task and gave them a lecture into the bargain, saying (he was quite a lecturer): "The devil take your fathers and mothers! Are you sages from the Houses of Shamai and Hillel arguing over a ritual egg for the holidays? Now get to your studies, troublemakers!"

That's my example and the object of the example, my dear wife, you yourself will have to understand. But here's the problem: what will the Turk get out of this? He stands to gain a great deal because until the conquered cities go over from the Balkan states to the high powers, plenty of blood will be spilled because the high powers themselves aren't so eager to share or give them up so quickly. And therein lies the real foresight and wisdom of my project that I propose to lay before the Turk. But as I don't have time now (I have to run to the editorial office to see what they are reporting from Vienna, Paris, and Berlin. Nowadays in one day the whole world can turn topsy-turvy!), I am making this short. God willing, in my next letter I will write you everything at length. In the meantime, may God grant us all health and success. Be well and kiss the children for me and send my best and most friendly regards to your mother, whom I honor, and to the whole family, each and every one!

From me your husband Menachem-Mendl

ALMOST FORGOT! As to what you wrote me about not asking enough money for my writing, please forgive me for saying this, my dear wife, but you write like an old woman. First of all, everything has a limit. You mustn't pull the string too tight or it will snap. And you must also put yourself in another's situation. People are sacrificing themselves, they have expenses, overhead for a big editorial office and printing presses, and paper does not come free. Let alone dispatches! What they spend for dispatches every day your Kasrilevka merchants couldn't hope to take in on a typical market day. And second of all, do you think I am writing simply for money? From writing alone, my little silly, no writer has ever built himself a mansion since the beginning of time.

As for me, what are my writings compared to the plans that are brewing in my head? And all because I am here and have become well respected in the editorial offices and am interested in politics. As your mother says, "Near a loaded wagon it's better to go on foot." My pet, if I were able to follow through on my great plans with those Turks, as I wrote you about, I would make enough for three mansions in Warsaw! May God have mercy on me and help me find the right person, who in addition to knowing the language must be a trustworthy man whom I can depend on not to use my ideas and say afterwards that they were his. Politics, you understand, is a delicate matter.

And as to your question regarding those at home who are signing up to leave, I have to make it clear to you that you mustn't talk like an old woman. There are societies called, "IKA," and "ITA." "IKA" is the one to which the Baron Hirsch donated his millions and from which no one has had any benefit except for a few trustees and ringleaders. And "ITA," is an altogether different society, a society of *territorialists* who are seeking a territory just for Jews. Their leader is Zangwill, who sits in London and is trying to find a territory for Jews anywhere in the world and can't find one. Why? It's elementary: in the territory the Jews want, they are not wanted and the territory where they are wanted is worthless. It's a pity I don't know English. If I knew English, I would write him a letter, that Zangwill, offering a plan for him too, a priceless plan!

As above.

8. Sheyne-Sheyndl from Kasrilevka to Her Husband, Menachem-Mendl, in Warsaw

To my dear, honored, renowned, generous, and wise husband, Menachem-Mendl, may his light shine forever.

FIRST OF ALL, let me tell you that we are, thank God, in the best of health. Pray God we hear the same from you, never worse.

SECOND OF ALL, I am writing you, my dear husband, that what you write me about looking for a partner for your big scheme doesn't sit well with me at all. I only hope you can find someone who will think about you and not just about his own affairs, although I cannot believe that among those big shots who know so many languages, you can't find an honest man. As my mother says, "It is written that man is like the animals in the forest and the fish in the sea." But these are far-off worries. The main thing is the scheme itself. I am talking about that big plan you tell me you have and which I don't begin to know what or who it's about. I only hear that you have it. Let's hope we live to see the day when we can learn what it's about. Who knows where you can fly off to? As my mother says, "It is written that a person's head doesn't know where his legs can carry him off to."

And as for the example you gave me, Mendl, about Ziml, the paper-bag cutter and Beyle-Leah, when I told my mother she called down wild curses on her enemies' heads. So long, she says, as Charneh with her foul mouth is ailing, Ziml won't allow her next door. And why, she says, you were pleased that Ziml out of the clear blue sky went berserk and threw Beyle-Leah out of the house, she can't begin to understand. Unless, she says, "that clever son-in-law of mine has nothing to do and wants to stir up trouble among neighbors." That's what my mother says, long life to her, and she asked me to write this to you. She doesn't know that her clever son-in-law is not like other sons-in-law. Sons-in-law the world over keep in mind that they have a wife, may she live till a hundred and twenty, and children, may they be well, and all you have on your mind is the Turk and worrying about the whole world, even America, where you say you learned a few things. In the meantime there's nothing to show for it. Maybe something will come of it in time, God willing, as my mother says, "It is written that as long as man roams the earth he will continue to do foolish things." These words should tell you she isn't terribly impressed with your talents. Don't be offended by her, you can't force someone to believe another on faith until he sees for himself the outcome with his own eyes. It's enough that your own wife has time and can wait. What other choice do I have? I am tied down to your children and to a widowed mother who can't be abandoned. And I can't take her along to Warsaw. She says Warsaw will never live to see her bones buried in a strange cemetery, away from Kasrilevka and her husband with whom she lived her whole life in peace and contentment, never saying a mean word to each other, and even if she did come out with a loud word, he ignored it because he knew, God rest his soul, may you live such a long life, that a wife must be appreciated and no matter how badly she treats her husband, she is, after all, a wife and a mother to his children, and a mother is not a father. A mother wracks her brains over each child, making sure it eats on time, doesn't go naked, learns how to pray, to study and write. And a father? Not a care! There you are sitting in that big city like a lord writing your little letters, the devil knows about what, day and night mixed up with kings and ministers, and if someone asks you out of curiosity whether you have children, what their names are, what they know—may the enemies of the Jews know what you begin to know about their health, or that your Moyshe-Hershele, a blessing on his head, is already grown up. I'll bet my life you wouldn't recognize him! First of all, he is, *kayn eyn horeh,* so handsome that God Himself and everybody else envy me. And second of all, you should hear how he chants the prayers and how he studies and how he speaks the Holy Tongue!

I enrolled him for the summer in the Mesukenem cheder that recently opened here. Everyone studies there. He speaks nothing but Hebrew ever since. "Shalom!" he says to me every time he leaves and comes back from cheder. That's how they say, "Good morning," and when I ask him something, he doesn't answer me but makes with his head up or down. I understand according to whether he nods or shakes his head whether it's a yes or a no. To get a word out of him, you practically have to pay for it! And sometimes when he latches on to me, babbling words and all in Hebrew, I plead with him to talk like the rest of us, so he laughs and shuts up-just like you, God bless him! He even takes after you in his writing. He has the same habit of scribbling. Since he was a child, as soon as he got hold of a piece of paper, he would scribble on it. He's scribbled on everything. I'm enclosing one of the writings he wrote for your sake so you can also have some pleasure from your son, the writer, though to tell the truth, I would rather he would be anything but a writer. As my mother says, "A good writer is a good pauper." Don't be insulted, Mendl, by my bothering you with this nonsense about your wife and children at a time when you are crowning and dethroning kings. I think it would be only right so long as you're already writing, to write about what is close to your heart. Your Turk, for whom you have so much pity that your heart is breaking for him, in the meantime has a home and a place to rest his head while our poor little Jews are wandering like lost sheep, roaming from place to place, not knowing where to run, as my mother says, "It's time for the Messiah because it is written," she says, "that when the Messiah comes, they will herd all the Jews together from all four corners of the world." Everyone says that since the beginning of time, Jews have never suffered as much as now. It's likely, they say in Kasrilevka, that the enemies of the Jews have decreed that pogroms can be brought down on all the Jews in the Diaspora. Write me if this is true. You know how our heavy hearts are wishing you all that is good and happiness to you always. From your truly faithful wife

Sheyne-Sheyndl

Oh, yes! What is this babble about "IKA" or "ITA"? May my enemies know who invented them and I don't begin to understand what you are talking about . . . Baron Hirsh . . . territory . . . millions! Right away you start in with the millions. As my mother says, "It is written that whatever man thinks about during the day, he dreams at night." Maybe if you would give me a thought or two during the day, heaven forbid I would come to you in a dream at night and maybe that would be a way for you to remember to come home. But wait! I completely forgot, as my mother says, "How can he come home, the world might go topsy-turvy where he is, the Turk might get into a fight with Mrs. Turk and Menachem-Mendl won't be there—that's no joking matter!"

9. Menachem-Mendl from Warsaw to His Wife, Sheyne-Sheyndl, in Kasrilevka

To my dear, wise, and modest wife, Sheyne-Sheyndl, may God grant her many years!

FIRST OF ALL, let me tell you that I am, blessed be His name, in good health and spirits, and may the blessed one grant that we hear from one another only good news of comfort and salvation for us and for all of Is-rael—Amen.

SECOND OF ALL, you should know, my dear wife, that my grand plan you keep asking about appears to have become a fearful tangle but which I can explain in two words, no more than two carefully chosen words, but on which the fate of the world depends—*peace* and *balance*.

Peace—without it the world could not survive. People would swallow one another alive, there would be no commerce, no trains, no ships, no cities, no money—chaos. That is as simple as a groshen a bagel and I don't have to belabor it, you yourself understand this. Kasrilevka is a perfect case. Just imagine if one fine morning it was decreed that all laws are abol-ished, everyone could do as he pleased or take whatever his heart desired! Do I need to describe to you how the town would end up? Or what would happen to the market, the shops, the houses, the owners, and especially the rich men? Within three or four days, my little silly, they would wipe one another out, plunder and burn the town and Kasrilevka would remain no more than a memory of a town called Kasrilevka that once stood on this spot. But as long as there is law and people live peacefully, as it is now, for better or worse, the town remains a town, Kasrilevka is Kasrilevka, and Kasrilevka will remain until the Messiah comes.

What is true for Kasrilevka is true for the whole world. As long as law prevails in Kasrilevka and in other towns, the world is at peace. So long as the peace is a peace, the world is a world. But if, God forbid, there is no peace and the nations all over the world go to war, the world will be annihilated—no more world.

Reason tells us there is one remedy. What is the remedy? Destroy the guns, dismantle the cannons, send home the soldiers—and done!—as our prophet Isaiah foretold long ago. But the problem is that this can only happen when the Messiah comes. In the meantime, the nations have another remedy: to hold onto their guns and soldiers, the more the better. Not for the sake of war, God forbid, but for the sake of peace, in order to feel secure with one's life and possessions and in order to be assured that no country will attack another country. And that is called the *balance of power*. Life hangs on that balance, the world teeters on a balance scale. And who is holding the scale? You'll never guess. It is precisely the Turk with the red yarmulke! And why him? Because his country borders the Black Sea and to the Black Sea is where all the big powers are pushing themselves. Everyone wants to gain access to the Black Sea. Everyone wants a passage for his ships and everyone would prefer to be the only player in the game. I know you will ask: isn't the sea large enough for everyone? Don't ask this question. Once you start asking questions, you can go on asking and asking. That's the way it is, forget your questions!

Still and all, the fact remains that Turkey is situated on the Black Sea on the Dardanelles and holds the balance scale in its hand. By rights the Black Sea should be everyone's sea and not just belong to one nation. You must also understand that for the Turk this is good. No one may touch him. That's how it's been from time immemorial. A hundred and fifty years ago, the big powers gathered in Paris and sat and deliberated how to make the sea everyone's sea without each one striving to be the only merchant in Moscow. It was agreed that only one solution was possible: the Turk should remain in charge of the sea and the Dardanelles and no one may touch him—hands off! All the heads of state signed this agreement and went home in peace. Naturally, the heads of state soon regretted this, each wanting to change his mind and to move closer to the Dardanelles, but they had signed. Too late! And, by the way, even if one head of state had wanted to go back on his word, the other heads of state would have stopped him—and so it has been to this day. This treasure is right in front of their eyes and each one is watching that the other doesn't make a grab for it. Some thirty years ago when we were at war with the Turk and had conquered Plehve, and Osman Pasha was already in our hands, Bismarck opened up the old document and reminded us—be careful!—and the Turk was left as before. After that the great powers haven't stuck to their agreement and they keep tearing away at him bit by bit. Franz Josef takes a bit, Victor Emmanuel another bit, and now the Balkan countries have joined together and have cut off a rather large piece. It's really a shame. But you're not through hearing what I have to say. Be patient. As I wrote you earlier, in the first place the Balkan countries won't be in a hurry to share among themselves, and in the second place, no one knows into whose pot the lion's share will fall. As your mother says, "You cooked it, I will eat it." But that's still not the main thing. The main thing is the balance of power, and here we come to the plan I will lay before the Turk.

The plan calls for the Turk to become soft as butter and give each and every one exactly what he demands. He should give in to the Balkan states, return what they want to them, except for reparations (when it comes to money you always have to hold back!). And besides this, I will propose another great idea that will maintain his honor and save his skin! Listen to this. First I will provide him with a few million through speculations and then afterwards arrange it so that all his cities and provinces that had little by little been chipped away in recent years will be returned to him. You will ask: How? Easy. First of all, he must send out his agents to all the main stock exchanges in all the major cities and order them to buy stocks, bonds, and as many lottery tickets as possible. This will send a clear message to the world that he, the red yarmulke, knows something and expects the market will be going up. Then, when he has bought up his fill, he must send out notes to the heads of the great powers and let them know the following: as I, the Turk, am old and weak and exhausted from the war the world is waging against me for years and years, as I am left without one intact bone in my body, and as you, the great powers, are young and strong and smart and educated, you have money and ships and soldiers and airplanes and all the modern tricks and devices, therefore I have decided not to drive myself crazy worrying in my old age about Istanbul, Bosporus, and the Dardanelles. I am handing them over to you gladly. Divide them amongst yourselves, do whatever you want with them and I will enjoy the rest of whatever years I have left in vast far-off Asia with my thousand wives and my water pipe. May you all live to be a hundred and twenty years in happiness and in harmony, as I wish you with all my heart, your truly faithful friend, Ishmael, son of Abraham, born of his servant, Hagar.

And immediately after he has sent this letter, he must get off a dispatch to his agents in the stock exchanges to let it be known that he is prepared to sell all his stocks, bonds, and lottery tickets, which will cause them to go down in value. Quite a coup. The Turk gets rid of Istanbul, Bosporus, the Dardanelles! And not only should they not sell what they have, no! They should rake in a huge profit by buying at the new low prices and make even more money. Why? Herein lies the heart of the matter! As soon as the Turk gets rid of Istanbul, Bosporus and the Dardanelles, and the heads of the great powers set sail on the Black Sea with their ships, a fire will be lit under them and a war will break out among them that will outdo all previous wars! Can you imagine, my dear wife, how much damage such a war would cause and how much money and how many people it would cost? This would not be just any war, my little silly, this could be, may the One Above protect us, a deluge, the second deluge on earth! One would have to be either blind or mad not to foresee what a slaughter this would lead to! And I am absolutely certain that the heads of the great powers themselves will back away from such a prospect and will beg him, the Turk, to have pity on the world and go back to his Istanbul and his Bosporus and his Dardanelles, and if that isn't enough, they might even give him back Adrianople and Scutari and Albania and everything he wants. And if Franz Josef, Victor Emmanuel, and the Balkan noisemakers complain, they'll be invited in! No harm meant, they were only intending to maintain peace and the balance of power on which the whole world depends!

As proof that I am not speaking idly, this very day there was a conference between the Germans and the French in Bern. They are the bloodiest of enemies on account of Alsace-Lorraine, which the Germans took away from the French, and not so much Alsace-Lorraine as the five million in reparations the French had to pay almost in a single day. What do you think they did in Bern? They searched for ways of forgetting Alsace-Lorraine and the five million and to declare a truce, meaning a halt to preparing for war, which would waste energy and money that could be better used for something more important. Do you realize what this means? They are beginning to gradually understand that the prophet Isaiah's words must at last be heeded or else it will be disaster! How much do you think it cost old Franz Josef before he sends out so much as one soldier to wage war? A million for each conscript! And the other countries? How many millions does this preparation for war cost? And this during peacetime! What then will it be, I ask you, during wartime? Where will they find so much money?

It's understood that this is still only the outline of my grand project. In addition there are many, many smaller projects and plans that must be carefully explained to you. But from this alone you can see that your Menachem-Mendl is not crazy, that he is speaking about one day owning three of his own mansions in Warsaw. When Khoskl Kotik heard of my plan he sprang up and covered me with kisses. "You are worth, Reb Menachem-Mendl, your weight in gold! You don't belong in Warsaw, you belong in Vienna, in Berlin, in Paris, or in London!" "Sha! Sha!" I said to him, "Don't get yourself worked up, Reb Khoskl, I know it myself without your telling me, that my place is there, not here, but what can I do? My brain is racing but my tongue is silenced!" Wait awhile, my dear wife, just let me find the right emissary and you will, with God's help, hear even greater things from me. And as I don't have enough time now, I am making this short. God willing, in my next letter I will write you everything at greater length. In the meantime, may God grant us all health and success. Kiss the children for me and send my best and most friendly regards to your mother, whom I honor, and to the whole family, each and every one.

From me your husband Menachem-Mendl

ALMOST FORGOT! My idea that the local Jews should repay the Poles for the boycott with their own boycott has finally caught on with the Polish Jews. The first boycott was against Polish carp. Radomer and Keltzer Jews stopped buying fish for *Shabbos,* and especially the live carp the landowners haul out of their ponds before *Shabbos* every week and which bring in a large income for them every year, no more and no less than a million and a quarter! (Khoskl Kotik and I added it up with a pencil). Serves them right! I wish our Jews would listen to me regarding other matters as well. Ah, you are wondering what do Jews do without fish on *Shabbos?* I'm surprised you should ask that. What do your Kasrilevka Jews do when they don't have challah either? You can get along very well without fish. For instance, take my landlady, where I eat every *Shabbos.* She makes "fish-potato-cakes" without so much as a speck of fish, good enough for kings! I asked her how she makes them. She takes, she says, potatoes boiled in water, fries some onions, and adds heapfuls of pepper till you smell fish all through the house and you die for a drink afterwards, just like after real fish. I have always argued that we should do the same sort of boycotting as the Poles, but no one listens to me! For instance, if the women around here would listen to me, they would do what the fine Polish ladies do and would give up many, many things. If it's good enough for the Polish ladies, it's good enough for the Jewish ladies. Recently the richest Polish ladies gathered in Krakow and promised to help boycott

Jews. I am of the opinion that we have to imitate the Polacks and do everything they do.

As above.

10. Sheyne-Sheyndl from Kasrilevka to Her Husband, Menachem-Mendl, in Warsaw

To my dear, honored, renowned, generous, and wise husband, Menachem-Mendl, may his light shine forever.

FIRST OF ALL, let me tell you that we are, thank God, in the best of health. Pray God we hear the same from you, never worse.

SECOND OF ALL, I am writing you, dear husband, not to be offended by what I am going to say but it seems to me you are not writing what you should be writing. You should know, for instance, what is happening here, how Jewish blood is running in the streets and there is no one here to help us, to give advice, to put in a good word. As my mother says, "It is written that we are like birds who have left their nests, or like stray sheep who have lost their shepherd." Anyone and everyone is taking a piece of our flesh. If just strangers were doing this, the hurt wouldn't be so bad. But our own Jews are profiting from it, may they choke on every groshen! How can God be silent? Yet, as my mother says, "It is written that heaven and earth have vowed that nothing is past hope . . ." Listen to this fine story that happened to our Shaye-Dovid's relative in your very own St. Petersburg among the big shots, as you call them.

Shaye-Dovid's relative, Yenkl Sharogrodsky, and his whole family, if you remember, lived not far from Dubno since God knows when, even before the first pogrom. Suddenly they were driven out right after Passover, bag and baggage, leaving them utterly destitute! So they came here. And Shaye-Dovid—that genius of a man!—advised them to spend some money, gather themselves up, and head for St. Petersburg. There, he said, are these arrangers who can make *trayf* kosher and can arrange to get those who have been driven out back in.

They let themselves be persuaded—if your own relative says so, you go!—sold off everything they had, and went off to St. Petersburg, where they found an arranger. The arranger welcomed them politely and told them to come back in the morning. The next morning he told them to come the next day. And so it went on day after day, day after day. You can imagine how much they suffered because they had no housing permit and there were living expenses! Then one day the arranger said to them that he had just barely managed to arrange for them to go back home but a permit had to be prepared that would cost three hundred or else, he said, it was doubt-ful that the minister would agree. Well, they began to weep and swore on their lives that they had no three hundred to speak of, not even one hun-dred—you might as well hang them right there on the spot!

To make it short, they negotiated and bargained and agreed on a hun-dred and fifty. It was left that the next day, God willing, they would come to him with the money. And so they wouldn't think they were dealing with a nobody, he said to them, "Just wait a minute, let me call in the minister for a moment." Hearing the word "minister," they gasped, almost fainted! The arranger then said, "Don't be afraid, I'll just speak three words to him." And without another thought, he faced the wall, turned a knob of some sort, called to the minister and had a conversation with him through the wall as if with a friend. They thought, I mean the Sharogrodskys, they would die on the spot! How were they to know it was no more than a show, may they all sink into the earth, and that this arranger, cursed be his name, knew the minister like I know the minister's mother-in-law. In the mean-time the money went down the drain for good and whom could they sue, to whom could they protest when they didn't have a residency permit, no money to live on, nothing at all? Nu, I ask you, my dear husband, shouldn't these arrangers all come to a bad end this very day? Aren't they right, the gentiles, when they say all kinds of terrible things about us? As my mother says, "Those sorts lengthen our exile."

So do you see, Mendl, that you are not writing in your newspaper about what you should. You should write about *those* things and maybe the arrangers would soon be buried ten feet deep. Instead, you take it into your head to pity the poor Turk! You want the Turk to make millions and you yourself are satisfied with three mansions in Warsaw. I only want to know what is so great about three mansions and why in Warsaw? You know very well that as long as my mother is alive—may she live and live—I won't budge from here. I haven't joined you in Warsaw just as I didn't join you in Odessa or in Yehupetz. You will have to drag me out by force with police like Leybele Bronshtein dragged his wife out of Yehupetz, she who is not worth my littlest fingernail, because since girlhood she was a ne'er-do-well. She even ran off with her teacher but they stopped them in the act. Then when she couldn't run away from her father and mother she ran away from her husband. As my mother says, "It is written that as a person conducts himself, that is the way God deals with him."

And now you've decided to go to the ends of the earth, anywhere but home and that's what you keep doing. If it's not Yehupetz, it's America, and if not America, it's Warsaw. It looks to me as if you'll remain in Warsaw. If not, you wouldn't be talking about three mansions in Warsaw. Why do you need mansions, Mendl? What security do they provide? And where is it written that mansions are the only security? As my mother says, "The best dairy meal is a piece of meat and the best security is money in your pocket." Speaking of money, let me make a suggestion even though you never ask my advice—after all, what am I compared to you? Still and all, I tell you as a true friend that if your dreams about the Turk have any possibility of coming true, you had better work it out ahead of time in no uncertain terms what your earnings will be, without tricks and half-words muttered through the nose, the way Jacob was tricked over Rachel and Leah. What is there to be ashamed of and on whose good will should you depend? I really must tell you the honest truth, that so long as you were dealing in stocks and bonds and brokering deals, I understood some of it— may my enemies not understand more. But since you started to work out deals with the Turk, the great powers, kings and kingdoms, I'm becoming afraid of where this might, God forbid, be leading you. As my mother says, "It is written that if a person is destined to succeed, it will come through the door, and if not through the door, then through the window, and if not through the window, then through the chimney."

Maybe I'm so small-townish that I am not worthy of understanding you, could that be? Yet isn't it possible for you to describe things so that I too could understand them? What would you do if you really had a wife who was an "old woman" as you call me? Are you telling me that in your eyes I've become an "old woman"? I would like to know what kind of a wife you want? Maybe like the one who cooks potato-fish cakes every Friday night over which you lick your fingers with pleasure? Who is this beauty? Is she a widow or divorced? What is her name? How old is she? And what does she look like? Why do you write me that she is your landlady and you eat there every *Shabbos*? Can it be that you have two there: one for *Shabbos* and one for the rest of the week? If that's the case, Warsaw deserves to sink into the earth with all her beautiful landladies who cook such delicious potato-fish cakes and then you won't need to lick your fingers and maybe then I too can also be respected, as I wish you all good things and eternal happiness, your true, faithful wife

Sheyne-Sheyndl

Yes. How about sending me a picture of yourself? Let me also have a look at the successful writer. They say that being a writer destroys your health, so maybe you shouldn't work so hard. Health is more important. As my mother says, "It is written that you can buy everything for money but not health and not years."

11. Menachem-Mendl from Warsaw to His Wife, Sheyne-Sheyndl, in Kasrilevka

To my dear, wise, and modest wife, Sheyne-Sheyndl, may God grant her many years!

FIRST OF ALL, let me tell you that I am, blessed be His name, in good health and spirits, and may the Blessed One grant that we hear from one another only good news of comfort and salvation for us and for all of Israel—Amen.

SECOND OF ALL, you should know, my dear wife, when I say something is gnawing at me, I know what I am talking about. Let other sharper minds who sit and wrack their brains in London hammer out a thousand peace treaties, I will still stick to my guns. So long as it doesn't strike me right, it's no good—*it cannot work out!* To my way of thinking, a peace that people exploit only for themselves is no peace at all. People have to reach the point where they realize there is nothing worth fighting over. With good will everything can be worked out. You cannot convince me that if two people have a disagreement and a third comes along to straighten them out, that they will be grateful to him and will part in peace and tranquility, kissing one another on the lips. Let that third person turn his back for a minute and you will see how brotherly their embrace will be and how soon it will be before they will bite off each other's noses! And especially when we have more than two!

The Bulgarian must be crazy, my little silly, to allow the Greek to throw his weight around in Macedonia any way that suits him. Poor Macedonia! For years and years it has been a powder keg ready to explode into a bloody war among the many different peoples that live there. Besides Turks you have Greeks, Bulgarians, Serbs, Albanians, Rumanians, and many more. Naturally there are Jews there too. You will ask, why do they need Jews there? For pogroms. What would the city of Salonika have done if there had been no Jews? Who would they offer as a thanksgiving sacrifice right after the victory God granted them over the Turk? And since we are speaking of peace—ask yourself what sense is there for King Ferdinand, may he forgive me, to move his soldiers closer to Macedonia? And what is the sense of his writing letters to the Turk about peace without consulting any of the other Balkan combatants? So long as they are in this all together, why all the secrecy? Or again, take the Serb, really an ally, and yet they've arranged a pact quietly with the Greek against their good friend, Ferdinand! As I wrote you, now the pot will begin boiling among the three Slav rulers and it will get to the point where each will invade the land he believes he alone can conquer with his prowess.

Why just these three? And what's happening with King Mikita of Montenegro? Do you really think that this cunning little king who quietly made clever speculations and earned a few groshens on the stock exchange will be satisfied with that? Rest assured he will not be satisfied with just a *gut shabbos* greeting. They'll have to pay him off too, if not payment-in-kind, then with hard cash. You can't get rid of him so easily! But wait, we're not through yet. So far we are talking just about the bride and groom; where are the relatives on the groom's side and on the bride's side? Reb Franz Josef? Reb Victor Emmanuel? Reb Wilhelm? How about the English? The French? And where are "we"? Have you forgotten about "us"? If you think "we" are going to stand by looking from afar at someone else's wedding, watching the relatives eat and drink and have a gay time while they just wish us a happy year, you are greatly mistaken! And especially now when there are rumors that Sezonov is resigning and that Witte will be taking his place. *"Our"* Witte! With him there will be different politics and a different order of things. Witte, you understand, is "one of ours." He knows very well the meaning of buying high and selling low and what a "stallage" means. He was, after all, minister of finance! He can wrap them all around his little finger!

So there you have the relatives. And what about the musicians, entertainers, matchmakers, servers, best men, and bridesmaids, as well as ordinary well-wishers and the needy hangers-on who also must be catered to? It is, after all, a celebration! God helped out and they married off the Turk and they're sharing his fortune, no small amount! Take Rumania, for example. Do you have any idea for what great deeds she deserves a piece of the pie? How much "butter" did Rumania contribute to the war? Don't fret over it—they'll cut off a hefty slice of Bulgarian Silestria for her, and the Turks and Bulgarians and Jews who live there will go over from Bulgaria to Rumania. The Jews are protesting—what do they have against them? They don't want to go over to Rumania. They would rather remain in Bulgaria because in Bulgaria they were, they claim, at least respected citizens. In Rumania, Jews and garbage are all the same! The great powers, acting as intercessors, assured the Jews, pledging stocks and investments, but who knows what these pledges are worth? The Rumanians Jews themselves have a Berlin treaty, a paper written and signed, with all the right stipulations and still have nothing to show for it, and crying *sh'ma yisroel* will not help!

But all of these matters are for me just trivialities. These Balkan alliances don't begin to bother me one bit because, as I already explained in my previous letters, the Turk loses very little because of them. On the contrary, he gains a good deal by not needing to spend money to support an army against those countries filled with his enemies. It turns out my worry over the Turk was for nothing. If anything, the Balkan war was the best thing for him. Now he can look around at home in Asia a little and, as they say in America, see where he stands and tend to his own business dealings a bit. They say, and it's true, that after a fire, you can become rich.

Still, something else is gnawing at me. I am not too happy about the great powers starting to play up to the Turk in Asia. I am referring to the Englishman and that treaty he secretly made with the Turk about the railway to Baghdad. You might think, why a train to Baghdad? The English don't have enough trains? But there is an entanglement here that can turn the whole politics of the area topsy-turvy. It's possible that all my schemes will go up in smoke. You will probably wonder what this railway to Baghdad has to do with my scheme? It's necessary to explain it to you slowly so you can digest it.

The English with their castles are the smartest nation in the world. Cunning, crafty people, old hands! They never fight you but always manage to get the biggest share. If two foes go to war, they stand off at a distance in their ships, keep their hands in their pockets, and calculate from which side they can profit the most. They set one side against the other, promising one side that in a pinch he can come to them and all will go well because who is equal to them? And especially at sea, where the largest fleet in the world is English. When the wheel turns and the other side is winning, and more can be made from him, they cozy up to that side, giving him the same assurance, that if they get into trouble they will be of help with their fleet which is the largest fleet in the world. Supposedly this is all arranged in the greatest secrecy but so that the whole world knows about it in order to intimidate everyone. Understand? This is called: letting other people do your dirty work. Till now they did what they could to weaken the Turk. But now that the Slavs have done too well with the Turk over the Balkans and the Turk has already suffered a big defeat, the English have suddenly started to smile at the defeated side, playing up to him, promising him loans and other favors, and the result is—a railroad to Baghdad. Besides opening a way to India, they are making themselves at home in Persia and they no longer need to make common cause with "us" as they did until now when they were dividing Persia in half, one half belonging to them, the other to "us."

And if they cool off toward "us," the French will also cool off and it will undo the whole arrangement, throwing the two "troikas" one against the other: "we," the French, and the English on one side against Franz Josef, Wilhelm, and Victor Emmanuel on the other side. And when it all comes undone, who can be so clever to foresee *who will be against whom?* Ay, you will ask: what has this to do with me? It actually has nothing to do with me, but it has a great deal to do with the Turk. I am afraid they might try to get at him in his own back yard and that would, God forbid, undo all my golden schemes that I have worked out on his behalf. He would no longer be a speculator and would lose the millions he could have made. But most important, peace could no longer be counted on, a real peace, like the one the prophet Isaiah prophesied. A shambles! This all begins to smell of the real war the world trembles in fear of and for which we all pay good money. Do you think the French raised the military conscription from two years to three years for nothing? True, the French rebel against this, they don't want to suffer, but who listens to them?

In short, my dear wife, I find myself feeling pessimistic. For a whole week we pored over the map, I and Khoskl Kotik. We were trying to find this Baghdad. What does Persia border on? And how far is it from there to India? We wanted to figure out exactly what kind of knavery was in that secret pact between the English and the Turk. It ended up in a serious argument. He, Khoskl Kotik, wanted to convince me of the opposite, that it's good for the English and the Turk to become bosom friends. What's so good about that? He believes the good is in this railway, it's a real blow to the Germans. They would be ready to butt heads with the English over it and as long as the Germans and the English are butting heads, that would be doing the Turk the greatest favor. I said to him, "Never mind such favors. If they want to butt heads, let them butt heads here, on this side of the Dardanelles, not on the other side, in his own back yard." He smiled at me and said, "Jew, what's the difference?" And I said back to him in his manner, "Jew, is it my fault if you understand politics as much as a goy understands the Talmud?" He got a little hot under the collar and said to me, "All right, if you understand more than I do, maybe you can help *me* understand too." So I gave him an example. If two people grab each other's throat, it's better that they wrestle outside the door, not inside my house. Have you chewed that over?" He fixed me with his eyes and said, "Do you know what I will say to you, Reb Menachem-Mendl? It seems to me you don't begin to know what's going on." So I said, "Why don't I begin to know what is going on?" He then said, "Because you don't understand." I said again, "Why don't I understand?" Said he, "Because you're an idiot." I really wanted to tell him off right then and there, calling him an even bigger idiot, but I stopped myself—today let it pass. Why should I get into a fight with a man who knows all my secrets? As your mother says, "With a Jew it's good to eat kugel." I just said, "Do you know what, Reb Khoskl? You're really a good man, may I have as good a year. But let's not talk politics any more. Let's talk about whatever you wish, but not about politics!" He said, "That's fine with me. God has brought me this far without politics, he can take me further without it too." And we became good friends as before and again chatted, again about the Turk and again about the Balkans and the great powers and the English with their pact and about all the other things that are happening now in the world, with others and with our brothers, the sons of Israel.

But as I have no time—I have to run to the post office and from there to the newspaper to read the latest wires from Tokyo—they say the Japanese Mikado is on his deathbed—I will make this short. God willing, in the next letter I will write you everything at greater length. In the meantime, may God grant us all all health and success. Kiss the children for me and send my best and most friendly regards to your mother, whom I honor, and to the whole family, each and every one.

From me your husband Menachem-Mendl

ALMOST FORGOT! Thank God I have found my go-between, just the right person to send to the sultan. He was recommended to me by no other than Khoskl Kotik himself. According to him, this person is made to order for me. First of all, he is a man of integrity, one in a million, a man, they say, who is educated and knowledgeable about politics. Second of all, they say he is a thoroughly honest man. That is the most important thing for me. He is a fanatic Zionist. And a man who has passion, no matter what he believes, is right for the job. They say he is good with languages, knows maybe seven languages. And he can talk a blue streak in any one of them! And not only in one language but in several at once. When he begins, he begins like a person should, in our mother tongue, Yiddish. But he soon jumps over to Russian, from Russian he leaps to Polish, from Polish he springs to German, and from German he throws himself into English. Finally he finishes off in Hebrew or even in biblical Aramaic. My bad luck he isn't in Warsaw just now. He's in America traveling around Columbus's land, making Zionists out of the Jews there. A waste of time. If he had asked me, I would have talked him out of that trip. I know more about American Jews than anyone. They need Zionism like you need a toothache. They'll applaud him, throw parties, (they call those "recep-tions" there), drink a *l'khayim* (there they call it a "shpritz"), and do every-thing his heart desires. And no sooner will he board the ship and hardly have left the shores of Neviyork than they will forget him with his lectures about Zionism and they will run to give new "receptions" and hear new "shpritzes" from those *against* Zionism. What a country! It's no wonder you hear from every peddler, *"America ganev, a curse on Columbus!"*

12. Sheyne-Sheyndl from Kasrilevka to Her Husband, Menachem-Mendl, in Warsaw

To my dear, honored, renowned, generous, and wise husband, Menachem-Mendl, may his light shine forever.

FIRST OF ALL, let me tell you that we are, thank God, in the best of health. Pray God we hear the same from you, never worse.

SECOND OF ALL, I am writing you, my dear husband, that once things start going badly for a person, trouble will come, as my mother says, "through doors and through gates, through shut windows and through a crack in the shutter . . ." You surely know whom I'm talking about. I'm talking about our Shaye-Dovid's father-in-law, Yenkl Sharogrodsky, and the tragedy that befell him! And whose fault was it if not Shaye-Dovid's himself, with his cockeyed notions and clever advice? As my mother says, "If it's your fate to get a blow on the back, it will come from one of your own . . ." Just listen to what a person is capable of doing!

When the Sharogrodskys came back from Petersburg with their tails between their legs, with nothing to show for their efforts in addition to having lost their last kopek, Shaye-Dovid wasn't at all sorry about the bad advice he had given them but gave them still another idea. Since it was the constable who had driven them out of the village, not the goyim—on the contrary, the goyim were ready to stick by them through thick and thin, in-sisting they shouldn't be bothered. The goyim said that Yenkl Sharogrod-sky was a good man and his wife, Khane-Mirl, was even better. How about that! May what Khane-Mirl lacks in goodness be mine. Last year when she came to us for the holidays she came to such blows with Shaye-Dovid's eldest daughter-in-law, Ettl-Beyle, that all the neighbors came running. And over what do you think they came to blows? Over something impor-tant? Not at all. Over a little book in Yiddish that Khane-Mirl's sons brought home from the village, a story book or a novel or the devil knows what! Ettl-Beyle's sons got their hands on it and started to read it one at a

time until it was time for Khane-Mirl to leave and by then the book had
vanished. What book are you talking about? Who ever heard of a book?
Gone. A whole to-do broke out over who had it last. Book! Book! One word
led to another, blows were struck, they barely pulled them apart! I won't
say it, but it is possible that Khane-Mirl wasn't as guilty as Ettl-Beyle and
her boys. You should see them, her boys, they have become such big shots.
They get together every Friday night for meetings, play a game of cards,
and put on such airs it's laughable! You think, Mendl, that our Kasrilevka
is the Kasrilevka it once was? In a million years you would not recognize it
if you came here! As my mother says, "It is written that a generation will
arise whose fathers will not know their children and the children will not
know their fathers . . ."

So, the gentile neighbors stood up for the Sharegradskis saying they
shouldn't be sent away. They had nothing against this Jew and had already
sent off a petition to the governor. But it did no good at all, it's the law—finished! So Shaye-Dovid gave them more of his good advice, may my enemies live as long! Some people! They like to give advice, whether you ask
them or not! When you were in America and when, may it never happen
again, there were no letters from you for a long time, Shaye-Dovid hit on an
idea and tried to put a bug in my father's ear, may he rest in peace-my father was still alive then—that he get a writ from the local rabbi who had
married us and send off this writ together with our marriage contract to the
rabbis in America saying that in case a young man by the name of Menachem-Mendl came to them and wanted to get married, they should know
he already had a wife and they mustn't perform a wedding ceremony. My
mother overheard them whispering together, Shaye-Dovid and my father,
and caught a few words, "Menachem-Mendl," "America," "wedding ceremony." She said to Shayeh-Dovid, "Tell me, I beg you, why do you need to
wrack your brains over my children? Whom are they bothering? Why are
they so important to you?" Shaye-Dovid wanted to explain himself, saying
he didn't intend, God forbid, to be harming anyone or to be doing it for
himself. On the contrary, he had no one else's benefit in mind except my
mother and her children. She thanked him for his good will and asked him
again to tell her just one thing: whom were her children harming? On
whose toes were they stepping? Whom were they inconveniencing? And
why were they so important to him? He begged her forgiveness, asking her
to forget what he had said, as if he hadn't said anything and hadn't even
thought anything! Do you think he was fooling her even though he swore
on his children's children? That's the kind of man he is! When you look at
him, it seems he's not a bad person, not bad at all, ready to go through fire

and water for anyone, but he's a real pain-in-the-neck, gets under your skin, and loves to give advice.

In short, what was the advice he gave his relatives? The advice was this: since there was a rumor going around and they were writing in the newspapers that the expulsion of the Jews would soon be stopped, he wondered how could this be used? Certainly it would be good for those who had not yet been expelled. But what about the others who had? Here was his idea. Shaye-Dovid thought it would be good if the expelled relatives, the Sharogrodskys, would pretend not to know what was going on and would as soon as possible sneak back into the village and hide from the constable for one or two nights. They needn't be afraid of the goyim. The most important thing was that the constable shouldn't find out until the new edict came out ordering a stop to the expulsions and then they could again show their faces to the constable. Ah, but wouldn't the constable then complain because he was the one who had driven them out? They would have to worry about that later, pay him off, how much can a constable cost? What was he? A governor?

And so they let themselves be convinced—after all, if a relative says— you listen! They quietly snuck back into the village, not all of them, just the father, Yenkl Sharogrodsky and the two sons-in-law, Motl and Meier, because all of them at once, a whole crowd coming in, would raise eyebrows. They stole into town at night and tiptoed into the house. They were apparently afraid to light a candle for fear somone would see people were living there. Soon they wanted to go to sleep but as it was cold as ice, this is what they decided to do: if they lit the stove, there would be smoke, and if at that very moment the constable drove by and saw smoke coming from the chimney, he might become suspicious. So they took a brazier—I don't know what brilliant mind thought that one up—poured coals in it, lit a little fire and began to warm themselves. And when they were good and warm, they fell asleep, but really sound asleep. The smoke filled the room, they suffocated, and—goodbye.

You can imagine, Mendl, what is going on here with us. The whole town is up in arms! Things are at the boiling point! When do you think we found out about it? Just this morning. It was from your very gazette that we found out. I am simply amazed that you didn't write me anything about this story in your last letter, not so much as a word, as if the Sharogrodskys didn't mean a thing to you. The Turk, apparently, is much more important to you than my father's family.

We learned all about it from your gazette, how they found all three of them, Yenkl Sharogrodsky and both his sons-in-law, dead next to the brazier and how they brought them to Dubno and what kind of a funeral they had. All Dubno was there! There was wailing, they write, the likes of which hadn't been heard since the Keshinev pogrom. So what has come of it? In the meantime poor Khane-Mirl almost went out of her mind. She was desperate to go to Dubno but they wouldn't let her. And Shaye-Dovid himself, well, I've seen nicer looking corpses. What devil made him give advice? And now he will be burdened with a widow and a whole troop of orphans. Serves him right, a Jew shouldn't have this vile habit of giving advice!

Then again, maybe he wasn't so guilty because how do we know that if not Shayeh-Dovid, it wouldn't have been someone else? Khane-Mirl herself tells about what happened to her husband a year ago. On the way from Dubno to their own town with hundreds in their pockets, Yenkl and the sons-in-law were set upon by peasants. They were tied hand and foot and would have been killed if a priest hadn't driven by. By this miracle they were saved and gave thanks to God. Go figure they would end up losing their lives and with a brazier! As my mother says, "It is written that every seventh day of Succos it is decided from above how every person must die . . ."

Don't be offended, Menachem-Mendl, but I am so broken up by this tragedy that I can't write you of anything more even though I have enough to write about! I can't put hand to pen and I'm not in the mood for anything. And not just I, but all of us are walking around in a daze, as I wish you all good things and eternal fortune from your truly faithful wife

Sheyne-Sheyndl

My dear husband! Maybe you could wake up your people who have suddenly fallen asleep? It seems they've gotten tired of sending me the hundreders for your writings. They're not too tired to put out a new gazette every day. May God help me, but I already knew it would be this way. As my mother says, "Taking money is easy. Giving money is hard . . ." When she says one of her sayings, all your expert friends are left in the dust!

13. Menachem-Mendl from Warsaw
to His Wife, Sheyne-Sheyndl, in Kasrilevka

To my dear, wise, and modest wife, Sheyne-Sheyndl, may God grant her many years!

FIRST OF ALL, let me tell you that I am, blessed be His name, in good health and spirits, and may the Blessed One grant that we hear from one another only good news of comfort and salvation for us and for all of Israel—Amen.

SECOND OF ALL, let me tell you, my dear wife, that the world is the same everywhere and what happens in politics is the same as on the stock exchange—exactly the same, not a hair's difference. On the stock exchange, the smartest broker has no way of knowing today where the wind will blow tomorrow, and stocks that yesterday reached all-time highs, tomorrow can hit bottom. So it is in politics. Only a fool would predict today what tomorrow will bring. Remember what was going on that time on the Yehupetz stock exchange, may it never happen again? Every half hour the dispatches were arriving from St. Petersburg saying that "Putilevers" were falling and from Warsaw they were telegraphing that "Lilliputs" were rising. Buy "Lilliputs" and only "Lilliputs"! Of course the crowd, I among them, ran immediately and bought up as many "Lilliputs" as possible. What was the outcome? The roof caved in! Within the hour a new dispatch arrived from St. Petersburg saying that "Putilevers" were going up-up. Buy "Putilevers"! And from Warsaw came a dispatch saying that "Lilliputs" stink from high heaven like old fish. The poor speculators, I among them, wracked our brains to scratch out so much as a ruble from it all. But we were all left with empty pockets. So what's the moral? The moral is that the stock exchange and politics are cut from the same cloth, a cloth so fine it is hard to place a price on it.

It's a blind business and you have to find your way blindly, without guidance. In politics, as in the stock exchange, you must have a bit of luck in finding the right way, and I hope to God that in my new business, politics, I have found, with God's help, the right way, the way to peace, to that peace all nations of the world look to and yearn for and wish for and are starving for! But that was not the peace that was signed a week ago Friday in London between those Balkan playboys and the Turk. Worthless! I wouldn't give you a groshen for that peace. Nothing will come of that peace. It can even lead to war, as I wrote you earlier. I don't want to repeat myself. Already the Turk has announced publicly that the Greeks should not dare go near the islands because he, the Turk, won't allow it. You will ask: but the Greeks have always held those islands firmly in their grasp, so why has the Turk kept quiet until now? The reason is that until now the Turk wasn't finished with the Bulgarians, hadn't known where he stood with them. Now that he's made a deal with the Bulgarians, even before signing that great peace treaty in London, it's another matter. Is this all clear to you? Be patient—we still have Serbs in the world who have a dozen grievances against the Bulgarians and the Bulgarians have as many grievances against them. Both want to fight more than they want to live because we are dealing here, you understand, not with victory or pride but with money, with fortunes!

In the Balkans, as everywhere in the world, everyone wants his own way, and between the two—the Serbs and the Bulgarians—there are old scores to settle, especially now after the war that was so profitable for them, even more so than they had figured. Into the Serbs' hands has fallen such a fortune that the Bulgarians will never in their lives allow them to keep it, although the Serbs helped them take Adrianople. If it were to go to trial, for example, and I were to be a witness, I would testify that the Bulgarians are right. They *did* sacrifice more people and more money—there's no question about it. Although there's a dispatch here from St. Petersburg saying we are prepared to participate in a peace between these two "good friends" who are sharpening their teeth against one another, it is on the condition that both sides put down their arms. You can see that it will never work because there is a Franz Josef in this world who wants only the Serbs to put down their arms so that he and his friend Victor Emmanuel can do with Albania whatever they want and for all the others to butt out.

Let fools celebrate the good news this day from Berlin, where the Germans "married" the English, and let them lick their fingers at the fine speeches that were held in honor of the new peace in the world, and let them be thrilled by the wedding presents from both sides given to the bride and groom. When the Berliner "ladies" saw the gifts, they fell over each other in astonishment. To my way of seeing it, the same way they see it in America, it is a big to-do over nothing, a swindle, a "bluff," as it is called in America. That is not the peace I have in mind. The peace I have in mind is a totally different peace. It is the peace our Isaiah prophesied over a thousand years ago. That is the peace we aspire to and to that peace all my thoughts are now directed and on that peace now depend all my schemes through which I must once and for all become, as you say, a mentsh, but a *mentsh* with a fortune and with a reputation, may it come to pass with God's help!

Ah, you're impatient, you want it to happen this very minute? As your mother says, "Money takes time to make." It's not my fault, my dear wife, that you don't understand me and think little of me. The same words that I write you now I spoke to a good friend, an old friend and an honest one, without pretensions, by nature a good, gentle person, one can say a person without guile.

We met the other day in Warsaw, on the Nalevkis. He stopped me and embraced me warmly. *"Sholom aleichem!* How are you, Menachem-Mendl?" *"Aleichem sholom!* How should I be?" I said, "How is it going for you?" Back and forth we went—how come he never sees me and how goes it and how do I like their Warsaw? Then he grabbed me by the lapel and started to lecture me:

"Tell me, where do you, Menachem-Mendl, come to politics? What are you, some kind of idler? You're a businessman, your place is in Yehupetz on the stock exchange, among businessmen, not here among idlers. Our faces are red with shame for you. It pains us to see what you are occupying yourself with and whom you are competing with. For God's sake, with ordinary *cheder* teachers, cheap word peddlers who know nothing from nothing and wiseacres who aren't worth your time."

And on and on he went with a barrage of more such sweet words all the while clasping my lapel. I let him speak, heard him out to the end, and finally, when he stopped, I said to him:

"Done? Have you finished? May I get a word in? If so, first of all, you are entitled to a thank-you for your compliments in raising me to the level of an intellectual. It's possible you are right, that they're impractical and ordinary *cheder* teachers and cheap word peddlers and idlers who are not worth my time. And it can also be just the opposite, that these wiseacres, as you call them, are really great experts and political scholars who have more understanding in their little finger than I have in my whole head. Truth be told, I don't know any of them, I don't know who they are or what they are. Second of all, I don't understand why your faces are red with shame over my current job. How is a speculator or a broker on the stock exchange better than a speculator or a broker in politics? On the contrary, a broker speculates to make or lose money and that's the end of it! But a politician like myself, besides trying to make money and besides hoping to make a good name for himself, can, if God allows it, do good things for people and bring about a long-hoped-for peace in the world. How am I to blame if *your* wiseacres are idiots and think that politics is like the Bible that has to be learned for its own sake and who don't begin to understand that politics is a stock exchange, that wars are speculations, that nations are speculators, and that diplomats are brokers?" I continued:

"God knows what He is doing. To one He grants no more than a fat finger for counting, to another a wagging tongue for gossip, and to me, blessed be His name, He granted a bit of talent in the things that have to do with speculation and a bit of understanding in order to come up with a plan to make something important happen. Certainly they should envy me as I envy Witte, who has in him a businessman's zeal and the good ideas of a real stock exchange broker, a born speculator. Would that it were true what they say, that he will soon be elevated. Then I would also be elevated. For him I have a special scheme and with him I would need no intercessor. I could explain it all myself, and very well. He was once in Odessa and, they say he understands Yiddish perfectly, and in a pinch he has a Jewish wife called Matilda. It's no secret, Hummel brokers know her. But in any case, I am waiting for a person whose name I cannot disclose, who is coming from America so that I can have someone to intercede for me and then it will really start working! I have such great schemes, not only for the Turk and not only for all the other nations of the world, but for us Jews as well. I have such schemes that your wiseacres will be floored and will no longer say that Menachem-Mendl is competing with just anyone."

Good—good, I really gave it to him! He let go of my lapel and remained standing speechless. We parted good friends, as before, meaning he held to his opinions and I held to mine, because if fifteen good friends were to come along, the finest people from Warsaw and from all over, from east and west, would they be able to convince me that I'm not following the right path? Would they be capable of pointing out to me that now is not the moment that I can raise myself up? How much longer can Menachem-Mendl roam this world, as you say, pursuing idolatries, wandering to the ends of the earth? I was in America—enough, beyond America there is nothing further—the end of the world! And as I have no time, I am running to the post office to see if there's a letter from you, I am making this short. God willing, in my next letter I will write you everything at length. In the meantime, may God grant us all health and success. Be well and kiss the children for me and send my best and most friendly regards to your mother, whom I honor, and to the whole family, each and every one!

From me your husband Menachem-Mendl

ALMOST FORGOT! I thought that only in Yehupetz betweeen speculators and brokers on the stock exchange was there this habit of swearing, cursing, and coming to blows. It turns out the Yehupetz speculators and brokers have a lot to learn from the Warsaw intellectuals. And the Warsaw intellectuals can't hold a candle to the Lodzer intellectuals. As much as they curse your Kasrilevka marketwomen who sell rotten apples, as many curses and insults as they earn, it's only a tenth of what flies through the air here! Ranting and raving! Shouting and storming! Hell itself! Every day, every day, it's a story without an end! I visit Khoskl Kotik and say to him, "Reb Khoskl, what is this all about?" He says to me, "Just wait, Reb Menachem-Mendl, this is nothing, they'll come to blows soon." Tell me, my dear wife, am I not correct in saying that the world is the same everywhere?

As above.

14. Sheyne-Sheyndl from Kasrilevka to Her Husband, Menachem-Mendl, in Warsaw

To my dear, honored, renowned, and wise husband, Menachem-Mendl, may his light shine forever.

FIRST OF ALL, let me tell you that we are, thank God, in the best of health. Pray God we hear the same from you, never worse.

SECOND OF ALL, I am writing you, my dear husband, that God is dealing with our Kasrilevka very badly. We still hadn't gotten over Shayeh-Dovid's father-in-law's tragedy with the Sharagrodskis when God dealt us a new blow. Do you remember Moishe-Nakhman Khortovoi? These days he's really poverty-stricken. He had to sell his apartment long ago. After his Khaye-Perl died, he remarried a wretch of a woman from another town, some slaughterer's widow. As my mother says, "If you can't get a bargain at home, you have to find it elsewhere . . ." His only meager means of support was his brother, Berl-Isaac. Berl-Isaac lived in a nearby village, made a living, and was able to help out his brother, sometimes with a sack of flour, sometimes with a sack of potatoes, and sometimes with a little money too. But this was all in the past when Berl-Isaac had a shop, earned money, and could spare some for his brother. But where is it written that Berl-Isaac can't be visited by misfortune? The goyim forced him to sell his shop for very little and there was no way he can earn a living. How long can you help out a brother? As my mother says, "A sack full of holes is hard to stuff." Sounds bad enough? What does God do? By some government decree Berl-Isaac was forced to leave the village in twenty-four hours. They were in a panic! And when do they throw them out? Right in the middle of the night, in pitch-black darkness, in the rain, in the mud, in the slush. As my mother says, "It is written that when the Jews fled from Egypt, it was so dark they might as well have been blind . . ."

Where could a Jew like Berl-Isaac go when he was driven out of his village? To the city, to Kasrilevka—where else?—where his brother, Moishe-Nakhman, lived. Ay, Moishe-Nakhman himself was starving from hunger? Was that Berl-Isaac's fault? Didn't he always help him when he, Berl-Isaac, had something? That's one consideration. And second, how would Berl-Isaac know his brother was so poor that he had nothing to keep body and soul together, and the Khortovois are, after all, a proud family? They would die three times over in a day from hunger before they would say, help me. What more do you need to know about these people? One brother will not ask the other, lend me, or give me credit. If you give it on your own—fine, and if you don't, that's also fine. A strange family. Not for nothing does my mother say, "A proud person is worse than a wastrel." Do you think Berl-Isaac went straight to his brother's, to Moishe-Nakhman? Not at all. Instead he went to an inn and had to take two rooms with six beds and mattresses, otherwise the innkeeper wouldn't let them in. Berl-Isaac was about to have the innkeeper light the samovar and serve dinner, when luckily his brother, Moishe-Nakhman, who had found out they were there, suddenly ran in, more dead than alive. "Berl-Isaac! In God's name! Why didn't you come straight to me?" Berl-Isaac pointed to the six beds as if to say, "Do you have enough room for this crowd when even here they are sleeping two to a mattress?"

But coming from that family, Moishe-Nakhman began to laugh, and said very generously, "Ach, what nonsense! So it will be without mattresses, a small problem! Gather up your crowd and come to me!" Do you have any idea where he would be able to get food for such a bunch—tea and sugar besides meals for them? But he was, after all, a Khortovoi. He pawned his gabardine and asked his wife to prepare supper. Berl-Isaac knew very well what kind of a rich man, God help us, his brother was and how much blood this supper cost him. His sister-in-law, the wretch, stuck her nose in the air and muttered, "Some herd you've coralled for me here." The next morning Berl-Isaac wanted to have breakfast at the inn and it was the same story all over again. Moishe-Nakhman arrived, argued, waving his hands in the air, "You can't do this, it's a shame for others, a brother comes and eats at a stranger's table. It's bad enough you're staying at an inn."

One day followed another. Berl-Isaac ran all over town looking for a way to earn some money. What money? What jobs? There are more than enough of people here looking for work without him! They refused to eat at the brother's. First of all, how long can one be a guest at another's table? And second of all, what was there for them to eat when his brother's wife and family were themselves dying for a crust of bread? To eat at the inn you have to pay. The innkeeper was no fool. He soon sniffed out that his guests smelled of poverty. That's no disgrace, the innkeeper himself was no rich man. As my mother says, "May we inherit the difference between him and Rothschild . . ." He was kind enough just to let them stay at the inn. Did I say he was letting them stay? It was more that he didn't know what to do with them! Should he tell them to leave? He did tell them that, not once but several times. But where could they go, for God's sake, disappear into thin air? They would gladly go to America but they had no means of getting there. Your comrades, the "Ikas" and the "Shmikas," make millions, you say, and hold on to them. Why don't they come here? What are they saving their millions for? Till the Messiah comes? They obviously don't know what my mother knows, "When the Messiah comes, what will we need them for?"

So, it's really bad! What to do? But listen to what a Khortovoi thinks up. Berl-Isaac had a long talk with his wife about things not working out. There was nothing to live on, moving to America they couldn't afford, you had to die in any case, so rather than die of hunger it was better to poison themselves. More than once his wife burst into tears and pointed to the children, as if to say, "What will happen to the children?" Berl-Isaac said, "We'll poison the children first and then we'll drink it ourselves." What do you think of a man's way of seeing things? Only a Khortovoi could think like that!

Nothing for it—only a woman, she gave in. As my mother says, "It is written, a woman's life is in her husband's hands . . ." Without further thought, he pawned some of his wife's clothes, went off to the market and bought fresh rolls, tea, and sugar, asked for the samovar to be heated for tea, gathered all the children, and served the tea and rolls. "Eat, children," he said, "for the last time!" What joy there was to eat at last! Then Berl-Isaac poured a powder into the tea. The smaller children complained that the tea tasted bitter, so he added more sugar and told them to drink. They drank and made faces, but they drank. The older children saw that their parents were whispering to one another, crying, and pouring something into the tea and they refused to drink. The parents begged them with tears in their eyes to drink. They themselves had to drink to show the children until all had drunk, except one, an older boy, a bar mitzvah, who was stubborn and refused to drink! And when the others finished drinking and began to feel sick, the bar mitzvah rushed out for help screaming that his parents had poisoned all the children and themselves with some powder in the tea! The whole town came running, brought doctors, tried to save them, wept and cried—it was no use!

What can I tell you, Mendl, whoever was not at that funeral will live twenty years longer. It was a funeral never to be forgotten! It was like *Tisha B'Av*, I tell you, the Destruction of the Temple! To this day I can see Berl-Isaac in my mind, with his poor worried face and glazed eyes, a person who has lost everything. I imagine that on his face it was long evident that he would die an unnatural death. But worst of all, he comes to all of us in our dreams, night after night! My mother says, "It is written that he who takes his own life cannot arrive as quickly to the next world . . ." So we don't sleep through the night, not I, not my mother, as I wish you only good things and eternal happiness, from me your true faithful wife

Sheyne-Sheyndl

I forgot to write you, Mendl, that this week I finally received money from your people, this time, thank God, with a note enclosed. Some note! May my enemies receive such a note—altogether one line. "We are sending you," they wrote, "payment on account, a hundreder." And that was it! First of all I would like to know, who is this "we"? It was signed by some official with a fancy signature. And second of all, what is this "payment on account"? What account? I would like to see how they figured this out with you—by weight or by size? And another thing: why do they have to write me that they are sending me a hundreder when they are sending me a hundreder? Can't I see for myself that it's a hundreder, not a thousander? As my mother says, "It makes as much sense as if they had slapped someone in the face and told him, 'Here, Shloime-Yosl, you've been slapped . . .'"

15. Menachem-Mendl from Warsaw
to His Wife, Sheyne-Sheyndl, in Kasrilevka

To my dear, wise, and modest wife, Sheyne-Sheyndl, may God grant her many years!

FIRST OF ALL, let me tell you that I am, blessed be His name, in good health and spirits, and may the Blessed One grant that we hear from one another only good news of comfort and salvation for us and for all of Israel—Amen.

SECOND OF ALL, let me tell you, my dear wife, that you can rest easy now. We have safeguarded the Turk. No one will bother him now or complain, God forbid, that his "crescent moon" is threatening anyone's honor. And they can no longer say that he, the wild Asiatic, isn't dealing, heaven forbid, properly with his "brothers," the Slavs. And no one can any longer come to the defense of the injured parties—that's all finished! They all embraced him in London, rolled out the red carpet, and confirmed the new borders exactly as it was for his land long ago so that the map has now taken on an altogether new face. And whom do you think he has to thank for that? The Balkan partners who defeated him? Not at all! It was really the big boys, the great powers, who waited till the Turk was thoroughly beaten. Then suddenly they became peacemakers, sat themselves down and worked out a peace between the Turk and the Balkan kings so that if you were to read over the treaty, you would certainly never think it had been the Balkan "brothers" who had waged this bloody war but they, the great powers who had started it all and then taken over. And that is why they are now involved in dividing up the spoils. It will be a pleasure, I tell you, to see them sit down, these fine people, all honorable men, roll up their sleeves, and get down to work distributing the spoils to that Balkan gang the way you distribute, forgive the comparison, honey cake in our shul Yom Kippur eve. And then they will simply walk off. Among the "brothers" a hue and cry will then break out, each will be unhappy with his share, little by little fights will erupt among them, and fresh blood will be shed, their own blood—and he, the Turk, will sit back and look on, smoking his water pipe, growing big with satisfaction. But there is only one thing—why did he have to lay down the lives of thousands of Turks, waste so much gunpowder, and spend so much money? He could have accomplished the same end peacefully—my very contention, my very words—but what's done is done! The most important thing is that now our Uncle Ishmael's hands are free, he can relax, see where he stands, and with a clear head carry out those great schemes I have come up with for his benefit. And because of that I myself have also become a bit more free and can devote myself to our own *Jewish* politics, to our own *Jewish* affairs. And, thank the Holy One, there's plenty to be done there.

True, we don't have the problems the Turk had but we have our own problems. And if you think about it, we have it worse than the Turk. A thousand times worse! The Turk, at least, has a home, a corner of his own, as your mother says, "A poor landlord, but still a landlord . . ." But what are we? We are little more than a fancy sabbath gabardine, threadbare and torn. But what do we have to show for ourselves? Nothing with nothing, even less than nothing, shame and worry and anguish and heartache is what we have! What more do you need to know, my little silly? One tiny parcel of *Eretz Yisroel* is all we have, for God's sake, and that too comes with trouble and factions and competitive organizations and wrangling and quarreling, intrigues, spite, and controversies! Since Theodore Herzl, of blessed memory, died, they can't agree on anything. Now as they all are getting ready for the Eleventh Congress in Vienna there are big scandals! Nordau, they say, won't be coming to the congress and a congress without Nordau is like the high holy days without a cantor. If they would listen to me, the Zionists, I have for them, with God's help, a special scheme that will open their eyes! But I won't talk about it ahead of time. I'm afraid there might be a dispute even before anything happens. I hope, God willing, to be in Vienna at the congress and can put it before them myself. For the Zionists I don't need any interpreters and can get along without Turkish or French. The Zionists conduct their business in German. They don't know any other language but German. When a Zionist is at a congress, they say, whether he comes from Shklov, Old-Kostetin, Kotzk, or Drozhne, the minute he gets to the congress he speaks no other language but German, and German is supposedly *our* language!

Are you ready for what I will tell you next? Be patient. Besides the Zionists we also have *territorialists*. I already wrote you who they are. They are called "ITA." Zangwill is their leader. He travels the world looking for a territory suitable for Jews and can't find one. There is no such territory, not one small piece of earth. None, you might as well lie down and die! That is to say, there is room enough in the world, more than enough, but not for us. Do you think for a moment that I sat idly by? Both of us, I and Khoskl Kotik, spent days poring over maps looking for some little corner—nothing! What I liked, he didn't. What he liked, I didn't.

But recently Zangwill barely managed to find a small piece of territory. Actually not so small, really a big piece! But they're not saying what it is, it's still a secret. I, of course, do know the name of the territory, but I don't dare mention it to you. I can only tell you one thing: it's *not close*, but *really* not close! This territory is all the way in Africa. They say it's a blessed land with all good things, a land flowing with milk and honey! That is to say, if we settle there, we'll *make* it into a land flowing with milk and honey. In any case, for our Kasrilevka Jews it is a stroke of luck! Is it better for them to remain in Kasrilevka till they perish like that generation in the desert? Especially since, as you write, they are being driven from their villages to suffocate in the towns, God forbid. Let's hope they will have enough sense, the Kasrilevker Jews, not to find fault as usual with this new land. Finding fault—at that your Kasrilevkers are experts! They're not happy with Israel either. You should know that the leaders of this project, the territory in Africa, are not wet behind the ears—Reb Yakov Schiff from America, Reb Leopold Rothschild from London, and Reb Leibish Brodsky from Kiev—Jews who are millionaires! And Reb Shrira from Baku is no shabby tailor and the others are also not babes-in-the-woods! These people, you understand, have come to the conclusion that it's time to do something for the Jews. How long can we be beggars, dragging ourselves around the world looking on as others prosper?

Know then, my dear wife, that this is a time of seeking hard-to-find land. The world is apparently becoming overcrowded. People are looking for land, nations are looking for space. Take the Slavs in the Balkans. They felt crowded. People wanted space. What did they do? They organized themselves against the Turk, armed themselves with steel and iron, risked their lives, and paid with blood, with real red blood. One wonders: when other people risk their lives, give their blood for a piece of earth, why shouldn't we risk our capital? Why shouldn't we gamble our money?

Money in its way is also blood, but it's not real blood. Money is money and blood is blood. But mostly I worry about just one thing—divisive quarrels.

For us Jews nothing can happen without quarrels. Among the young people especially, it's become a fashion that no matter what you say they bring up the language problem and before you know it you're involved in a dispute. If you talk about universities in Israel, the first thing brought up is language—in which language will students study? If you talk about colonies in Argentina—in which language will they speak? If you talk about schools in the Pale—again language. Whatever you talk about—it's language. That's the primary thing. If one says, "Hebrew," the other says, "Russian." If one says, "Russian," the other says, "Polish." If one says, "Polish," the other says, "Spanish." If one says, "Spanish," the other says, "Turkish." Yiddish no one wants to hear about. Yiddish—God protect us! They hear the word Yiddish, "Zhargon," they have a fit! And it's possible they aren't so far from wrong because how does it look for Jews to speak Yiddish? It would be a fine thing, do you hear, if a quarrel were to break out over language. In which language will we speak in the new land in Africa? It would be even worse if the Jews who were driven out of their villages, those now in Kasrilevka would, God willing, arrive in the new Jewish land and be required to speak African or Hebrew or even Russian, anything but Yiddish! This would not be revenge on goyim, but revenge on Jews. It's a cockeyed world with cockeyed people with cockeyed minds! I figure I will soon get to these people and clear out their minds a bit. But now isn't the time for it. Their heads are elsewhere. They harry us, persecute us, chase us, suffocate us, oppress us, squeeze us, hound us, poison us and burn us. Yet they stand and point their finger at us laughing at our sore wounds. You write me about the tragedies befalling the Sharogrodskys and the Khortovois who perished so shabbily. What do you know about such things, my little silly? That is but an eighth of an eighth of what is going on today in the rest of the world!

Take, for example, another Sodom story that took place not far from Warsaw in a town called Pontev, perhaps you have already read about it in the newspapers. Polish goyim, evildoers, set fire to a Jewish prayer house, poured naphtha around the walls beforehand, didn't allow anyone to be rescued and then stood by laughing and watching as Jews roasted to death. Eight souls were consumed in smoke and flames! We live in a time, my little silly, of torment and humiliation, a time drenched in blood and steeped in poison, a time of forced conversions and the iron fist. But for us this is nothing new. We have survived worse times, greater woes, and we will survive these as well, God willing. You'll see!

In short, my dear wife, you yourself can see that I have enough to do here in Warsaw and am not, as you think, entirely taken up with the Turk. And as I have no time now I will make this short. With God's help, in my next letter I will write everything in greater detail. In the meantime may God grant us all health and success. Kiss the children for me, send regards to your mother and all the family in the most friendly way.

From me your husband Menachem-Mendl

16. Menachem-Mendl from Warsaw to His Wife, Sheyne-Sheyndl, in Kasrilevka

To my dear, wise, and modest wife, Sheyne-Sheyndl, may God grant her many years!

FIRST OF ALL, let me tell you that I am, blessed be His name, in good health and spirits, and may the Blessed One grant that we hear from one another only good news of comfort and salvation for us and all of Israel— Amen.

SECOND OF ALL, let me tell you, my dear wife, that I am not getting involved in the Duma. I don't hold with deputies and I hate windbags. I am of the opinion that it is a waste of time on the part of good people who want to do us a favor and defend us against what others say about us. I believe that for us it is, on the contrary, the worst disservice. If, for example, I were a deputy in the Duma, I would wait till Purishkevitch and Markov and Zamislavski talked till they were blue in the face, and when they stopped talking I would stand up and say to them straight out:

"Finished? You're through speaking? May I perhaps say a word too? If you'll allow me, I must tell you, gentlemen and scholars, that you are entirely correct in every way. Let us discuss the matter, point for point and you will see that I concede everything:

1. You claim that you must drive us from our villages because we are a sober people. True, confirmed, correct, and honest. We are a sober people. Too sober! Take a village of three thousand Russians and if among them you find one Jew, he will be sober. Always sober! You won't ever catch him stumbling on his feet or approaching anyone with a mean word. Never mind taking a club and hitting someone over the head for no reason at all. It's understood that someone like that is dangerous. How can you allow him to remain?

2. You claim you must bar us from any trade because we are too shrewd a people, we can make rubber out of snow or two rubles from one and it's difficult for you to compete with us. True, confirmed, correct, and

honest. Naturally this is unacceptable. But who is responsible for this disaster, gentlemen and scholars, if not you yourselves, by forbidding us to follow any other livelihood but trade?

3. You claim that you forbid us to undertake any other livelihood because we are too clever for you and we could in a short time, God forbid, provide you with the best officers, the greatest generals, the finest police officers, gymnasium directors, investigators, attorneys, governors, and ministers. True, confirmed, correct, and honest. Would it were so, although it is unlikely . . .

4. You claim that though you forbid us to do anything else and though you drive us out, harry us and persecute us and come up daily with new lies and punishing edicts, still and all you can't get rid of us. Despite that, you claim, we play the most important roles. The richest manufacturers, you claim, are Jews, the finest bankers are Jews, the biggest exporters are Jews. No need to mention the speculators on the stock exchange. Aside from us you wouldn't find a lost dog on the exchange—true, confirmed, correct, and honest. Let me put it in your own words, 'That's the way it has always been and that's the way it always will be.' It's a foregone conclusion and you yourselves are responsible, as I just told you.

5. You claim that even in literature and journalism, as well as in song and theater we occupy the highest places. But for that you are not responsible. Those are God-given gifts and no man can do anything about it. With force one can drive out a poor Jew from a village, throw out a sick woman, bag and baggage; one can with cleverness take away the last mouthful of food. One can make life so bitter for another that he will flee to the ends of the earth. But to tear out another's brain, rip the pen from his hand, the voice from his throat—that is impossible!

6. You claim that our children are too eager to study in your schools and that they outdistance your children who can never catch up to us. True, confirmed, correct, and honest. Our children, besides having good minds, are also very hardworking—you have made them hard-working. You yourselves! And now you are seeking remedies: quotas, quotas, and more quotas until we are altogether squeezed out. Of course this is a good remedy and who would say that you are, God forbid, wrong? It's the same with the younger ones in the gymnasiums and universities and with the older ones in the workplace. You say you have to throw us out of the workplace altogether and I am sorry to say you are right. Why do you need to have us always complaining to you about paying taxes and providing you with soldiers while we are treated like stepchildren? Ah, where is justice? Where is humanity? Where is God? But who talks of such things these days? But you have one more claim.

7. That's the claim that we murder your young children and use their blood for Passover. That claim we will leave for another time. Why should we delude ourselves? As my late rebbe used to say when Thursday arrived and we needed to recite our weekly readings and didn't know them, *and* we would nevertheless rock back and forth and sing loudly so he would think we did know them: *"You* know, little rascals, that *I* know you *don't* know your Gemorah, so why on earth are you rocking back and forth so hard?" With these same words I wish to tell you, gentlemen and scholars, that *you* know that *I* know that *you* know that it's all a bluff, so why are you making up stories? Only because you need it to justify yourselves for appearance' sake before the world by saying you have to drive us out because we are still a primitive people with primitive customs from the past. "Imagine—they use blood for Passover!" Ah, the world really knows better than that? What difference does that make? In the meantime there's an uproar. In the meantime you bring forward somebody's sister who is ready to testify in court against her own brother. She really isn't his sister? That's his problem! In short, gentlemen and scholars, as you see, I have conceded every point. Now but one thing remains: what do you need us for? Is it not more reasonable for you to be rid of such a blight? Think about it, gentlemen and scholars, what a life it would it be if you were to wake up one fine morning and there would be not one Jew, not a one! How could this be accomplished? Ask me and I will present to you a plan, a simple and honorable plan in all good faith. Why should you eat your hearts out with aggravation and run up expenses? Why not proclaim in all the synagogues and study houses that every Jew who wishes to emigrate may go in good health in the name of God, here's a train ticket third class to the border in your pocket plus a hundred for expenses. If you add it up, gentlemen and scholars, what do you think it will cost you altogether? Truly, nothing at all! Well, the train doesn't count—it's your train, so all that remains is the money for expenses. So what is there to fuss about? Let's say six million Jews at a hundred per Jew, and we have a total of six hundred million. That's only four hundred million short of a billion. Isn't it worth a billion to get rid of such a dead weight of Jews, *kayn eyn horeh?* Consider it, gentlemen and scholars, I give you a year to think it over."

That, my dear wife, is the way I would address them if I were a deputy. But you will ask what would happen if they would really like my plan and adopt my project? Where will we all go? Khoskl Kotik asked me that same question. That man has the habit of asking questions and always challenging everything. Whatever you say to him he has to say the opposite! I told him of my plan, good and fine as it should be and he wouldn't let me finish before he started right in cross-examining me: "First of all, what will happen if they won't let us out? Second of all, maybe our Jews won't want to go? Third of all, even if both sides do agree, where will they get enough money and wagons and food and other necessary equipment to transfer, *kayn eyn horeh*, six million people?" And more and more questions like that! I let him go on—a Jew likes to talk, why shouldn't I let him? He talked and talked and talked. And when he stopped talking, I answered each and every question and made short work of all his arguments, as you know I can do! He saw it wasn't going his way so he came up with a wild question: "What will happen, Reb Menachem-Mendl, if there is a pogrom, not now, but much later, in a hundred years from now? Where will they find a Jew?" I said to him, "If that is your only reservation, all right then, although you could come up with a better one. But if you really mean it, there's an answer to that too: since they recently began attacking our converts and treating them more like Jews, it's likely they are also beginning to feel, as we do, the sting of quotas and more quotas. And since the converts have remained, when it comes down to it, they will be able to make do very nicely in place of real Jews. Are you satisfied or not?" He backed off a bit and said, "Words, Reb Menachem-Mendl, just words. Let us return to the beginning," and he started again with his questions. I was going out of my mind and said to him, "How many times have I asked you, Reb Khoskl, not to talk to me about these matters!" He then said to me with a smile, "Who came to whom—I to you or you to me?" What a stubborn Jew! As you know, he couldn't fool me. I really showed him up! If I were to tell you everything that I made him realize, you would really enjoy it. But as I have no time, I will make this short. With God's help, in my next letter I will write you everything in greater detail. In the meantime may God grant us all health and success. Kiss the children for me, send regards to your mother and all the family in the most friendly way.

From me, your husband Menachem-Mendl

17. Sheyne-Sheyndl from Kasrilevka to Her Husband, Menachem-Mendl, in Warsaw

To my dear, honored, renowned, generous, and wise husband, Menachem-Mendl, may his light shine forever.

FIRST OF ALL, let me tell you that we are, thank God, in the best of health. Pray God we hear the same from you, never worse.

SECOND OF ALL, I am writing you, my dear husband, that they are beating down our doors, mine and my mother's, not just relatives, not just neighbors, or friends and acquaintances, but total strangers, people I never saw before in my life, mostly those fleeing the villages from which they were driven out. They don't give us a moment's peace, they can't wait to know more about this new land for Jews you write so much about. They want to know where it is—further or closer than America? How many days does it take to get there? And how do you get there—by sea or by land? And whom do they let in—only married men or bachelors as well? And what about military conscription? Will they let them off or will they still have to pay the three-hundred-ruble fine? Your gazette writes that the fine has been lifted but it turns out they don't know what they're talking about. Just last week our Shaye-Dovid's brother-in-law, Dodya Nebish, had to sell his chairs and pillows and the samovar and even his old prayer books to pay his stepbrother's fine. Why? Just listen. His father in his old age decided to remarry. He joined his new wife in Rakhmestrivke and after a while good fortune smiled on him and he had a baby girl, Basya. He went to the local rabbiner to register the little girl and told the rabbiner explicitly, "Register her, if you don't mind, with the name Basya." The rabbiner, apparently absentminded or just plain deaf, registered her among the boys and instead of Basya put down Masya. From Masya it became Mosya and from Mosya—Moishe. Then his father goes and decides to die, his widow and children leave for America to join a brother of hers, and here they are looking for a Moishe to conscript into the army. Of course there never was a Moishe in the first place. When a Moishe didn't show up, they declared a three-hundred-ruble fine. But whom could they ask for it? After all, Dodya was a brother, not from the same mother, but still a brother! Dodya claimed he never had a brother, he could prove with a hundred witnesses that he was an only child of his mother! They paid no attention to him and told him to pay the money. Had Dodya known how to handle himself, he would have dug up the Rakhmestrivke papers showing that Moishe was not Moishe but Basya. But we have a Shaye-Dovid in our midst, a Jew who loves to give advice and he came running over just as a police officer arrived to confiscate everything, bag and baggage. Shaye-Dovid called Dodya off to the side and began telling him something in secret. The police officer said, "What's all this whispering?"

Shaye-Dovid told him impertinently that the fines had been lifted and waved the gazette—*your* gazette—right in his face and pointed to the place where it said that the three-hundred-ruble fine had been forgiven and repeated that there was no more fine. The police officer did not appreciate this at all and said, "Just wait and I'll show you a 'no more fine,' " took the gazette, stamped all over it, arrested them, and sat them in jail for two days. It cost good money to get them out. What will happen about the gazette article we still don't know. They're even saying nothing will come of it. But, I ask you, who needed this? Here you have your consolation, as my mother says, "It is written, who needs others people's troubles, you have enough troubles of your own."

At any rate, our house is like a circus these days. This one out, that one in. We can't get rid of these Jews! They're all ready this very day to move to the new country with wives, children, bedding, and even the Passover dishes. They badger me to tell them the name of the country! I tell them, "Leave me alone, I beg you, I myself don't know!" They don't believe me. "What do you mean," they say, "you're the wife, till a hundred and twenty years, your husband knows and you don't?" I'm really embarrassed and ashamed, I must tell you! But what can I do? I don't say anything. As my mother says, "Swallow your pride and smile and let them think you swallowed a bone . . ."

And what you write me, my dear husband, of your millionaires, the Rothschilds and the Brodskys and the rest of them who've finally looked around and seen there are poor people in the world, that's very well and good on their part, but I would just like to know one thing—where were they till now, why were they silent? They apparently reminded themselves a bit late, but they did remind themselves that there is Another World with a *gehennum* and a paradise and an Angel of Death. As my mother says,"It is written that happy is the person who doesn't forget he must die . . ." Something must have bothered those millionaires to make them do good all of a sudden so that sugar wouldn't melt in their mouths. I'm just afraid, Mendl, may I be lying, that it might happen with them what happened with our wealthy neighbor's wife, Mikhl Shteinberg's Dvoire-Ettl, when her husband was barely alive on his deathbed (it shouldn't happen to anyone). They brought a professor from Yehupetz to operate on him, to cut out his intestines and his stomach and his bowels and whatever else was there! So Dvoire-Ettl sent for the rabbi and vowed to give half her fortune to the poor if her Mikhl would survive this operation and would live and be well. The rabbi thought it over and gathered all the Talmud Torah students in the synagogue to study and pray. The whole town came together to pray to God on the rich man's behalf. It was a big event—after all, a person has vowed to give half a fortune! And God helped, they performed a fine operation on Mikhl. They say they cut him to ribbons and, what can I tell you, he survived and was cured—may it happen to my loved ones. He eats and drinks and walks around just like everyone else!

Naturally the whole town was overjoyed. First of all, a Jew was cured and was recovering, had survived such an operation! And second of all, money would be coming to the town. No small thing—half a fortune! They held a meeting at the rabbi's to decide what to do with the money. There was some quarreling too, almost leading to blows and it was decided that first they would take the money, then they would quarrel. They went to Dvoire-Ettl's, the rabbi and his assistant along with the finest elders of the town, to congratulate her and her guest, she had such a wonderful guest— her Mikhl, thank God, had torn himself out of the hands of the Angel of Death, blessed are those who are revived from the dead! Dvoire-Ettl laid out honey cake and brandy and a little jam for them and asked them to sit and have a bite and to taste her jam. They thanked her very warmly for the jam and started to chat about the operation, professors, cutting, and about the donation of half her fortune that she had vowed to give and for which reason they had come. She didn't hesitate, Dvoire-Ettl, untied her purse and brought over to them a big twenty-fiver! They were all dumbstruck. "But Dvoire-Ettl, God be with you! What is this? Your husband doesn't have more than fifty? Is it possible?" She wasn't at all put out and answered coolly, "What does this have to do with my husband's fortune? I vowed to give half of *my* fortune, not my husband's and I have fulfilled that vow." What generosity! What do you say to that? They get away with anything. Even tricking God, if he allows it. As my mother says, "If a rich man stood on his head, they would say it was normal . . ." A plague should befall all rich people in the world and then maybe the poor would prosper, as I wish you all good things and eternal happiness, your loyal wife,

Sheyne-Sheyndl

By the way, how come you aren't writing me about Mendl Beiliss? How is it going to turn out, how long can they hold him in prison and for what reason? Let them make up their minds, as my mother says, "Either give me honey cake or send me away . . ." She's very right—either put him on trial or let him out! Everyone knows he is innocent as a lamb. Do you know, Menachem-Mendl, that he is distantly related to you, this Beiliss? Would you like to know how? I'll work it out for you: my father's aunt, Sheyndl, whom I'm named after, had a daughter, Lifshe, who was engaged to be married to a cousin of Mendl Beiliss's who was also named Mendl and also Beiliss, but the match was called off, for what reason I don't know because we weren't that close, but we were on friendly terms. As my mother says, "We get along like Aunt Kreni's dairy noodlepot's lid with the other lids . . ."

18. Menachem-Mendl from Warsaw to His Wife, Sheyne-Sheyndl, in Kasrilevka

To my dear, wise, and modest wife, Sheyne-Sheyndl, may God grant her many years!

FIRST OF ALL, let me tell you that I am, blessed be His name, in good health and spirits, and may the Blessed One grant that we hear from one another only good news of comfort and salvation for us and for all of Israel—Amen.

SECOND OF ALL, you should know, my dear wife, that with God's help war could still be averted. Oh, but there will be a war, I could win money on that! And not just one war—but many wars, and great ones, as I already wrote you. But the war everyone thought would break out at any moment among the "good friends," those who recently joined hands against the Turk—that war apparently has, thank God, almost been averted unless something happens, something unforeseen—who can tell with those Balkan headbangers? If they were really *brothers,* it would be another matter. In the meantime one has to hope it will remain quiet. And this might already be assured since "we" have mixed in and sent out word for it to be quiet, and that should be enough! Of course these Balkan headbanger are heroes, of course they are clever, of course they conquered the Turk, yet still and all as soon as they received "our" telegram saying it wasn't proper for brothers who are partners to fight over an inheritance and it would be much nicer if they were to trust each other a little, the telegraph wires began humming from one partner to another explaining how they were very pleased with how things were working out and that they hadn't contemplated any other means except peaceful ones! On the contrary, they wished to express the greatest thanks. True, this happened in the heat of the moment. A day later, when it was proposed to them that the brothers who had rolled up their sleeves and were ready for a fight should be so kind as to roll their sleeves back down again, they began singing a different tune. And one still cannot say at this time whether *all* four partners will send their prime ministers to St. Petersburg, and even if they do send them, whether they will smooth things out with each other. One can't be a prophet and predict what can come of this attempted solution or be so smart as to guess what Franz Josef will say if the conflict among the "good friends" is smoothed out without his knowledge because what is good for you is not good for me and what is breath to one is death to another. But in the meantime it's worthwhile reading the telegrams from the "good friends" who just yesterday were at each others' throats, ready to fire off the first shot and today they are outshouting one another, insisting vehemently that they intend, God forbid, no harm, on the contrary, just the very opposite!

When I read these Bulgarian and Serbian dispatches—it was late at night in the editorial offices when not even a stray dog wanders in—I went downstairs to the typesetters. I peek in there every once in a while. I like the typesetters. They are an easygoing bunch. A typesetter has the habit that whatever you give him to print he will print it and no matter what you say to him, he will hear you out, never contradict or doubt you. It's not Khoskl Kotik who has to challenge everything with a "what if" and a "how do you know this?" and a "then again."

So I sat myself down with the typesetters for a little chat about this and that and about the responses that had arrived from the Bulgarians and the Serbs and I said to them: "Do you know, boys, what I am reminded of by these Balkan telegrams? I am reminded of the time I was once at a trial before our rabbi in Kasrilevka. You should have bought tickets for it. Two butchers had a falling out over an animal hide. One brought a hundred proofs and a thousand items of evidence and letters from eyewitnesses swearing that the pelt was his and the other brought even more proofs and witnesses that it was all lies and falshoods—it was definitely his hide. But the proofs and evidence and letters from eyewitnesses weren't as enjoyable as the arguments the two made. I remember it as if it were today. One was called Zimmel, the other—Leybe. This was what Zimmel argued before the rabbi:

"Listen, dear Rabbi, you are a wise Jew, this is what happened. I have nothing against Leybe. What can I have against him? A butcher like myself, works hard to earn a crust of bread, and I swear by whatever you hold dear that I am very satisfied that he came with me to you, leaving it up to your sense of justice. Rest assured that no matter how you decide, it will be good, I will not, you can believe me, say a bad word against anyone. But first, I must tell you one thing, Rabbi, you are not an expert on who this Leybe is, a devil unto his furthest ancestors! This is a crook, a *momzer* and a *trayfnik*, slippery, bad from top to bottom, dead meat to throw to the dogs! Not only must you decide that the hide is my hide, you must also fine him, the thief, to pay me what the hide is worth plus all expenses so that he'll remember for next time and tell his children's children!"

That is what Zimmel argued in a rather loud voice. And Leybe argued in the same vein, only louder:

"Hear me out, Rebbenyu, this is ridiculous. I am not grasping and insolent like Zimmel and I don't have a foul mouth like him and so I will not speak badly of him. I admit that we are both butchers, a butcher shop next to a butcher shop. Never, do you hear, did we quarrel, never said a bad word. Even now there would be nothing bad between us if not for the business of the hide that brought us to you for a judgment and which really is a fair way to do it, hearing people out and letting the rabbi decide according to the law which one of us is right and which one is wrong. That's why you are the rabbi and a man of the Torah and a wise Jew while we are just ordinary Jews. I will certainly obey you and Zimmel will probably also obey you. Why shouldn't he obey you when he himself knows that the hide is as much his hide as it is your hide? It's just a sham on his part. He thinks maybe it will go his way and you will decide that the hide is his. After you hear my side, you yourself will see whose hide it is and who has to pay whom three times as much and who will remember not to steal someone else's hide, that *ganev*-son-of-a-*ganev*, that *momzer*-son-of-a-*momzer*, that no-good *treyfnik*, may the devil throw his father out of Hell and throw *him* in, God in heaven, may we live to see it, amen!"

"Do you want to know, boys, how the hearing ended up? It came to a bad end. The two butchers argued and threw insults at each other until they finally grabbed each others' beards and the rabbi was glad to see them on the other side of the door . . ."

So I'm afraid, dear wife, that we might have the same thing here, particularly when it is not a question of two butchers, but really four, and besides the four there are provocateurs, outsiders always on the lookout to spur a fight among the "brothers" so they can get a little something for themselves. But I don't think it will come to that. Our Sezenov won't allow it to happen. The only problem is that he isn't quite well. He caught a cold, that's one problem. The second problem is that our ministers are now very busy with boycotting the Duma. It's become a custom nowadays, praise be God, that as soon as anything happens—boycott! If you say an angry word to me, I don't answer back, I boycott you, that means I don't hear you and I don't see you and I don't know you and I don't even know that you're alive!

The Poles when they started boycotting Jews were right on the mark. Everyone saw what they were doing and did the same. Zionists boycotted the congress. Ministers boycotted the Duma. Soon wives will start boycotting their husbands, children—their parents, students—their teachers, servants girls—their mistresses, horses—their drivers—in short, everybody will be boycotting everybody else! But the best boycott is our ministers' boycott. How did this start, you may want to know? From a nothing. The devil put a bug in the ear of this deputy from the Black Party—Markov Number Two they call him—to come out with a tactless comment in the

Duma. He reminded the Duma that it is written somewhere, "Thou shalt not steal," and that stealing is forbidden, as if they, the Blacks, have a monopoly and only they can interpret "Thou shalt not steal" as they see fit. And I will tell you the truth—I agree with them, with the Blacks, because whatever they may say, they say what they mean, without tricks. For instance, they want Beiliss found guilty even though he is completely innocent. They claim, "We really know and you know and the whole world knows that you need our children's blood like we need it, but we want you to confess that you do need it and if not all of you, then a sect among you. Why does it trouble you to say it? Strange Jews that you are! You don't have to say that you slaughter our children for Passover. No. You just have to say that according to your law you would really need it but you don't do it because you have lived among us for so long that you have absorbed our refinement and civility and have become like us . . ."

Now you see, my dear wife, why I agree with Markov and especially with Purishkevitch? If I were in the Duma, do you hear, I wouldn't let anyone speak but those two. Twenty Milikovs and thirty Chekhidzes wouldn't say in a year's time what a Markov or a Purishkevitch can say in half a minute! I have a bit of work for them in the Duma, an entire scheme. But as I have no time—I have to think about getting some sleep—I will make this short. God willing, in my next letter I will write you everything at length. May God grant us all health and success. Be well and kiss the children for me and send my best and most friendly regards to your mother, whom I honor, and to the whole family whom I greet in the most friendly way.

From me, your husband, Menachem-Mendl

19. Sheyne-Sheyndl from Kasrilevka to Her Husband, Menachem-Mendl, in Warsaw

To my dear, honored, renowned, generous, and wise husband, Menachem-Mendl, may his light shine forever.

FIRST OF ALL, let me tell you that we are, thank God, in the best of health. Pray God we hear the same from you, never worse.

SECOND OF ALL, I am writing you, my dear husband, that I don't know if there is another town on earth that has ever had the troubles we are going through here in Kasrilevka. What has happened here recently has never happened anywhere since the world was created. We are still living in fear and dread. God has sent us a Haman of a police commissioner who wants to take revenge on us. And who do you think is responsible? Our own rich people. And not so much the rich people as those idlers, the writers who write for the papers. They have nothing else to do so they jump on every bit of nonsense, spread it all over the pages and make of it, as my mother says: "A whole *tzimmes* smeared over seven platters . . ." If not for them, nothing would have happened. That Haman of a police commissioner would probably have ranted and raved and finally worn himself out. But I am putting the cart before the horse, completely forgetting that first I have to tell you the story. The story is short and sweet. I can tell it to you in three words if you have the time to hear me out to the end, if you can put aside for a minute your big deals and your Turks and your kings and your millionaires and remember you have a wife, till a hundred and twenty years, who can't write as fancy as her husband the writer, though telling a story even a peasant in a haystack can also do.

You must remember Levi, the deaf man's son, Shlomo-Velvel Charlatan? Today he's become a regular big shot, a rich man with a fancy buggy. The only rich man in town with a buggy! How he got rich no one knows. Some say from railroads, some say in Yehupetz, others say—gambling. Whatever way it was, he built himself a little house in the market square, with a little garden, with an awning, a lantern on the balcony, and, brought in from Yehupetz, an iron cupboard that ten men could barely carry in. The whole town gathered to gape in astonishment. Soon he began to show off for the whole town, dispensing charity with an open hand so that all would know he was doing it and everybody would be talking about him— Shlomo-Velvel! Shlomo-Velvel! Who would have guessed that this would happen to Levi, the deaf man's son, whom no one would ever think it worthy of speaking a word to? As my mother says, "It is written, you can't know today who tomorrow will come riding high on a horse . . ." So far so good, no? But what should happen? He gets it into his head to become cozy with the authorities. He becomes fast friends with the police commissioner who had been placed over us and invites him Friday night for fish—once and twice and three times, so the whole town will see it all and respect him. No small thing, this Haman eats fish at Shlomo-Velvel's! The police commissioner, no fool himself, one day sends a policeman to Shlomo-Velvel carrying some kind of cage with a strange bird inside. Shlomo-Velvel looks at it: "What's this?" The policeman says, "It's a parrot." "What's a parrot?" The policeman says, "A bird that talks." Shlomo-Velvel asks him, "Why a talking bird all of a sudden?" The policeman tells him, "The police commissioner sent you this as a gift." Shlomo-Velvel is very pleased and asks the policeman, "What will I do with it, with the parrot?" The policeman says, "You'll feed it and, if you please, pay me a hundred and fifty rubles plus a fiver for the cage." Now Shlomo-Velvel is becoming upset: "A hun-

dred and fifty rubles! For what?" The policeman says, "For the parrot."
This makes Shlomo-Velvel really angry and he says to the policeman that
he won't pay even a hundred and fifty kopeks. The policeman says, "As
you wish!"—turns away and goes, leaving the parrot with Shlomo-Velvel.

Quickly harnessing his horse to the buggy, Shlomo-Velvel tears off to
the police commissioner and in his great haste forgets the bird. He arrives
at the police commissioner's exclaiming, "My lord master, what have you
sent me?" He replies, "A parrot." Shlomo-Velvel asks him, "What do I need
a parrot for?" The police commissioner answers, "If you have such a grand
house with a balcony and a lantern and an iron cupboard and you drive
around in a fancy buggy, it befits you to have a parrot too." Shlomo-Velvel
then says to him, "Fine. But a hundred and fifty rubles?" That Haman
replies, "Did you expect such a rare bird to be given you free of charge?"
Shlomo-Velvel tells him, "Thank you, but I wouldn't want it for free and
even if you pay me, I still wouldn't want it!" The police commissioner says
to him, "Listen Shlomo-Volka, you don't know what kind of bird this is. He
speaks like a person." Shlomo-Velvel says, "He can talk till he's blue in the
face, I don't want him in my house!" This finally gets to that Haman who
points his finger at him and says, "Look here, Volka, you'll be sorry for
this." Shlomo-Velvel replies, "I am never sorry." The police commissioner
says, "If that's the case, you'll pay not a hundred and fifty rubles but two
hundred." Shlomo-Velvel replies, "We'll see about that!" The police commissioner replies, "We'll see about that!" And Shlomo-Velvel slams the
door, seats himself in his buggy and drives home. You think that was the
end of it? Wait, the story is just beginning.

Arriving home in a fury, Shlomo-Velvel finds his house and balcony
and courtyard full of men, women and children. What is this? What's this
crowd doing here? They've come to look at the miracle of a bird that talks
like a person. We were there too, I and my mother, and we heard how the
parrot spoke, said every word like a person, "Silly parrot! " and not a word
more. My mother says: "It is written that the animals and the birds have
their own language but a human being cannot understand it. Still and all,"
she says, "I wouldn't want to have such a bird in my house for anything. A
silent person," she says, "and a talking bird are both good for nothing . . ."

And so when he saw all these people in his house, Shlomo-Velvel became even more infuriated and began shouting, "Why have you all come
here, as if something terrible has happened? Haven't you ever seen a parrot before?" What do you say about him? As if he never saw anything but
parrots at his father, Levi the deaf's. So my mother really gave him a lecture! She reminded him that she still remembered his father, was on familiar terms with him, though he could hardly hear her. And, she added, "It is

written that an ox must not be too proud of his fine horns, a pig of his spiky hairs, or a person of his easy money because these are all things one can lose." Well, that didn't sit too well with Shlomo-Velvel and he said angrily, "It is also written that you should go on home." So we went home. But now he has a pack of troubles for which he would gladly pay twice a hundred and fifty, but it's too late. Even the police commissioner himself can't help him now. An official from the capital arrived to investigate the matter to see if it was true that the police commissioner had forced a parrot on a Jew and then demanded a hundred and fifty rubles for it.

About three hundred witnesses were ready to say it was as true as God Himself. And it is likely, people say, that they will dismiss the police commissioner. But the police commissioner says that whether they dismiss him or not, he cannot guarantee that there won't be a pogrom in the town. And this Haman is capable of doing that! The whole town descended on Shlomo-Velvel. "Over you and your parrot we will have a pogrom!" Shlomo-Velvel complained, "How is it my fault? It's the newspapers that are guilty. If the newspapers hadn't raised a fuss, the police commissioner and I would have come to an agreement and the town would have been spared a pogrom." It's possible Shlomo-Velvel is right. In the meantime it's no good. What can I tell you? Let's hope we either get rid of that Haman or if he stays, we can grease his hand enough so that he'll forget about the parrot, may they both suffer a miserable death, the police commissioner and the parrot together with Shlomo-Velvel Charlatan and the newspapers and these idle writers, as I wish you all good things and eternal happiness your true faithful wife

Sheyne-Sheyndl

What you write me about your immigration plan, in which everyone is paid a hundred rubles apiece except for railroad tickets, would be a marvel and the arrangement you're suggesting in your letter is also not a bad deal. As my mother says, "The amount makes sense, but when will we see the money?" The problem is that you spread yourself too thin. The minute you get going on one plan, there you are with a new plan. That's well and good, my dear husband, and it's fine for you to be so concerned about all of Israel. But you might also sometimes give a thought to your wife and your own children. What will be the outcome of a life like ours, an exile like ours, and all this wandering over the face of the earth? But that doesn't even occur to you! What do you care about a wife? What do you care about children when you've become such good friends with the Rothschilds and the Brodskys and all you think about are wars and Turks and ministers?

20. Menachem-Mendl from Warsaw to His Wife, Sheyne-Sheyndl, in Kasrilevka

To my dear, wise, and modest wife, Sheyne-Sheyndl, may God grant her many years!

FIRST OF ALL, let me tell you that I am, blessed be His name, in good health and spirits, and may the Blessed One grant that we hear from one another only good news of comfort and salvation for us and for all of Israel—Amen.

SECOND OF ALL, you should know, my dear wife, it's been hanging by a hair. When I wrote you my previous letter, the Serbs were holding an important meeting. At this meeting they had to choose—war or peace. With the Serbs, as with all nations, you must know, even though it is a small country, there are nevertheless factions. Whatever one says, the other one says the opposite. If one says peace, the other one says war. Mostly, as I've observed since I've been dabbling in politics, the kings are in favor of peace and the sons of kings are in favor of war. Young people, you understand, are ambitious, want to make a name for themselves. Isn't it the same thing with Franz-Josef? If Franz-Josef weren't around, God forbid, his son, the prince, Franz-Ferdinand, would long have cooked up a stew. And it's the same with Wilhelm II. I have nothing against him, let him grow old in peace. But I say between us, let the emperor try shutting one eye and you will see how his son will soon stir up a war. But you will ask, if that is so, how can we be sure of our lives? The explanation is this: there is a God on earth, a guardian of Israel, and he extends the years of kings so long that when the princes finally do ascend the throne, they are themselves fathers and have princes of their own. Do you understand? The father, the king, is a peace promoter and his son is a Junker. And thus the wheel turns from the beginning of time and it will probably continue to do so.

In short, the prince of Serbia really wants to wage war with the Bulgarians. And a war would have broken out between them long ago over what they inherited from the Turk, as I've written you many times, and from this war would probably have sprung a smaller war, and from that war another little war and then a big war. It would have been, you can be certain, quite lively! Luckily "we" intervened in time and invited all four Balkan leaders to St. Petersburg to straighten things out among themselves and to listen to responsible people. But this didn't sit well with the Serbian prince. Alexander is his name. He is desperate to go to war. So much for listening to responsible people! He's stirring up his faction: "We don't have to listen to anybody! We have to teach the Bulgarians a lesson to keep their hands off Macedonia! They took Adrianople—that's enough for them!" But another Serbian faction strongly advocates peace. And at the head of this faction stands the minister Pashitz. He is the minister-president, as we have our Kokovtzev. But if the prince wants war, is there a choice? So the minister Pashitz thought it over and said goodbye. The king—he is for peace, like all fathers—also thought it over and wouldn't allow it. Pashitz reconsidered and said: "Do you know what? Let's hear what the Duma will say." (There it's called *skuptshineh*, not Duma).

That was the important meeting of the *skuptshineh* I was telling you about, and at that meeting everyone agreed with Pashitz and felt he should remain minister. And as Pashitz is still the minister, they are going to St. Petersburg, and if they go to St. Petersburg they pray to God there will be peace. Now do you understand?

That's the way it is, my dear wife, if you observe how the world works. It's a never-ending circle. Wise people turn the wheel. Just like it was, forgive the comparison, with us in the good years during the feuds between the Talner Chassidim and the Rzshishchevers. Over a nothing, you would think, over some arcane interpretation, the greatest scandal could erupt. The rabble who stood on the sidelines were crying for blood, each defending his interpretation while the insiders knew the whole thing amounted to nothing. It simmered and simmered and eventually blew over.

That's the way it is now too. There in Kasrilevka, when the newspaper arrives and you read the telegrams from Sofia and from Belgrade, you must surely think that any minute now they will be fighting and you are scared to death. And we who sit at the very source, we read the telegrams even before we give them over to be printed, and we know it isn't so serious. So what's happening? The prince is tugging at the reins? He wants to go to war? Don't worry, he'll keep wanting so long until he loses the desire. Several frightening dispatches have already reported shooting. Khoskl Kotik was rejoicing when he read these dispatches: "So," he said to me, "where is your peace, Reb Menachem-Mendl?" I said to him, "Trust me, Reb Khoskl, the peace is still a peace." He said to me again, "What do you mean? Don't you hear they are shooting?" "I don't," I said, "maybe you hear. You have a good sense of hearing." He became enraged, he's a hothead, watch out!—and shoved the newspaper right under my nose. "There, read. There, see. They write from London that the Serbs are taking over cities. There, read, they write further that the important meeting among the Serbs, was a waste. There will probably have to be another meeting. And here they write that they've heard shooting at the border."

"Te-te-te-," I said to him, "All of this I read before you did. I am, you know, from the newspaper. Believe me, Reb Kotik, the shooting they write about in the newspaper isn't worth an ounce of gunpowder. The shooting is being done by correspondents who are trying to make money on it. Don't worry, when it will come to the real shooting, you'll fall off your chair." He said: "Bite your tongue. You are a person who obviously loves to be an alarmist." I said: "On the contrary, I am by nature a man of peace. Alarming people, that is *your* specialty." One word led to another—we got into a really good fight, I grabbed my walking stick and was prepared to go back to the newspaper office when he said to me: "What's your hurry, Reb Menachem-Mendl? Let's put aside politics, to the devil with all of them, and let's better talk about *our* issues." By that he meant our own Jewish matters: Duma, deputies, immigration, Zionism, a land for Jews—there is, thank God, enough to talk about. But as I have no time now—it's likely that a person I'm waiting for has already left America and today or tomorrow will be arriving in Warsaw, and so I am making it short. I hope in the next letter, after I've met with him, I will write you everything in detail. In the meantime, may God grant us all health and success. Be well and kiss the children for me and send my best and most friendly regards to your mother, whom I honor, and to the whole family, each and every one!

From me your husband Menachem-Mendl

ALMOST FORGOT: What do you say to this, my dear wife? Khoskl Kotik hit it right this time. There *is* shooting in Salonika and in Ishtiv as well as in other places. I can just imagine how that man will crow! I won't be able to get near him at the cafe on the Nalevkis.

21. Sheyne-Sheyndl from Kasrilevka to Her Husband, Menachem-Mendl, in Warsaw

To my dear, honored, renowned, generous, and wise husband, Menachem-Mendl, may his light shine forever.

FIRST OF ALL, let me tell you that we are, thank God, in the best of health. Pray God we hear the same from you, never worse.

SECOND OF ALL, I am writing you, my dear husband, I must tell you again, and I don't care if you get angry, but you don't write about what you ought to. Tell me, I ask you, what good is it if they give all the Jews free train tickets and a hundred apiece when there's no telling what will happen at the border? I don't mean just at the border but with the customs officials and the Aid Committees and the other do-gooders. And especially with the German Jews on the other side of the border, may a pogrom descend upon them, Lord in heaven, may they feel the taste of exile and maybe become better for it! You should read, Mendl, the letters we receive here in Kasrilevka from the miserable emigrants, I tell you a stone would melt reading them. It's really the end of the world, time for the coming of the Messiah, that's the truth! There is no justice, there is no mercy, there is no God, there is nothing. As my mother says: "It is written that since the destruction of the Temple people's hearts have turned to stone and their foreheads to copper . . ."

Who would have expected your German Jews in Kinisberg, in Hambur and in Bremel (God knows if that's what they're called), may they fall frothing at the mouth, would behave like policemen and treat our Kasrilevka emigrants even worse than our own Kishinev hooligans? Just listen to this terrible letter written by Maier Popelov's children. It's almost a year since they left for America and disappeared as if they had sunk into the ocean. The family had already mourned them here thinking they were no longer in this world. At long last the letter carrier arrived with a letter, not from America, but from Kinisburg, a fine letter—woe unto their parents who had to live to read this! As my mother says, "Lucky is he who lies under the earth and doesn't see what is happening under the sky . . ." I was barely able to convince Kreni, Maier Popelov's wife, to let me have the letter for half an hour so I could sit down and read it. It should interest you, so I copied it out word for word. See for yourself and then think twice about your German Jews, may a plague suddenly befall them so they won't know what hit them, may they perish, God in heaven, may they suddenly be afflicted and slaughtered one at a time from the oldest to the youngest. Amen! Amen! Amen! Now listen to the letter:

"To our dear beloved father Maier may he live and be well and to our dear beloved mother Kreni may she live and be well and to our dear beloved brothers and sisters may they live and be well and to all our dear and beloved friends may they live and be well and you shouldn't worry that we haven't written in such a long time because we kept putting everything off from day to day and we kept thinking any minute now we will be making money and any minute now we will be free to go because the agents just took our money and our things and they abandoned us and the aid committees are a thousand times worse than the agents because they don't want to ever let us go they are holding us until we are all cured and even when we are cured they will still have to hold us because we don't have any money to move with they took every last groshen from us at the very beginning when we crossed the border in good health and to this day we haven't stopped paying and at first they stripped us all naked in Hambur searched us for money to exchange and we told them we didn't have any but they didn't believe us and stripped us naked and took our Russian money and shoved their money at us the German money as much of an exchange as they wanted and they held us and held us and held us and held us and made us pay for everything for rent food water so we began to cry and begged to be sent on our way and they laughed at us and now we really became angry and they said that if we don't shut up they will beat us we saw it was bad so we shut up and waited and waited and waited till they finally sent us to Bremel because in Bremel they told us another party of emigrants like us was waiting and we would be sent on together and when we arrived in Bremel they asked us if we had Russian money to exchange and we told them we didn't they already exchanged our money for us but they didn't believe us they stripped us naked again and searched us one at a time and found nothing but in the meantime the other party of emigrants that had waited for us couldn't wait any more and had left and we were pushed into a stable and held for three days and nights and only then taken to the doctor and they stripped us naked again and found the we are all thank God healthy and strong except for Khaya and Leibl who have sick eyes and with sick eyes they don't let you on the ship then we began crying and pleading what will happen to us they laughed at us so we became angry and told them to make up their minds one way or the other and they told us that if we kept on complaining they'd break our bones so we had to shut up and again had to wait and we waited and waited and waited until finally they sent us to Kinisburg because in Kinisburg they told us they cure sick eyes and when we arrived in Kinisburg they asked us if we had Russian money and we told them not to bother us with their Russian money they long ago exchanged it but they didn't believe us and again stripped us naked and searched us one at a time and found nothing and kept us apart on account of Khaya and Leibl till their sick eyes would be cured and they asked to be paid for everything for rent separately for food separately and for water separately and they began to feed us this fish that you had to hold your nose because meat they don't give you only fish and then not every day only *Shabbos* and they keep the fish from *Shabbos* to *Shabbos* so we all got sick and we made a fuss and they warned us that if we make a fuss they will throw us out the healthy ones together with the sick ones so we were afraid it might be true and what will we do with the sick ones because while we're living here all together Bertshik and Godl and Maryasha also became sick in the eyes and so we are five people with sick eyes and there's no way we can budge from this spot and we sit here like in prison and don't know what will be because being good doesn't help and we're afraid of getting angry so we decided that rather than keeping quiet so long we had better write you the whole truth because we can't stand it any more we miss you so terribly our dear and beloved parents our dear and beloved sisters and brothers our dear and beloved friends and at least write us a letter how you are doing and of your health and of everyone's health and maybe by the time your letter arrives the One Above will take pity after all and the sick ones will become well in their eyes and we will finally be able to tear ourselves out of here to America because we've already worn out the last shirt on our backs and we look only to God to take pity and perform a miracle or else we are lost God forbid all of us from the youngest to the oldest . . ."

What do you say, Mendl, to that *megillah*? Can't your spleen burst, may they all burst into pieces, into small pieces, dear God! As my mother, may she live long, says, "It isn't any worse among the wolves in the forest . . ." Do you think you're finished? Just wait. That's just the beginning. Popelov's letter is heaven compared to the letters that Feitl-Moshe Bass receives from her brother, Noah, and that Borukh-Leib writes to his mother, Perkele the widow, where it is really as my mother says: "Heaven open your gates and *gehennum* be astounded!" But as I promised Kreni that in half an hour I will give back her children's *megillah*, I'm afraid she'll come running here raising a fuss—if she wants to, she knows how!—so I close my letter with a blessing on the Germans: may they either be struck by lightning on a clear day or may they go begging from house to house and suffer from boils on their faces, not have a crust of bread, or may the earth open and swallow them all, like Korakh, with their children and with their bed linens and even with their Passover dishes, so there would be neither hide nor hair of them left the following morning, not a memory, not a trace of any German, as I wish you all good things and eternal happiness, your truly loyal wife

Sheyne-Sheyndl

Dear husband! The children write you separately, as usual. Moyshe-Hershele, may he live long, writes you in Hebrew, God bless him, and the others, may they be well, write you in Yiddish. They ask you to send them books from Warsaw. Do that for them, you are certainly in the best place where they print books so it won't cost you too much money. As my mother says, "If you make jam, your fingers get sticky, and if you fry shmaltz your lips get greasy . . ."

22. Menachem-Mendl from Warsaw
to His Wife, Sheyne-Sheyndl, in Kasrilevka

To my dear, wise, and modest wife, Sheyne-Sheyndl, may God grant her many years!

FIRST OF ALL, let me tell you that I am, blessed be His name, in good health and spirits, and may the Blessed One grant that we hear from one another only good news of comfort and salvation for us and for all of Israel—Amen.

SECOND OF ALL, you should know, my dear wife, that your Menachem-Mendl is really quite a prophet. What I predicted to you has proven true practically point for point. Only the squabbling started a bit too early. Unexpectedly the poor Balkan relatives have been grabbing each other by the throats over their rich Turkish inheritance even before they started handing out the shares. They couldn't contain themselves, even out of respect, for the brief time until they arrived by invitation in St. Petersburg. No sooner did they give one another a *sholom aleikhem* than—aha, they were maiming each other and the blood was flowing—Bulgarians, Serbs, and Greeks—brothers, God in heaven, their own brothers! It is a disgrace, I tell you, my dear wife, one's face reddens with shame when you read the dispatches flying from Sofia and from Belgrade. Each blames the other for the bloodbath while each one maintains he is completely innocent, had no intention of fighting but was forced to fight, what could he do? And the way each side is boasting and gloating while swearing that the other side killed fifteen thousand people, and the other side denies it, swearing that the opposite side has lied in its teeth, they are the ones who have lost twenty-five thousand men besides prisoners. And all this among one's own, among brothers and among partners who just yesterday went arm in arm to wage war on *God's behalf* to fight against an alien religion! Do you think they had anything else in mind other than to free the poor Slavs from the Turkish yoke? Was there ever any other intention but cleansing the Balkans of the unclean Turk? And everything you read about the fifteen thousand and about the five thousand is still without a war! For the time being, that's the way it's playing itself out, it's just a rehearsal, a disgrace, as I live, a disgrace! Just to read the names of the places where the fighting is going on, I tell you, is enough to make you laugh. Look, we also have enough places with crazy names. For example listen to these names— Pereshchepeni, Treskizilia, Zsherebyatnik, Djonskivolya, Khatzepetevka, Petekhatka, Tzekhatzinek, and so forth—they are nothing compared to the ridiculous names of those places where the Bulgarians, the Serbs, and the

Greeks are having a go at it now! You wake up in the morning and start reading dispatches that in Katchana and in Kilkitch they have laid out so many and so many people, and in Ishtiv and in Trokholya they have slaughtered so many and so many people, and in Krivolkavrika and in Redkibayuki and in Karvekitka the blood is running like water. So, I ask you, can't the names alone turn your stomach?

But that's the least of it! Khoskl Kotik may be rejoicing, he may even be doing a little dance, but I am still of the opinion that this is not yet the real war. The real war will be not among these small nations who are like flies on the wall compared to those gigantic elephants who in the meantime are standing on the side looking on as the children are playing. The real war will not be with Rumania, which in preparation is massing its meager troops at the border. The real war won't even be with the Turk, who is barely able to hold himself in as he looks with one eye at Adrianople and with the other at Salonika, anxious to make a move. If the Turk would ask me, I would tell him to wait a bit—it's still too early. The real war will be among the great powers when they finally show their hand and settle things among the little brothers who are scratching each other's eyes out. Each of the great powers will undoubtedly take one of the little brothers under its wing and that will lead to a real free-for-all!

For now, don't worry—it's not at that point yet. For now each one is tending to his own business. The diplomats are sharpening their tongues and arranging visits to one another and the great powers are sharpening their swords, building ships and airplanes, because the coming war—I mean the big war—will not be fought on the sea or on land but in the air. It will really be *some* war! But then again, the best part is that it won't last long. The first explosion will be followed by such outrage that the world will tremble and then we will have peace, joy, and light among all people. And then, at long last, the time will come for our brethren, the children of Israel. Others, little silly, will come to our aid. Enemies will become good friends. The word *"zhid"* will never be heard again. The Polacks will undo themselves completely with their boycotting. They will be ashamed to say they had once boycotted us. And many, many others will be abashed and will regret that they had shed our blood for no rhyme or reason. But that is still off in the future.

In the meantime it is bad for us, my dear wife, very bad! You write that I don't write you what I should write. Believe me, I know it very well and even before you wrote me I myself had in mind to get to work first thing on the emigration question. I have already worked out a whole plan with all kinds of guidelines on how our emigrants should be protected from the agents, thieves, bandits, and do-gooders on *this* side of the border and on the *other* side of the border till they reach their destination. The plan with all the guidelines is all prepared and I mean to publish it in a separate book. With God's help, I will print six million copies and distribute them free to all the Jews in the Diaspora! This will run into money. Printing the book, you understand, will cost more than a few kopeks! Actually, the printing alone is nothing. That won't cost me anything. I had a chat with my friends, the typesetters, showed them the plan on paper, and they said it should take them no more than an hour or two and they would typeset it free for my sake and because it was for the public good. But there remains one thing—the printing and the paper. I don't know yet how much paper is needed. So I ran over to Khoskl Kotik. He's already published many books and is in these matters very knowledgable. We both figured it out and it turns out that the paper alone for six million books would have to cost a fortune! He's afraid, he says, that it might run into the many thousands—so that's bad! Where does one get so much money?

So I came up with a scheme, a scheme that you yourself will say is re-markable. But you will ask, what kind of scheme? To that I will answer with one word: "advertisements." You will ask: What is the meaning of "advertisements"? I need to make it clear to you so you will know that everything today depends on "advertisements." For instance, when you buy a newspaper you surely think the editor depends on your four groshen? The four groshen are just the beginning! The main thing for him is the last page, the "advertisements." The "advertisements," little silly, bring in for him hundreds, thousands! If not for the "advertisements," he might as well close up shop. That's the way it is in America and that's the way it is with us. In America the editor is so in love with "advertisements," he puts out one page of newspaper and three pages of "advertisements." In America there are newspapers where all four pages are "advertise-ments" and there is no newspaper. These newspapers are distributed free. Others pay you to take them because the more newspapers they print, the more they get for the "advertisements."

Now will you be able to appreciate my scheme, my dear wife? Since my book won't cost anything and six million copies will be printed at one time, I will be able to cram in more and more expensive advertisements be-cause who won't want to put in an advertisement in such a book that costs nothing and has so many copies in print? I am sure they will be fighting to place their advertisements! Everyone will be pushing for their "advertise-ment" and there won't be enough space. The money from the advertise-ments will cover not only the expenses of the printing and the paper, there might even be a few thousand if not more left over. One has to be a fool not to understand it. But—you need people who will be willing to work on it, which means collecting the advertisements. One person alone can't do everything. And especially when that's not my only scheme. I have more! At this time I am working on a scheme that concerns us directly, I mean our Jewish writers who are dispersed everywhere, this one in Lisi, that one in Strisi. They have no permanent place where they can gather together, to have a glass of coffee or just sit and chat. I will sell shares to finance it. That will be a gold mine! But as I have no time now—I must run to read what they are writing from Sofia and from Belgrade and from Trokholya and from Krivolakavdika and from Redkibuk and from Kaverkitka—I will make it short. God willing, in my next letter I will write you everything at greater length. In the meantime, may God grant us all health and success. Kiss the children for me and send my best and most friendly regards to your mother, whom I honor, and to the whole family, each and every one.

From me your husband Menachem-Mendl

ALMOST FORGOT! I am sending you the books the children asked for. But I don't know if those are the ones they need. Today there are as many editions as stars in the sky! We have: Hebrew with Hebrew, Hebrew with Yiddish, Yiddish with Hebrew, Yiddish with Russian, Yiddish with Yiddish, Russian with Hebrew, Russian with Yiddish, and Russian with Russian. And as for the Torahs the children ask for, I don't know which ones to send: the regular Torahs or the modern Torahs, the new ones? And among the modern Torahs alone there are all kinds. For instance, some Torahs are shortened a little and some Torahs are very much shortened. We have complete Torahs, Torahs cut to shreds, Torahs chopped to pieces, Torahs sliced up—you're fooling around with Warsaw!

23. Sheyne-Sheyndl from Kasrilevka to Her Husband, Menachem-Mendl, in Warsaw

To my dear, honored, renowned, generous, and wise husband, Menachem-Mendl, may his light shine forever.

FIRST OF ALL, let me tell you that we are, thank God, in the best of health. Pray God we hear the same from you, never worse.

SECOND OF ALL, I am writing you, my dear husband, about those fine Germans, may they enjoy living on this earth as I enjoy writing you again about how they are treating our emigrants, worse than vermin. Instead of writing about them, I would like to write them off, may they die painful deaths. I don't even want to talk about them, may they only talk from fever.

And I certainly don't want to curse them, may they be cursed by God, may all calamities befall them for all our blood flowing without pity in all the streets of all the towns all over the world, amen, God of the Universe! But as I promised I would write you everything, I can't go back on my promise, as my mother says, long may she live: "It is written that if a wife gives her husband her word, she must keep it because a mouth is not an empty boot." And since you are now, with God's help, a writer among writers who writes in the newspapers and you need something to write about, instead of writing about the devil knows what, wars and schemes and this and that, better you should write in your newspaper about what Noakh wrote to his brother, Feitl-Moshe Bass and about the letter Borukh-Leib wrote to his mother, Perkele the widow. That is more important than all your scribblings. I'll tell you about them in brief because I don't have time to put down everything they write, the children will soon be waking up, they need to be given breakfast and sent off to cheder.

Well, the torment that both of them, Noakh and Borukh-Leib went through until they reached the border, I'll leave out. Feitl-Moshe Bass is no liar and even Perkele the widow, who my mother calls a "great weeper" for her crying and for the sad faces she makes, will also not say what is not true. When his Noakh got to the border—so tells Feitl-Moshe Bass—he soon realized that the devil was at work. The agents took him over hand and foot, promised him the sun and the stars, and then left him with nothing, no tickets, no money, no help to sneak across the border—nothing! But Noakh is not a small man, twice as big as Feitl, and he began shouting at the top of his lungs that he would do this and that to them. So they began beating him up. Luckily his Blyuma got into it and his children also raised a terrible fuss. People came running and he was spared. But God sent him other agents who trundled him over the border where they cleaned him out of the rest of his bit of money and left him with nothing. With luck he reached the Aid Committee, which sent him on further but with such haste that while boarding a moving wagon, Feygele, a lovely little girl of a year and a half, slipped out of Blyuma's hands. Blyuma almost went out of her mind and Noakh yelled and screamed and tried to get help, but they beat him up again. They were still among Jews and they advised him to go to court and demand damages—after all, a child, although he has enough. May I not be committing a sin but, as my mother says: "The rich man has millions and the poor man has children—who can say which is more dear . . ." He followed their advice and complained but nothing came of it because if you don't speak the language, a person is useless. As my mother says: "It is written that when God wanted to punish man, He took away his language so that if one man said give me bread, he got a stone in the head and if he asked for a drink, he was stuck with a knife . . ." The point is Blyuma fell sick with grief and Noakh couldn't go any further without her and the children, so he is sitting in misery writing letters to his brother Feitl to help him in whatever way he can. Feitl wrote him that he should try very hard to find the money for fare back home. But Noakh wrote back that he would rather die than come home. My mother is right. She says: "That Americhka has such power that once you decide to go there, you'd rather die than turn back . . ."

That takes care of Noakh. Now you'll hear a fine tale Borukh-Leib writes to his mother, Perkele the widow. But with Perkele it's hard to make head or tail of what she says because she herself is hoarse from so much talking. She grinds it out like a mill. She either cries or makes such faces that no matter how sad it is, you can't help laughing. Of all the stories she tells about her son, her daughter-in-law, and her grandchildren you come out with just one thing—they were living together with Noakh in Kinisberg somewhere in a pig sty, sleeping on rotten straw, eating wormy bread once a day and one child or another kept coming down with sick eyes. Finally, with much trouble, they were able to get to London and when they got to London, that's when the real hell started for them. Borukh-Leib writes that as long as they were among the Germans, at least the Germans managed to understand them because our Yiddish, he writes, and their German is like a Pole talking to a Litvak. True, it's unpleasant to hear a Litvak call *broit-brayt* and *fleish-fleis* and *milkh-milekh,* but still and all you try to understand what he is saying and that's the way it is with the Germans too. They laugh at the way we talk and hate us as if we were pigs, but if you pay them money, they understand. But in London, he says, it's a catastrophe. He says we are worse than mutes there. And worst of all is that the Jews there make believe not to understand us, or maybe they really don't understand us. But that, he writes, is still not all of it. If only that London had sunk into the earth like Sodom before he came there, he would still have a son, Menasha. Menasha was his pride and joy and on him he placed all his hopes. But he had to bring him to London and in London, mostly hanging around the poor emigrants, are people who are trying to convert Jews. They see poor Jews suffering, starving for days on end and they trick them, promise them mountains of gold, give them food and drink, provide them with a doctor for free plus whatever cures they need and it sounds good. At first, he writes, they didn't know what was going on with Menasha. He seemed always to be deep in thought and troubled, leaving the house without so much as a good-bye until finally one time he left and didn't come back. But he did send a letter to them saying not to worry about him and not to look for him and not to wait for him, he would never come back again because he was no longer who he used to be. You can imagine what news that was for his parents! He writes that they pray for death every day, but death won't come. As my mother says: "It is written, that the One Above made a deal with the Angel of Death that he wouldn't go where he was called, but only where they were hiding from him . . ." Just like Papa, of blessed memory. Would it have bothered God, she says, if Papa had lived another twenty years? Whom was he bothering and whose bread was he eating? But when it is fated, Grandma Rikl became blind and deaf and now she drags herself around while Papa lies in the ground! Just like Fruma-Gitl, our Aunt Leah's daughter, decided last week to up and die. Guess from what? From fright. She was going home from the market with her basket when she saw people running and looking up. She thought who knows what—a pogrom, a fire, a plague. It turned out it was a balloon flying over Kasrilevka! May my woes and your woes and all of our woes be on the heads of those balloonists! Because of a balloon poor Reuven is now a widower and his children are orphans. What is even worse is that a man like Reuven, may his face break out in boils and may I have gold, if he won't marry again, as I wish you all good things and eternal happiness, your true, faithful wife

Sheyne-Sheyndl

The books that you write you've sent out to the children are still not here. I don't understand why. Either they robbed the train carrying them or they are coming by foot . . .

24. Menachem-Mendl from Warsaw to His Wife, Sheyne-Sheyndl, in Kasrilevka

To my dear, wise, and modest wife, Sheyne-Sheyndl, may God grant her many years!

FIRST OF ALL, let me tell you that I am, blessed be His name, in good health and spirits, and may the Blessed One grant that we hear from one another only good news of comfort and salvation for us and for all of Israel—Amen.

SECOND OF ALL, let me tell you, that your letters about our emigrants who are suffering at the hands of agents on the both sides of the border have done a great favor for all Jews because I will write it down exactly as you describe in my book which I am preparing to publish in six million copies and will distribute free of charge thoughout the Jewish world.

Money to publish the book, as I wrote you, I will have more than enough from the advertisements I will sell. I already have several dozen advertisements but those, for the time being, are swaps, advertisements traded for other advertisements. Let me explain. You put out a book, I put out a book. You want me to advertise your book, I want you to advertise my book. What do we do? We make an exchange. My book advertises your book and your book advertises my book. Plain as a groshen buys a bagel. No money comes in from these advertisement trade-offs but they attract many other advertisements that do bring in money, a lot of money. From the ship companies alone you can take in a tidy sum. Wait till they sniff out that the book I am publishing is about Jewish emigration and that six million copies are being printed. As soon as the first few zlotys begin to come in, I will hire several salesmen to travel the world selling advertising.

In short, as you see, my dear wife, I am almost finished with my book and am now devoting myself to my second scheme which I wrote you about in my previous letter. This is the scheme about us Jewish writers, both here in Warsaw and everywhere. They need to become one soul, one spirit, not to be dispersed and spread out and they must have the power to work for the good of all. From this can come the greatest benefit, both for us writers and for all our brothers in Israel, here and everywhere. You will ask where I got this idea? I have to admit that for this I must thank the Polacks and their boycott of Jews. How did this happen? Let me tell you.

When the hullaballoo over the boycott began, all the Jewish writers, your husband among them, protested, wrote fiery articles in the newspapers explaining our views and said in so many words—let's not fool ourselves, we will be worse than worse if we don't unite and come out against the enemy's boycott with our own boycott. There were those sages who came out with a different point of view in articles and in speeches, "Who has ever heard of Jews using the same weapons as their enemies to protect themselves?" they argued, "Think! If someone were to tell us to repay a pogrom with a pogrom, wouldn't we say that person was crazy?" That's one of their arguments. Secondly, they said, "What's so terrible if a few shopkeepers took steps against a few Jewish shopkeeper *bourjhukes*—they call them *bourjhukes* in Polish—what's so bad? Let the little shopkeepers fight each other, let them bite each other, what has that to do with the rest of us?"

But more than anything, they were upset with me. How come, one of them said, Menachem-Mendl, who was never a *bourjhuke* but a speculator, is sticking up now for the *bourjhukes* and supporting a Jewish boycott? I answered that accuser with a long letter and really laid it on! But my editor rejected it. Editors have a habit of rejecting. He found it too insulting. I tried telling him that sometimes he himself does a pretty good job of being insulting. He responded by saying that that's why he was an editor. If I become an editor, then I too could be insulting.

In short, the articles flew back and forth and to this day we writers haven't stopped raising a hue and cry. "How is it possible, Jews, how can you be silent? How can you not see what's going on? How can you not do anything about it?" And finally, I must tell you the whole truth. May no shame come to them, our own writers, they write and they write and in the end—they take themselves to the Polish cafes to drink tea, even though people look at them there like at a dog eating Purim pastries, but as your mother says; "The Jew is *trayf*, his groshen is kosher . . ."

I pleaded with them, "Brothers, how is it possible? How can you do that? It's a shame, an embarrassment before the whole world! I don't mean only our Jews, a Jew is hardly embarrassed by another Jew, but they, the Polacks themselves who point their finger at you!" They said, "What can we do when we have no choice? There's no proper Jewish coffee house in Warsaw." I said, "If there isn't one, we should see to it that there is one." They said, "You are a man with schemes, Menachem-Mendl himself, why don't you come up with a scheme for one?" And I said, "Give me one week." They said, "We'll give you two."

So off I went and worked out a project on ten sheets of paper for a Jewish coffeehouse financed by stocks. The cafe would be both for writers and for non-writers where one could not only get a cheap cup of coffee, tea, chocolate, bread and butter, and so forth, but also at cost, food and drink and a glass of beer, a cigarette, a hat if you need it, a shirt, a suit, a shoe, a bath, our own *minyan,* our own theater too with our own chorus, and Jewish concerts as well. With the profits remaining after the stockholders' dividends, we could support all the needy writers in Warsaw as well as in the whole world. All the editors would come there, of course Yiddish ones, where they could write. Inexpensive apartments would be available for rent to Jewish writers only. In the coffeehouse is where they would gather, discussing the plight of the Jews and seeking solutions, in a word—devoting themselves to the good of the community. When all the rest of the Warsaw Jews see what we have done, maybe they will also create their own societies—shopkeepers separately, craftsmen separately, bankers separately, teachers separately—each society would have its own coffeehouse with its own business, with its own interests, and all together we would be so powerful that the Polacks would bury themselves alive from shame and would come to us saying they had sinned—then we would know how to deal with them.

For now I am keeping this project a secret. I only outlined it in general for Khoskl Kotik, and as soon as he heard the word, "society," he sprang up and smothered me with advice on how to put the project into action. He had already, he said, organized many such societies, more than the hairs on his head. He has a real knack for organizing societies. One society he organized is called, "Society for Helping the Poor." If I liked, he said, he would give me a book, two books, three books about his "Society for Helping the Poor" so I could learn from him and not make foolish mistakes. I thanked him very much and told him to grow old in good health, but I would get along without his "Society for Helping the Poor".

In the meantime it's still very hot out and everyone has gone off to the dachas. In fact, they go to Polish dachas, although the Polacks chase them away with sticks. But Jews aren't discouraged by this. Come summer they run to the dachas. As soon as it gets a little cooler and the crowds start coming back home from the dachas, I will call them together, God willing, to give a lecture on my project for a Jewish coffee house. I hope they will all come and be enthusiastic about my project and take it up eagerly.

But now I must run to the editorial office to check out what's happening with the war between the Bulgarians, the Serbs, and the Greeks—who is burying whom and who is being destroyed? If you read what they say, it seems they are destroying each other. When you read how "brothers" are burying one another alive, a chill passes over the body. It's hard to believe. Picture it! Because of the great heat, the armies have thrown off their clothes and are fighting stark naked. And when they invade one or another village or town, they slaughter everyone including women and children. They commit atrocities not to be believed! You can understand how bad things are when the Greek king called out to the world for justice, complaining that the Bulgarians entered a Greek village, raped all the girls, and tore children to pieces! Exactly the same as a Jewish pogrom, but Jews have no one to appeal to for justice. What do you think the Bulgarians are doing? They also came out with a plea to the world for justice because the Rumanians want to attack them and take away everything they have. And what do you think the Rumanians are doing? They also cry for justice! They plead for justice while blood is flowing like water. In the newspapers they describe how not a drop of water is to be found where the battles are being fought, only blood. It's a fine time we are living in, my dear wife, no question about it! Let us hope we survive it! And as I have no time now, I will make this short. God willing, in my next letter I will write you everything at length. May God grant us all health and success. Be well and kiss the children for me and send my best and most friendly regards to your mother, whom I honor, and to the whole family whom I greet in the most friendly way.

From me your husband Menachem-Mendl

ALMOST FORGOT. What do you say to the Turk? They report from Sofia that he has decided to attack Adrianople after all. A big mistake on his part. I am of the opinion that it isn't the right time yet. Let us hope it will work out for him.

As above.

25. Sheyne-Sheyndl from Kasrilevka to Her Husband, Menachem-Mendl, in Warsaw

To my dear, honored, renowned, generous, and wise husband, Menachem-Mendl, may his light shine forever.

FIRST OF ALL, let me tell you that we are, thank God, in the best of health. Pray God we hear the same from you, never worse.

SECOND OF ALL, I am writing you, my dear husband, that your new plan for the coffeehouse you want to open in Warsaw doesn't begin to please me. You know why? Because nothing will come of it. It'll just be talk and more talk and that's how it will end. All Jewish undertakings are like that. Do you think it's any better here? Our Kasrilevkers have the same habit. At first they're all excited, then when it gets down to business, no one's at home. You'll be lucky if it doesn't end in blows. As my mother says: "It is written that if there were even a smidgen of agreement among Jews, the Messiah would have come long ago . . ." And especially when it comes to money. It's always like that. As soon as money is needed, all the rich people in town suddenly die off like fish when the lake water falls too low. That's how the rich are all over the world. They won't give to anyone else and they don't begrudge themselves anything, but no sooner does a rabbi, a miracle worker, a cantor, a doctor, a preacher, a fiery Jerusalem Jew, a nuisance, the devil knows who—come to town than they shower him with coins. You don't know where all this money in town is suddenly coming from.

Just last week this rabbi descended on us. He is as much a rabbi as I am a *rebbitzin* but he made himself out to be a rabbi. He came to us from God knows where! He lodged himself in a fancy room—it was at Chana-Malkeh, the blabbermouth, and let it be known he was half do-gooder and half doctor who heals the sick, makes children healthy, and lengthens everyone's years—even revives the dead! In all the synagogues and study houses he hung up notices listing all the sicknesses he healed, you name it. Do you have the chills, do you have headaches, do you have heartache, bellyache, eye pain? He cures it. And whoever has bad feet or a bad liver or gallstones or chronic rheumatism or is coughing from consumption or is simply crippled, they should all come to him. He will produce a complete recovery, may God produce a sickness in him on behalf of all Jews who are in fear and awe of him. You should see this Jew with his beard and side-locks, wearing a long tasseled undergarment down to his knees, talking with God and is sweet as sugar. With women he is distant, (may he be afflicted with boils), doesn't look you in the face, (may his eyes fall out), gives everyone a packet of herbs, (may God give him Job's trials), warns you at least ten times over not to eat on an empty stomach, not to think of anything at all and most important, not to speak the whole time you are taking his remedy. All the while he is wishing everyone well, smiling and sighing, and taking as much as they want to give him (may it take him by the belly). He doesn't bargain unless he thinks someone has more and is holding out on him. How does he know who has more and who hasn't, you will ask? Can't you figure it out, my all-wise husband? We have a Chana-Malkeh on this planet, may a boil fester on her face! It's likely the blabbermouth, may she suffer for it, split everything down the middle with him, but they only found out about it much later.

At first it didn't occur to anyone to ask how come the blabbermouth was scurrying around like a poisoned mouse, trumpeting the rabbi's miracles and wonders all over town, swearing on her life how the rabbi, that miracle worker, who was lodging at her inn, before her very eyes healed a boy of nineteen who coughed so hard you could hear it three streets away with a little bit of herbs. He also cured a lad who had consumption whom no one expected to live, and an old lady who complained about everything, and another old lady who was terribly hoarse, and still another old lady whose neck was turned to the side. And eyes, God in heaven, how many eyes this man has already cured! That's what Chana-Malkeh, the blabbermouth, broadcast all over town, may Pharaoh's plagues and Haman's end befall her. You don't know what he can do, she says! One after the other, one after the other! And mostly sick eyes, and mostly those coming in from the villages, those poor folks who want to go to America and are afraid of having sick eyes. They run to him with their eyes, the sick ones, the healthy ones, and he daubs on some kind of water—and that's it!

Chana-Malkeh blabbered on and on to everyone she met, young and old, rich and poor, wiping her lips and raising her wide-open eyes to the heavens, swearing she received nothing for her pains, at least not in this life. If not for her, I wouldn't have gone to this *shlimmazel,* may he lie in God's earth! I thought it was nonsense when Chana-Malkeh first began shooting off her mouth. I came home and told my mother, who said to me: "You can't know for sure, maybe this Jew has in him certain powers, because it is written that what someone can't do, another one can . . ." And she talked me into going to see him. What harm would it do if he gave me something for my back spasms so they wouldn't return? I told her I could spare him my spasms, I would rather have him see Moyshe-Hershele, may he thrive. He is so emaciated and so pale that I don't know what the matter is with him. Is it because of his studies? He studies and studies day and night. Or is it because he is growing? He's growing as fast and tall as a sunflower. That's what I said to my mother but she interrupted me and insisted that I myself had better see him. I am a mother, she said, so I am more important. She argued so long until we both went to see him. He looked us over carefully with one eye (may it come out the other side of his head) and honored us with a few herbs, which had the worst taste. May everything he tastes taste that way, Lord of the universe, and warned us not to eat on an empty stomach, not to think of anything at all and, most important, not to speak the whole time we were taking his remedy.

May he live as long as we took his remedy! We threw his herbs out the window as soon as the newspaper arrived warning us against this rabbi who was going from town to town and pretending to be a doctor, because he was just gouging money out of people and not helping them one bit—that's what they said in the papers. Such brains! What took them so long to realize it? If they had written about it a week earlier, I would now be a few rubles richer, may he spend it on a real doctor, may he break every bone in his body in a fall and may he not live to get to where he wants to go! Now my mother says she knew right away he was a thief. As proof—how come he told everyone not to speak the whole time they were taking his herbs? So I wondered, if she did know, why didn't she say something? She said: "How could I speak when he told me to be silent?" May he be silent forever, sweet God! As if there weren't enough things to throw away two silver rubles on! It would have been a lot better to spend that money on the children considering that you yourself don't ever think of sending them something from Warsaw. They say everything there is almost free. As my mother says, "It is written, if it is far from your eyes, it is far from your heart" . . . At least it's good you sent them the few books and that you don't forget to remind your newspaper people you have a wife, till a hundred and twenty years, who keeps an eye peeled every month for the mail carrier who delivers the little money to the house. I almost die when I think they might have let you go, or maybe the newspaper has gone under. These days when so many tragedies are happening to Jews, you wake up in the morning and look in the mirror and if you see you are still here—you are grateful and praise God. As my mother says: "Don't complain, let's hope it won't get worse . . ." As I wish you all good things and eternal happiness, your true, faithful wife

Sheyne-Sheyndl

26. Menachem-Mendl from Warsaw to His Wife, Sheyne-Sheyndl, in Kasrilevka

To my dear, wise, and modest wife, Sheyne-Sheyndl, may God grant her many years!

FIRST OF ALL, let me tell you that I am, blessed be His name, in good health and spirits, and may the Blessed One grant that we hear from one another only good news of comfort and salvation for us and for all of Israel—Amen.

SECOND OF ALL, let me tell you, my dear wife, there is no end to it. I am talking about the fighting in the Balkans. All you hear is: "Brothers, let's fight!" You can almost hear the bones cracking, see blood spurting, and what does the world say? Nothing! The world looks on as if it were a show and applauds! It's like in Warsaw when we watch the athletes competing. There is one athlete among them, a Royal Guard, Vildman is his name, and his name fits him—he is a wild strongman, though one of ours, a Jew. He is of that line of strongmen in Israel, from the tribe of Judah, they say. Night after night he puts on a show, flexes his muscles, puts away the Gentile strongmen one after another like little lambs. You should see how the Warsaw Jews take pride in him, what pleasure they have, clapping and beaming from ear to ear! I picture what would happen if this wild fellow, while all fired up, instead of showing his tricks on stage, would be let out naked in public on the Warsaw streets at the height of his power, and told: "Punch away, brother Vildman, as you love God!" Oh my, what havoc he would wreak in Warsaw!

It's the same with the Balkan "brothers." The difference is that our Warsaw hero is a Jew and fights for a living and it isn't as dangerous. I have a feeling that if this Jewish strongman were to see blood from a cut finger, he would faint away. He is the kind of man who, if you say to him, "Stop," would stand stock still. But with those wild Balkan "brothers," I'm afraid, "stop" won't work. You'll have to hit them over the head with a club, by which I mean you'll have to convince them with a few good volleys from real cannons, or send a few battleships against them . Only when they hear a real "bang-bang" will they stop to consider what they're doing and sober up. In the meantime they are drunk on Turkish blood still fresh in their nostrils while they keep bragging about the exploits they have performed. One reports coldbloodedly: "Today I attacked my older brother and knocked out his eye . . ." Another, with a fearsome look on his face says: "Today, thank the Lord, I tore off my younger brother's arm." A third, full of enthusiasm, is quoted in the newspapers: "Today I was lucky to tear out the bowels of my middle brother . . ."

What such boasting can lead to we can see in the case of Ferdinand, the king of Bulgaria, may all the enemies of Israel have the dismal end he had! They broke his bones, utterly destroyed him, the Serbs on one side, the Greeks on the other. Now Rumania is beginning to stir and worst of all, a threatening cloud is moving toward them—the Turk. He is fully armed and marching on Kirkeles and on Adrianople. If what the newspapers say is true, he should already have entered Adrianople. I hope I am wrong but I'm worried for Uncle Ishmael, I tremble for him! He showed his hand too early. According to my plan, if you remember, he should have laid low a good long time until the big powers themselves began bumping their heads together. Then it would be a different story. He should use his brains and not listen to the "young Turks" who are itching for a fight, but he should wait until my emissary arrives in Warsaw. He left America long ago but is busy somewhere in Berlin, in London, and in Paris. He's still very involved with the Zionist Congress, which will soon take place, with God's help, in Vienna. There we will finally see one another face-to-face and see what's what.

In the meantime I can devote myself to my other affairs and schemes. But first of all I want to finish up the book I plan to distribute, all six million copies free for the benefit of the emigrants. I have already prepared an advertisement for the newspapers and in rhyme at that! It's become quite the style these days to advertise in rhyme. Cigarettes, sausages, remedies, bandages—all are advertised in rhyme. It reads easier and it's much nicer. The readers likes it. Because of the popularity of these advertisements, several agencies are offering to set your advertisement in rhyme for a small fee, and the people love it! I went to one of these advertising services called, "Rhyme Anytime," and he put together for my book a rhyming advertisement to end

all rhyming advertisements called, *"L'kha Dodi—Go, my beloved."* This man
has rhymes pouring out of his sleeve, I tell you! Here it is, word for word:

Go, My Beloved, Greet the Bride
Jews come listen and take great pride,
Hear of deeds I will now retell
That in our Warsaw town befell.
Menachem-Mendl, what a Jew!
Trader, speculator, writer too.
(You know him? It's worth the bother,
Has a wife, who has a mother . . .)
In Odessa he had his start
At learning others to outsmart,
Knocking heads with other brokers,
Mostly rich Yehupetz jokers.
Low he bought and high he sold,
Money flowed, showers of gold.
Night and day he plied his trade-
Never sleeping, bed unmade,
Pulling off great combinations.
Stocks, bonds, obligations,
Money lent, interest returned,
Coupons clipped, dividends earned.
Selling buildings, settling estates,
Menachem never hesitates.
Rubles, kopecks up to his ears,
The very best of financiers,
Collecting many a business fee
From famous, rich old Brodsky.
And with Rothschild only
Was he an old-time crony?
A tricky deal in Baku or Kavkaz,
A broker dreaming of arbitrage?
Telegraph quick to London, Paris,
Send dispatches to find out where is
Sharpster Menachem-Mendl now.
You say he last was seen in Moscow?

But that was long ago by years,
Menachem-Mendl has changed careers.
Aha! No longer the same man anymore,
Never again seen on the trading floor.
He's a writer now! Only he could do it,
Writer, commentator, occasional poet.

On matters political
As well as rabbinical,
On wars and Jewish woes
His range of topics grows.
On what can he not deliver an opinion,
He's known wherever there's a minyan.
That he makes some money from his job,
Why not? As the saying goes, who does he rob?
But take my word, money is not his aim,
He's written a book will win him fame.
Not since the writings of our fathers of old,
Not since Egypt has such a tale been told
As you will find in this marvelous book,
You won't put it down once you take a look.
And best of all, my friends, the book is free.
It will bring you up to date, it's timely-
Describing how our Jews, poor souls, escaping
One disaster for the next, scraping
All they have together to leave at last,
Sighing with relief once the border's past,
On to Vienna, Konigsberg, Bremen
Are set upon by Jewish vermin
Who rob them blind of all their wordly goods,
Leave them like sheep wandering in the woods.
You'll be brought to tears and laughter
Enough to last you into the hereafter.
Menachem-Mendl doesn't select,
Everything is there—complete, correct.

In short, whoever loves God, hates sin.
Doesn't want a life of torment to begin,
But desires a blessing,
Don't wait till morning-
A stamp is all the expense,
Think what you'll get in recompense!
"Go, Beloved," is all you need to write,
Two words, a nothing in God's sight.
As Jews you will take great pride!
Go, beloved, greet the bride.

Well, dear wife, is there any doubt
That my book will not quickly sell out?
Won't Jews from everywhere
Agree that nothing can compare

With my *"Go, beloved"* and it's free,
A stamp, and it's all yours to see.
Who will not jump at a free ride?
Go, beloved, greet the bride.

Oh, the devil with it! Look what's it's done to me! That man with his rhymes has got me doing it. I can't stop myself and it's driving me crazy and besides I have no time and so I am making this short. With God's help, in my next letter I will write you everything in greater detail. In the meantime may God grant us all health and success. Kiss the children for me, send regards to your mother, whom I honor, and all the family in the most friendly way.

From me your husband Menachem-Mendl

27. Sheyne-Sheyndl from Kasrilevka to Her Husband, Menachem-Mendl, in Warsaw

To my dear, honored, renowned, generous, and wise husband, Menachem-Mendl, may his light shine forever.

FIRST OF ALL, let me tell you that we are, thank God, in the best of health. Pray God we hear the same from you, never worse.

SECOND OF ALL, I am writing you, my dear husband, that your rhymester, whose fingers you so enjoy licking, should have died a miserable death before you made his acquaintance, or half an hour after, and then he would not have put my mother and me to shame and disgrace (may ten boils disgrace his face), he who isn't worth the laces of our old shoes lying around the attic. Look how he writes about how Menachem-Mendl (may his right hand wither) "has a wife and she has a mother." Have you ever heard language like that except from an apostate? I don't know why that scoundrel begrudges you having a wife and your wife a mother, (may he have fevers and convulsions for a full year, God of mercy!) Would he be happier if you didn't have a wife, God forbid, and I didn't have a mother (may he not have a soul!)? What does he have against me and my mother to put us in his rhymes (may his head be put from his shoulders)? Let him suffer so that he'll never want to rhyme as long as he lives!

May God also grant you other ideas and other preoccupations, so you won't bother yourself with the devil-knows-what, and not become friends with the devil-knows-who, with entertainers, rhyme-makers, comedians and other such ne'er-do-wells. As my mother says: "God created plenty of *shlimmazels* and your husband finds them all . . ." She is very right. Not enough that I, Sheyne-Sheyndl, woe unto me, have to have a husband who lives in Warsaw, spends his time scribbling and bothers himself with Turks and Tartars. For what? For a crust of bread he barely earns? As my mother says: "There is no shameful job . . ." But still, do I need for you to start hanging around with rhymesters, song-makers, and actors who go all over the world and cheat people out of money? Really something to be proud of! We had a troupe of those fine people here this last summer. They rented a hall from Feivl Mezhebinsky and put on shows. They lodged at the blabbermouth's, naturally, stuffed themselves with potatoes, swilled beer and tea and left without paying—serves her right! She shouldn't have run all over town, her little tongue wagging, telling everyone she could about their wonderful singing and dancing and acting. You'd think that was enough. But with her hoarse voice and thin lips she told everyone, including me, that it was a pity on the actors, they had nothing to eat because the police didn't let them perform in the big cities so they had to go around to all the little towns and display their tricks. Tell me, where is it written that they have to live by doing tricks? Aren't there enough Jews in the world who have no work at all and are dying from hunger? But as my mother says—she always has a good word for everyone: "It is written that God hands out a livelihood to everyone, to the people on earth, to the animals in the forest as well as to the birds in the sky . . ."

I must tell you, my dear husband, that I would rather die of hunger three times a day, I would rather remain a widow before I see you in such a line of work! My face was burning with shame when I saw how Jews, husbands and fathers, made themselves up, glued on beards, and masqueraded as God-knows-who and performed God-knows-what, dancing and clapping their hands even as they were fainting from hunger while making funny faces and poking fun at Jews (may they break out in boils!) One saving grace they do have—their songs! The songs they sing are delightful, they melt your heart! One song they sang was to the tune the cantor chants in synagogue at *Succos* for the second *shmone-esre*, the eighteen blessings. The song is called, "Oy, I'm so happy! Oy, I'm so gay!" Everyone in Kasrilevka, old and young, is singing it now. I don't know who wrote that song, but he has to be a real devil, may he be cursed! I was ashamed of myself afterwards because I allowed myself to be persuaded by the blabbermouth and my mother to see their performance. My mother kept at me, "Go on over, what harm will it do if you go? Everyone is going, you go too. And especially when your husband makes a living in a way not too different from theirs." As she says, "One catches the fish, one cooks the fish, and another comes along and eats it up . . ." What she meant by that, I don't understand, but when I began to make excuses, saying I had no desire to go and that I'm doing fine without shows and so on, she burst out laughing and said I was a fool, how did I know where my husband was just that moment? "Maybe at this very moment he's going to a show himself. Do you think he sits day and night and laments over the Destruction of the Temple? Little silly, if I were you, I would long ago have gone to Warsaw. And I would arrive unexpected, on a dark night at the end of the month when no moon is in the sky. Not because I'm suspicious, God forbid, but just like this. I would come take a look out of curiosity from a distance, with one eye, so to speak, to see how things were going with him, that rascal, and how he was and what he was doing and how homesick the poor fellow was . . ."

I don't need to write you how those words broke my heart. I think that if someone would come and curse me up and down, it would be much easier to take. But when a mother speaks, you have to listen. After all, she's not my enemy. Nor yours either, though she buries you behind my back three times a day, actually with words of praise, as you have well earned and as I wish you all good things and eternal happiness, your true and faithful wife

Sheyne-Sheyndl

Everyone knows about the book you are writing which you say will benefit the whole world and yourself, and they are all looking forward to it. Many people have already asked me about it and I don't know what to tell them, may I know as much about troubles. They want you to send it directly to me in order to spare themselves writing you letters and using stamps. They are so smart! Not enough that it's free, they want it delivered free to their homes. As my mother says: "They expect their eggs shelled and placed right in their mouths . . ."

28. Menachem-Mendl from Warsaw to His Wife, Sheyne-Sheyndl, in Kasrilevka

To my dear, wise, and modest wife, Sheyne-Sheyndl, may God grant her many years!

FIRST OF ALL, let me tell you that I am, blessed be His name, in good health and spirits, and may the Blessed One grant that we hear from one another only good news of comfort and salvation for us and for all of Israel—Amen!

SECOND OF ALL, you should know, my dear wife, that the Turk, be-sides bringing misfortune on himself, has demolished all my wonderful plans. He should not have let himself be persuaded by his young people to move so quickly into Adrianople and Kirkiles and to other places from which they recently smoked him out, not even allowing, as they say, the smoke to clear. I hope I am wrong but he shouldn't have done that because it won't go smoothly for him. The big powers are seeking an honorable way for him to withdraw and retreat to his old home.

True, it's hard to hold a grudge against him. The passion for revenge is great especially when one see all ones wordly goods scattered all over the streets like after a pogrom, everyone helping himself. And here God helped out, the pogromtchiks themselves quarreled over the spoils and began to kill each other. When would you ever see such just desserts? As your mother says: "A kosher pot goes with a kosher spoon." But one mustn't forget that although his enemies have beaten each other black and blue, standing right behind them, egging them on, are such big bullies as the English, for example, with their checkered pants, or the Germans with their loud mouths, who have no interest in seeing the pogrom-bloodied Turk ever rise from the dead, reclaim everything, and stand on his own feet. Why is it worth their while to act that way, you ask? There's a simple reason, my little silly. I'll explain it to you with an illustration:

Say you have a rich old uncle whose inheritance you are aching for. God helps and he becomes sick so there's hope he will shut his eyes for good. He will be mourned, not spared a tear, given a decent burial service, delivered to the Holy Place, Talmud Torah boys will be hired to sing his praises, some small change distributed to the poor, and a cemetery plot bought for him. He will be put to rest among the finest rich men in town, the rabbi will orate a proper eulogy beginning with a peppery verse and ending with a shout of, "Go, little uncle, go and beat a path straight to par-adise—that is your proper place—and then the Kaddish will be recited. Then you will go home, take off your boots, sit shiva, the women will cook slippery noodles for the mourners' meal, friends and neighbors will pay their respects, and as is the custom, arrive without saying good-day, stay a short time and then get up and leave without saying good—bye, muttering under their breath, "For Zion and Jerusalem." Then you will lock the door, draw shut the drapes, and take out the will to see who got what. But imag-ine, my dear wife, if you can, the opposite, that the sick man starts getting well, asks for bread and butter, plum jam, and other food and wants to see a mirror to examine his tongue, becomes talkative, and comes alive. Can you imagine how dejected those poor relatives will be? They are smiling, pretending to be happy their uncle is, thank God, better, but what they wish him in their hearts should be sunk deep in the ocean!

That's the illustration. And the moral, I know, will be clear to you. It is not necessary to chew it for you and put it in your mouth. But there is one thing you will want to know: what about justice? Where is God? Why shouldn't the poor Turk take back his stolen fortune? Whom should it bother? I asked the same question, my silly, but just at first. If you were here in my place and had read everything that I read in the editorial office, the dispatches and the letters from all over the world, the lies that go back and forth, the falsehoods and accusations people make up which are immediately denied and the blood that runs in rivers in all the streets, you would also stop asking questions, as I stopped asking. I cannot bear it any more when someone asks me a question, and for that reason, I have stopped going to see Khoskl Kotik at the cafe so he'll leave me alone and stop berating me with questions like: how come they are silent and why do they allow the Balkan people to slaughter one another like oxen? Well, if the "half moon"—that's how he refers to the Turk—invades the Slovenes, that, he says, he understands. But how do the Slovene rulers allow their own brothers, the Slovenes themselves, to annihilate one another? Of justice, he says, he is no longer speaking. He just wants to know one thing—that I tell him what the sense is in all of this. And this Jew, you must know, when he latches onto something, you can't get rid of him so quickly. Now he's latched onto me about that Jewish coffeehouse I want to open with the sale of stocks, saying I should use the "by-laws" he has worked out for me. Everything, he says, needs by-laws, and once you have them, you don't need anything else. He has worked out a set of by-laws for my book on emigrants as well. A man has fallen in love with "by-laws" . . .

In the meantime I can write you, my dear wife, that my book is creating a sensation! Not the book itself, there is as yet no book, but the *"L'kha Dodi"* advertisement I had printed has stirred everyone up. I receive hundreds of letters from all corners of the world. One asks when the book will be coming out. Another asks if the book will be printed in rhyme like the *"L'kha Dodi."* And still another asks how I can afford to give the book away. And yet another asks—since I am giving the book away free, how come I require a stamp? Make up your mind, is it free or not? A greedy people, our Jews, I tell you! To reply to each one you need Brodsky's fortune in stamps alone! And as I have no time I am making this short. With God's help, in my next letter I will write you everything in greater detail. In the meantime may God grant us all health and success. Kiss the children for me, send regards to your mother, whom I honor, and all the family in the most friendly way.

From me your husband Menachem-Mendl

ALMOST FORGOT: You are eating your heart out, my dear wife, because the writer of the *"L'kha Dodi,"* put your mother in his rhymes. This is
the reason. At first he wrote it like this: "You know him? He's worth the
bother, has a wife, wouldn't have another." But I didn't allow it because I
knew you don't like such frivolous talk. He had to put in "mother" because
he didn't have another rhyme for the word "bother." So you needn't be
angry with him. He's is nothing more than a rhyme-maker and rhyme-
makers, as a rule, in order to get a good rhyme, will give away their mother
and father. You don't need much proof. We have a great rhymester here in
Warsaw, really a great one who has been writing songs in Russian and Yiddish for ages. Suddenly he got this crazy idea to poke fun at our Yiddish
language, making it sound ridiculous, calling it all kinds of insulting
names, cursing it out in Russian and finally ending with this rhyme:

> Yiddish—as a language it's a joke.
> If it were a business it would go broke.
> It's not worth a pair of old galoshes
> A curse on it! To speak it makes me nauseous.

My-my, what went on at the newspapers! How much ink was wasted!
Young people delivered fiery protests: "What an outrage! A Jew writing
Yiddish for so many years—and such fine writing at that—suddenly spits
on it and compares it to a pair of old galoshes and curses it too!" Young
folks—fools! They don't know how delicious it is for a rhymester to bring
off a rhyme!

29. Sheyne-Sheyndl from Kasrilevka
to Her Husband, Menachem-Mendl, in Warsaw

To my dear, honored, renowned, generous, and wise husband, Menachem-
Mendl, may his light shine forever.

FIRST OF ALL, let me tell you that we are, thank God, in the best of
health. Pray God we hear the same from you, never worse.

SECOND OF ALL, I am writing you, my dear husband, that if you do
write me, don't bother writing me about your *shlimazels,* those song writers—I don't care if they are big song writers—let them end up in purgatory
with their rhymes, may they have my migraines and my pains so they

won't be able to rhyme any more. May they be able to eat as I am now able to write you a letter when, if you must know, the whole house is spinning around me and I see spots before my eyes. What's going on? A few people asked me this morning to write you about something that has happened here. It's as if the whole town has gotten stuck in mud, can't move this way or that way, and they are hoping you can help them with advice, although I don't know why you've suddenly become the great sage to them, a deep thinker and adviser. But as my mother says: "Please God, don't give me brains or understanding, but just a bit of luck . . ." Here's the story:

We have a brand new Bridal Society, called by the Hebrew name, *"Haknesset Kalah,"* whose purpose is providing dowries for all the girls. As soon as God helps and a girl becomes a bride, she receives three hundred rubles from the Society! The father can be anyone—a merchant or a craftsman, a storekeeper or a teacher, rich or poor. As long as he's a member of the Society, that's enough. And a member can be anyone, you don't need any brains or ability. All you need is a fiver, and anyone who has it and can afford it and wants to give a fiver becomes a member of the Society and as soon as his daughter becomes a bride she is assured of receiving three hundred rubles dowry saved up from the fivers every member has paid in. Well, so many fivers came in the first year they didn't know what to do with all the money! Thousands of fathers, thousands of fivers. Quite a bargain, for a fiver a father is relieved of the burden of paying a dowry and can arrange the best marriage! My uncle, Avraham-Moishe, if you remember him, has three daughters, *kayn eyn horeh,* all three of whom should long ago have been led to the wedding canopy. As soon as he heard about the new Society he ran off and paid the five rubles to become a member and immediately engaged a matchmaker to find him three bridegrooms in one fell swoop. If someone has three daughters and all three become brides, according to the rule, the Society gives him three times the three hundred rubles dowry. And if someone has four daughters and all four become brides, they have to give him four times three hundred rubles dowry. And if another has been blessed with five daughters, they have to give him five times three hundred rubles dowry. In sum, the more daughters the better, as my mother says: "It is written that there will come a time when a father won't have to worry about having too many children and a mother won't cry over having too many daughters . . ."

But it suddenly occurred to the Society, a plague on them,—what would they do if somone had seven daughters, ten daughters, thirteen daughters—is there any doubt it can happen? Here in Kasrilevka we had a cobbler, Yidl Bezdetnik he was called, and God favored him with eighteen children from two wives, and all girls! Luckily he emigrated to America just in time. Whether he arrived there with his entire gang or whether they died one by one on this side of the border or on the other side of the border—no one knows. Who bothers thinking about a cobbler? Don't we have enough cobblers and tailors and other ordinary Jews who died before they reached their destination so they could toil like workhorses in order not to die of hunger? But the Society began to consider—what would happen if such a Bezdetnik, for example, were also to become a member and *didn't* go to America and all his eighteen girls grew up and became brides? Where would they get so much money? So they came up with an idea (may their eyes drop out of their heads), and they made this ruling: whoever pays *one* fiver a year can marry off only one daughter, and whoever has two daughters must pay two fivers a year and whoever has three daughters—three fivers, four daughters—four fivers, ten daughters—ten fivers (may they have ten black years on their heads!) There was nothing for it. Poor Uncle Avraham-Moishe had to cough up another two fivers, did he have any other choice? As my mother says: "Whoever likes a fatty kugel must also like to put schmaltz in it . . ." Are you ready for this? Have patience. The good part is just starting.

Anyhow, my uncle Avraham-Moishe didn't waste any time and made matches for all three daughters and got for them three excellent bridegrooms, one better than the next. What's so remarkable? For money these days, you get a good deal. The dowry is guaranteed as if in the bank, and the Society is trusted because the organizers and the really influential people are in tight with each other. You will understand when I tell you that Reb Yehoshua-Heshl himself is also one of the Society big shots. That's good, no? Just wait, you'll hear more.

The matches were arranged but he delayed the wedding for two weeks so that all three would take place on the same day. What was the reason behind that? The reasoning was simple and went like this: he would marry off all three daughters at one time so he could save himself three wedding dinners, three klezmer bands and three sleepless nights. It's too bad he couldn't save himself paying three matchmaking fees. It turns out Uncle Avraham-Moishe is no fool. Uncle Avraham-Moishe, in fact, didn't pay the matchmaking fee either. He decided to put it off till after the wedding in order to pay it, you understand, with the dowry money that the Society would give him. As my mother says: "It's good to smear your bread with someone else's butter . . ." You would think he would be satisfied, no? But Uncle Avraham-Moishe is not that kind of man. He is never satisfied. "What's the matter, Uncle? Why are you looking so unhappy?" He groaned: "After all, I have to part with my three children in a week because all the bridegrooms decided among themselves that a week after the wedding they would all leave for America. Since they each have three hundred rubles, why should they stay here?"

Well, Uncle Avraham-Moishe was in the depths of despair. A calamity! Here he finally lived to see a bit of pleasure from his children and they all pick up and fly off in a week! If they would at least let him enjoy it a little! That's how the poor man was bewailing his lot, but in truth you could see that the marriages were making him very happy indeed. After all, a man has such a weight lifted from his shoulders—three grown daughters in one day! But my mother cannot bear any complaining and hates when a person has deceitful eyes and doesn't say what he means, so she berated him, saying he had no reason to cry. "We have a strong, powerful God who can perform miracles," she said, "they might remain here and not go away because it is written that a person has only one way and God has endless ways." Uncle Avraham-Moishe became angry and said to her: "Somehow you've started talking too much to me about God! . . ." So, who was right? Naturally, my mother!

His three daughters were married in one day as I am a rabbi. When the time came for the wedding and the bridegrooms came to claim the dowries, Uncle Avraham-Moishe ran off to the Society to collect the money. It turns out there first had to be a meeting of the Society. He immediately became downhearted but if they say a meeting, let there be meeting. When would the meeting be? Saturday night after dark, we should live and be well. "But Saturday night is the wedding party and Tuesday is the ceremony, three ceremonies!" he protested. Well, you can protest today, protest tomorrow—you can't take on the whole town. Finally Saturday night arrived, the Society gathered for the meeting at Reb Avraham-Moishe's house, and they decided the following—wait till you hear this. Even though quite a few fivers had been collected, so many people were marrying off their daughters, and all at the same time, it was likely that by *Rosh Hashanah Elul* there would be a big backlog of maybe hundreds of weddings. They figured out that if they distributed a dowry to everyone, Rothschild's fortune wouldn't be enough and they might even go bankrupt. So they decided to wait and for now not give anyone a groshen until they came up with a solution, either to divide up the collected money among the brides who had married before *Rosh Hashanah Elul*, or to return the fivers to the members, and that would be an end to it! How do you like that story? May a plague befall them even before the first of Elul. Here they got the whole town all excited, and for what? As my mother says: "If you build on sand, it has to fall, and if you build on snow, it always melts away . . ."

Can you imagine the uproar? And the sorrow of the brides? And the pity on the poor fathers? Some are screaming bloody murder, threatening to make a scandal! Others are ashamed to go out in the street. And they, the organizers of the Society, a curse on their heads, they know just one thing—to hold meetings! Another meeting and another meeting and another meeting—may they choke on meetings, God in heaven! Meanwhile it was decided that they would send letters to all the big cities where there are also such Societies and ask their advice what to do. And since you are now in a big city like Warsaw, and you are acquainted with somebody you call Khoskl who is involved, you say, in organizing societies, my Uncle Avraham-Moishe and his children, who read your newspaper, have asked me to write to you so that you should visit this man and write me right away what that Khoskl has to say. Is there a solution to this or should we stop wasting our time? I'm afraid it's *really* a waste of time and we should all give it up as a lost cause. As my mother says: "It is written that woe unto the sick man when you have to save him with smelling salts . . ." As I wish you all good things and eternal happiness from your true and faithful wife

Sheyne-Sheyndl

30. Menachem-Mendl from Warsaw to His Wife, Sheyne-Sheyndl, in Kasrilevka

To my dear, wise, and modest wife, Sheyne-Sheyndl, may God grant her many years!

FIRST OF ALL, let me tell you that I am, blessed be His name, in good health and spirits, and may the Blessed One grant that we hear from one another only good news of comfort and salvation for us and for all of Israel—Amen.

SECOND OF ALL, let me tell you, my dear wife, as soon as I received your letter about you Kasrilevka "*Haknesset Kalah*" society, I ran right off to my friend Khoskl Kotik and found him at work making by-laws for a new society. What kind of society it is he won't tell me. He says it's a secret for now. But when people find out, he says, it will cause an uproar. There's never been anything like it anywhere. Anyhow, I told him the story of your "*Haknesset Kalah*," and read him your letter. He burst into laughter, but what laughter! He held his sides and was almost rolling on the floor. I thought the man would explode with laughter! When he had laughed himself out I said to him, "Maybe you can tell me, my dear Reb Khoskl, what about my wife's letter brought on such a fit of laughter?" He replied, "I'm not laughing at your wife or at what she writes, but at your idiotic Kasrilevka Jews who know nothing about anything and take it upon themselves to organize a society! To organize a society and to work out by-laws you have to ask *me* and *I* will give them the answers!" "That's the very reason I came here," I said. "My Kasrilevka big shots are stuck deep in mud and I want you to give me the best advice on how to pull them out!" "Ach!" he said, "Advice? Why not, with the greatest of pleasure! So long as they don't behave like fools and do what they are told. Your Kasrilevkers are always finding fault in whatever you tell them and are always ready to criticize." "How do you know our Kasrilevkers so well?" I asked. "It's enough," he said, "that I know you, and you're certainly a Kasrilevker. But come now, we're wasting our time talking like this. Let's think of something for your people, some really good plan. It's a waste of their money. It breaks my heart!"

With those words he stood up, rubbed his forehead, paced back and forth across the room a few times, and not thinking too long, stopped and said to me, "I'm almost ready. But tell me something, Reb Menachem-Mendl—do you have the time now?" "What's the difference whether I have time or not?" I said. "I really don't have the time. But if it's important, I can find half an hour." "If so, good," he said. "Here's a sheet of paper. There's pen and ink, sit down, I will dictate to you and you will be so kind as to write." "What can you dictate to me? And so quickly? Without giving it much thought?" I asked. He laughed out loud, "You think this is my first by-law for a '*Haknesset-Kalah?*' Sit down please, take the pen, write and don't ask questions." I obeyed, sat down at the table, dipped the pen in ink, and was ready. Do you think it took long, or that he consulted a book or notes? Not at all. Entirely off-the-cuff and without thinking long, he simply furrowed his brow and, just as I am writing you now, that is how it went for him, smooth as silk, perfectly phrased, straightforward, clear—pearls, not words!

He dictated and I wrote. "First of all," he said, "roll up your sleeves, dip the pen in the inkwell and put down in your fine handwriting as follows: THE ARTICLES OF THE BY-LAWS OF THE KASRILEVKA SOCIETY, "HAKNESSET-KALAH," to be confirmed by the Crown and declared legal:

PARAGRAPH NUMBER ONE: In the town of Kasrilevka is hereby organized the Society "*Haknesset-Kalah,*" whose purpose it is to provide Jewish girls with dowries on their marriage so that every Jew who has a daughter—and daughters have a habit of growing up—should not have to worry where to get the money for the dowry and for wedding expenses when they reach the age of eighteen or, God forbid, older.

PARAGRAPH NUMBER TWO: The Society, "*Haknesset-Kalah,*" is made up of a COMMITTEE and a COMMISSION. The COMMITTEE solicits membership, collects money, and processes applications, and the COMMISSION double checks all the applications, makes inquiries in town, listens to complaints, and supervises the COMMITTEE.

PARAGRAPH NUMBER THREE: The COMMITTEE is made up of three elected elders from among the finest and most respected men in town. They choose from among themselves a PRESIDENT who has two assistants. The COMMISSION is made up of seven elected officials, all young men, enlightened and dignified, smart and honest. All the elected officials making up the COMMITTEE and the COMMISSION work for nothing, but in good faith, with truth and justice for the good of all.

PARAGRAPH NUMBER FOUR: Each Jew who is married and has a daughter can become a member of the Society and must contribute, as soon as a daughter is born to him, one fiver, but on the condition that as soon as the girl is one year old, he must contribute an additional ruble, that is, six rubles. The following year he must contribute seven rubles, on the third year eight rubles. On the fourth year—nine rubles. On the fifth—ten rubles. On the sixth—eleven rubles. And so forth until the nineteenth year when she receives her dowry of THREE HUNDRED RUBLES and then she must marry.

PARAGRAPH NUMBER FIVE: The girl who doesn't wish to marry cannot be forced to do so. But then what? She loses her claim to the three hundred rubles dowry. Thereby three goals are achieved at once: (1) Jews learn how to save. (2) Our custom of needing to collect money for poor brides disappears; and (3) We no longer have any old maids.

PARAGRAPH NUMBER SIX: Every year before *Succos*, a new COMMITTEE and a new COMMISSION will be chosen to lead the Society in a peaceful, honest, and just manner for the well-being and pride of all Jews, amen . . ."

"Amen v'amen," I said, "That is all well and good, but what do we do with those who have already paid in the first fiver in the first Society and are left high and dry?" I asked. He answered, "There's your trouble! A man never has time! We are just at the beginning and you're already asking questions. Believe me, I haven't forgotten anyone. I've also thought of them. Now write, please,"

PARAGRAPH NUMBER SEVEN: Whoever has contributed the first five rubles and doesn't wish to pay in further, or cannot pay, or has forgotten to pay, will get his money back, and why not? Not right away, but in eighteen years—so that your uncle, whatever his name is, can relax. Now," he said, "gird your loins, my dear Menachem-Mendl, we have just begun. We have much more to talk about—about management, administration, and bookkeeping. We have at least sixty or more paragraphs to go."

When I heard "at least sixty or more paragraphs to go," my heart sank, I glanced at my watch, and begged a thousand pardons of him. I had no time, I would look in on him another time, I was in a terrible hurry, I was not my own man, I said, I must run to the editorial office. Who knows, I said, what's doing there now? Here we are, I said, sitting making friendly talk and out there the world could be turning upside down.

I managed to tear myself away and sped off to the editorial office and—sure enough, as if I were a prophet, I found dispatches piled high and all of them from one city, from Bucharest. Of all places! Bucharest! That's the place where world peace must come from now, where the biggest Balkan diplomats are meeting to work out a treaty to settle the conflicts among the brothers who are unable to divide Uncle Ishmael's inheritance among themselves. It's no laughing matter, I tell you! Bucharest! You call that a city! Rumania! You call that a country! Moldavia and Wallachia! You call them nations! They are now the arbitrators, the defenders of justice! They are supposed to work out a treaty and make sure everyone abides by it! You will ask, maybe they will obey what is stated in the treaty? If so, why haven't the Rumanians adhered to the treaty worked out in Berlin before Bismarck's time, in which it is stated in plain black and white that Jews should have equal rights in Rumania? People who do not pay their debts should not ask others to sign their promissory notes. This begins to look to me like nothing more than a mockery. I cannot believe that anything can come of this Bucharest conference and from their treaties. From one side the Greeks and the Bulgarians are haggling like at a market, setting forth their conditions for Macedonia, and from the other side Macedonia is asking to be left alone, it would rather be independent and wishes the Greeks and Bulgarians would go to the devil. And then there's the Turk with his Adrianople! He isn't moving from the spot so much as a hair although the great powers long ago let it be known that he had better retreat peacefully, and the sooner the better, or else they would drive him out by force, just as they once made King Mikita of Montenegro clear out of Scutari. I cannot begin to describe to you, my dear wife, the anguish and the heartache this has caused me. On the face of it, why should I care whether Adrianople, which according to law and according to justice and according to basic humanity and everything else—should belong to the Turk and to no one else? But what does your mother say? "If you can't go over, you must go under . . ." And it's true. Before anyone takes something away by force, it seems it would be a thousand times better if he, the Turk, would hand it over to the Bulgarian nicely, "Here, choke on it!" Do you understand what I am saying? I have a whole scheme for this Adrianople. What is my scheme? I must make it clear to you. The matter is as simple as two plus two. Since King Ferdinand of Bulgaria is now defeated—and with someone defeated it is good to do business—the Turk should become very congenial, the closest of friends and present him Adrianople as a gift and confide in him that he, the Turk, should be compensated for the fine war they waged against him in which they broke his bones, but it should be the Slovenes who should accommodate the Turk with a generous fortune for Adrianople and Macedonia and Albania. Now do you understand? Then he will appear like a decent person and will also get a nice pocketful of money. God willing, I figure to quickly get to work on this plan along with my other projects that have piled up here. But as I have no time I making this short. God willing, in my next letter I will write you everything at greater length. In the meantime, may God grant us all health and success. Kiss the children for me and send my best and most friendly regards to your mother, whom I honor, and to the whole family, each and every one.

From me your husband Menachem-Mendl

31. Sheyne-Sheyndl from Kasrilevka to Her Husband, Menachem-Mendl, in Warsaw

To my dear, honored, renowned, generous, and wise husband, Menachem-Mendl, may his light shine forever.

FIRST OF ALL, let me tell you that we are, thank God, in the best of health. Pray God we hear the same from you, never worse.

SECOND OF ALL, I am writing you, my dear husband, that those who read your letter pleaded with God to inflict hideous nightmares on this Khoskl Kotik of yours for the outrageous arrangement he worked out for us! They figured out that if they were to pay what he wants plus interest it will come out that we would end up paying in twice as much, maybe three times as much as we can ever get back, even if we were to live long enough to get it back. Who wants to wait eighteen years! It's easy for him to say eighteen years, may there be eighteen plagues on my enemies. As my mother says, "If you wait till Friday, then you'll eat pot roast . . ." No, Mendl, when you see him, your Kotik, tell him we are not such idiots as he thinks and we won't let ourselves be led by the nose to pay and pay as much as he says. He should know that since Kasrilevka is a town, there has never existed the amount of money he calls for, and even if there were, we can find better things to do with it than what he proposes.

And as to the advice he gives Uncle Avraham-Moishe, that he wait for a hundred years till those do-gooders remind themselves to return his fivers, please give him a big thank-you, your friend Kotik. Also ask him out of curiosity, as he is such a great adviser, to give you advice about what

Uncle Avraham-Moishe should now do with his three daughters, who be-sides being, just between us, full of years, are, *kayn eyn horeh,* so matured that when they walk down the street, no one would say these are still un-married girls. Should he salt them down like meat to preserve them or should he sell them as cut-rate merchandise? Now they don't have any bridegrooms any more because all three bridegrooms sent back the en-gagement contracts, may God send them pains, woes, and diseases! I don't like to curse but I wish with all my heart that they don't live to marry as long as they live, and if they ever do marry, may their wives in short order become widows and their children orphans! To add to the shame and heartache, they had already photographed all three couples in one portrait and had sent the pictures out to all the relatives from both sides, the brides' and the bridegrooms. If that were not enough, they sent pictures to Odessa, Vilna, America, and who knows where else! Men—they get away with everything! Let a bride say she doesn't want the bridegroom and she will be ridden out of town!

Look at Aunt Kreni's only daughter, the one who is so well educated. She knows how to dance, she's lively, dresses in the latest styles. She came this close to marrying Sholem-Zeidl's son. You don't know him, he studied in Yehupetz to be a pharmacist and returned a nothing, a failure! Under-stand, not a thing had yet happened between them, they hadn't even bro-ken the betrothal platter when Sholem-Zeidl's son couldn't wait and told the bride a few racy stories and she said to her mother that even if he were made of gold, she wouldn't marry him! What stories he could have told her, no one can get out of her for anything, but she put her foot down—no, no, and no again! An only daughter—what can you do? Well, that was the end of the match. As my mother says: "A bride no more, a spinster again . . ." What does a man like Sholem-Zeidl do? You'll never guess! He de-cides to noise it around that it was he who didn't want the match. Why? His sonny boy doesn't want the bride because she doesn't speak Russian well enough. What would he do, he said, if his son finished his pharmacy studies and became a pharmacist and had a wife who couldn't speak Russ-ian well? What do you say about him? Shouldn't a father like that be better off first burying the son and then himself dying a violent death?

Who do you think is responsible if not she herself, Aunt Kreni's edu-cated only daughter? Would *I* speak Russian with such a charlatan? I would have to be out of my mind to speak Russian with him! And do you think she's the only one? All the girls have become like that. If you go out for a stroll on *Shabbos* afternoon, you hear no other language but Russian: "How are you, Rosetchke?" "How are you, Sonyatchke?" "Good day, Rosetchke!" "Thank you, Sonyatchke!" It makes you sick to your stomach!

Why is this happening? Because in Yehupetz all the girls are Russified ladies, and speak in Russian, and our Kasrilevka girls also have to act like ladies and babble in Russian too. Whatever they do in Yehupetz, they have to do here too. For instance in Yehupetz every summer all the Jews leave for their dachas in Boiberik. What can Kasrilevka do if it has no Boiberik? God granted it a Zladyevka, so they go to Zladyevka to their so-called dachas. They are dachas like I am a dacha. But it's an excuse—where else would they go? They go to Zladyevka and act like they have dachas there. What does it mean to act like they have dachas? They rent a little hut from a Russian peasant and buy out all his milk, pay him off with grain and berries, throw off their gabardines and stretch themselves out on the green grass beneath God's sky—after all, what harm is there in that? But no! An edict is suddenly issued forbidding Jews from renting Boiberik dachas. Hearing this great news, the officials in Zladyevka also prohibited Jews from renting dachas. The Kasrilevka Jews should have responded with a "You don't want us? We don't need you either. Keep your dachas." But they are, after all, Jews. Just because *you* don't want *us, we* want *you!* Everything that is forbidden is sweeter. As my mother says: "You never want a piece of meat as much as when it is forbidden to eat it . . ." Suddenly everyone is talking about dachas. There have never been as many eager customers for dachas as this summer. Right after *Shevuos* they took off for Zladyevka as if something marvelous were awaiting them. Instead they found it was the constable himself waiting for them with two assistants. The constable announced that if someone is really sick and must have fresh air and if he brings a certificate from a doctor saying he is at death's door, he will be allowed to stay. Naturally, everyone got certificates from doctors. As my mother says: "For money you can even get shrouds . . ." Wouldn't you think that would be enough? The constable, may his name and memory be erased, reconsiders and says that a doctor's certificate isn't enough for him. He wants to see for himself who is pretending to be sick and who is really sick. He makes everyone undress, both the men and the women, those idiots. It seems to me, even if I knew I were dying, God forbid, I wouldn't embarrass myself like that. But for them anything is acceptable, so long as it gets what they want. Well, if the Yehupetz aristocrats are willing to sacrifice themselves for a dacha, that's to be expected—they have money, they can get it. But Kasrilevkers? What's so great about their Zladyevka hovels? As my mother says: "It is written, the reason the Messiah isn't coming is because the poor man imitates the rich man . . ." It's a lucky thing that in Yehupetz they don't cut off their noses. In Kasrilevka we wouldn't have one person left with a nose, as I wish you all good things and eternal happiness from your true and faithful wife

Sheyne-Sheyndl

Wait, Mendl, I forgot to write you that they are banging my door down again asking about your book with the *"L'kho Dodi."* They love it, a plague on them! Not so much the book, as the *"L'kho Dodi.".* And not so much the *"L'kho Dodi,"* as the fact that it doesn't cost a kopek. For nothing there are plenty of interested customers. Why you needed this mess, I will never know. Think about it, you were doing well, you finally succeeded at something that everyone was enjoying, so why couldn't you also make some money on it, maybe make a good profit? Suddenly you had to become a big philanthropist and do-gooder with a generous open hand. Tell me what's the big glory in it? What is the idea of giving it away free? As my mother says: "For free you don't get anything but fever and the evil eye for a whole week . . .

32. Menachem-Mendl from Warsaw to His Wife, Sheyne-Sheyndl, in Kasrilevka

To my dear, wise, and modest wife, Sheyne-Sheyndl, may God grant her many years!

FIRST OF ALL, let me tell you that I am, blessed be His name, in good health and spirits, and may the Blessed One grant that we hear from one another only good news of comfort and salvation for us and for all of Israel—Amen!

SECOND OF ALL, let me tell you, my dear wife, I am not opposed to the peace the Balkan brothers have finally made. Peace is one of the three things on which the world stands, and if you would ask *me*, and if it were up to *me*, all the nations of the world would have to live in peace and tranquility. When the Messiah comes, God willing, that's the way it will be. The only thing I am bothered by is that the peace was signed in Bucharest, in the capital of that country called Rumania. I don't know about you, but when someone mentions the name Rumania, I start boiling! It's foolish, I know—there are plenty of countries where our Jewish brethren aren't exactly licking honey. In those places they say it openly: "*You* are Jews—and *we* would just as soon you were dead!" But Rumania—that's another story. They talk a good game and say they believe in equality, but how different it is when they actually deal with us! On paper Jews have the same rights as everybody, not a hair's difference. But when it comes right down to it, they say we are "foreigners" and to "foreigners," altogether different laws apply. Then again, you can't blame them. Why should Rumania be guilty when we really *are* foreigners? If you want to know, we are a little guilty ourselves because of our ancestors. When they fled Egypt, if they had settled in Rumania instead of Canaan, we wouldn't be "foreigners" in Rumania. If that is so, then can't all countries say we are "foreigners" in their lands? Listen, that's what they *do* say! What's more, there are many different ways they say it. He who is blunt says it bluntly, with a wooden club to the head. Another who is genteel says it politely, disguised so it is hard to know what he means.

Be that as it may, so long as the peace is a peace, may it last many years and may no new conflict or new complication develop, God forbid, to cause the brothers to grab one another by the throat—amen. Now only one thing remains—what will happen with the Turk? Will he obey the leader of the young Turks who stands adamant as steel and says that not until his last soldier is killed will he give up Adrianople? Or will he follow my plan and give it up peacefully? It drives me mad when I see from afar how this one is making hopeless mistakes, another is drowning and I can't do anything to help! But I believe that in the end the Turk himself will figure it out. The Turk, you understand, is a businessman and a businessman sniffs out what another can only see with his eyes. You have to be a complete ass not to understand that now, while the Slavs are again bosom buddies, it is for the Turk a disaster. No, they cannot convince me that he is not his own worst enemy and is slaughtering himself without a knife because he won't give up Adrianople. The evidence is in the feelers the Turk is sending out to learn what might happen if he were to retreat from Adrianople.. Oh, he isn't actually saying he will retreat, God forbid. He would simply like to learn how much it would be worth if he swallowed that bad medicine. In business talk it's called putting yourself up against the wall for a price.

In short, it will eventually sort itself out. Some kind of order will prevail and we pray to the Lord above that there will truly be peace on earth—if only for a while—and then the nations will stop making a din about vain and idle matters and we will at last be able to pay attention to problems that are more important and closer to our hearts. For example, take Angola. Angola is the name of the country I once wrote you about that they are proposing for Jews to settle. It's no longer a secret. Whoever let the secret out I cannot tell you, but it's a good proposition. I like it. It is in Portugal. I mean to say, it is in Africa but it belongs to Portugal. The land is vast, even too big, I'm afraid, and rich in resources, as I already wrote you, truly a land of milk and honey. What is the problem? It's still very primitive, barren and unexciting. It has to be settled but no one wants to go there. Once it is settled, it will be a paradise, and for Jews a kind of *Eretz Yisroel*. You will ask, how did this land come to us? I must make clear to you precisely how that happened.

The land was a land like all desolate lands in wild Africa when the Portugese from Portugal arrived and took it over. But since Portugal is a small country, smaller than one of our provinces and hasn't many people or much money, the land remained undeveloped. But it was fated that something would come of this land. The owners of the land, the Portugese, found out that there was in the world the Jewish people who were lost, straying, wandering, and dragging themselves all over for two thousand years and could not find a resting place anywhere. Then the Portugese heard that in London there was a Jew named Zangwill. He, this Zangwill, I must tell you, is partly a writer, partly a businessman, like myself. But there's a bit of a difference. I write in Yiddish and he writes in English, so he probably earns a little more than I do because English is not Yiddish. How can you compare us, you little silly? Him they pay by the line. But how much do they pay him? It's likely they pay him a ducat a line! So many lines, so many ducats. Not a bad deal, don't you think? Well, that's not my point.

Anyhow, the Portugese found out that this Zangwill I am telling you about is the leader of the territorialists. He travels over the world seeking a territory, some land where a Jew can settle, become master of his own piece of earth and not be afraid that he will be driven out the next day. When they found out about him, the Portugese sent brokers to see Zangwill and he received them. They came in, sat down, smoked a cigarette and said to him: "We are from the land of Portugal. Our great-great-grandfathers did not treat you well. Even though it's been several hundred years ago, the fact remains they didn't treat you well at all! We are not guilty ourselves but our close neighbors, the Spaniards, are really the guilty ones. It was they who convinced our great-great-grandfathers to drive out the Jews." And so it went—a conversation of maybe half an hour. But Zangwill, who is not one of your dull minds, soon sensed what was going on and said to them: "Nonsense! Why talk of things that happened long ago? We have long forgotten it! By temperament a Jew is not vindictive. It is written in our Torah: 'You must not take revenge.' If we wanted to take revenge on all those who have done us harm, ha-ha-ha—we would be at it constantly. For who hasn't had a turn at hurting us? Take the Germans, or the French—fine people, you would think? How did they treat us, may it not happen again? Or, please forgive me, take our own Englishmen. Didn't they expel us and persecute us and commit all the evils people have always visited upon Jews? It's nothing, one forgets. A Jew has the memory of a cat. But you must have come for some reason and here we are talking about bygone days! Tell me, gentlemen, in a few words, what it is you want."

To make a long story short, they felt each other out about this, about that, and finally they came out with it: "The story is this, Sir Zangwill. They say you are seeking a land for your several million unfortunate Jews who are desperately trying to survive and find a tiny corner to lay their heads, and we have a land called Angola. It is in Africa and is vast, simply huge! Much bigger than your Israel! Your Israel could get lost in it. Perhaps we can do business . . ." But Zangwill is no fool, he is one of ours, you understand, and plays dumb, puts on an act, cool as a cucumber, strokes his beard and asks: "Exactly what business do you have in mind?" They said: "What is so hard to understand? It's good merchandise. We are a country without people, you are a people without a country, a kosher spoon matching a kosher pot. We offer you a territory, a bargain, something that doesn't come along but once in a hundred years. It's a golden opportunity and you should take advantage of it. We are giving it away very cheaply, half-price, practically free!" Naturally this was music to Zangwill's ears. What was there to talk about? He was delighted, but to get overly excited, to display his enthusiasm, was not wise. He was, after all, a businessman! He acted hard to get. He thanked them very much for the offer of the territory but he had, he said, enough territories—that was not the problem. May he have more such problems. Are there not enough territories in the world? There's America . . . They interrupted him: "Eh! How can you compare Africa to America! That's like comparing a pig to a horse! That is America, this is Africa—the land of milk and honey! You have no idea what a treasure it is, this Angola! We wouldn't give it to you for all the money in the world, but since our great-great-grandfathers . . ." Zangwill interrupted, saying: "Enough about your great-great-grandfathers. Let them rest in that paradise they earned from God because in God's name they burned us at the stake and in God's name they flayed us alive . . . but never mind! Who is talking about that? I told you that a Jew is not one to bear a grudge. A Jew has the memory of a cat. What once was, is not now. Now we are talking business. And business is business. It's an open-and-shut case. God has favored you with a land called Angola. I am not asking you how you got it, by inheritance or by force—that is not my business. I only know that your land is located somewhere far away, off in Africa, and you are, forgive my saying this, a bit short on funds and don't have the money or people to settle the land. So you want us Jews to come and settle your land. Have I understood you correctly?" They saw they weren't dealing with a child and said to him: "God bless us, how clever you are. But what do you say to our offer?" Zangwill again stroked his beard and said to them: "What can I say about it? Happily this business can come to something. But we have to work out all the details. First, a Jew has to see what he's dealing with. We have to see what Angola looks like, where it is situated and what it is worth. Sight unseen you don't do business. And second, be so kind as to put down on paper, written and signed, that we are in complete possession of the land and don't have to worry about your interfering with us." Here they sat up: "What has it got to do with being in complete possession? You'll be renters." Then Zangwill said: "Let it be renters but we will install ourselves as if we were in our own home. We won't pay you big taxes, we won't provide you with soldiers, we will maintain our own army, we will speak our own language, institute our own laws, have our own schools and synagogues. We will make it into a kind of *Eretz Yisroel.* Do you understand what I am saying? Moreover, the land will belong to you in name and for the property we will pay you not all at once—who has that kind of money nowadays?—but gradually, in installments. I believe you will be satisfied with this arrangement and we will both be happy! After all, how long can a land just lie there unused? It will lie there so long until your neighbors will take it away from right under your nose—the French, or even our English with their checkered pants."

In short, Zangwill really laid it on thick, as only he knows how! Afterward he convened a conference in London of the very greatest territorialists, including Rothschild from London, Schiff from America, Brodsky from Kiev, Teitl from Saratov, Yatzkan from Warsaw, and Schrier from Baku, and it was decided they would first send people to look over the land. They went and looked it over and brought back good news. The land was indeed ten times as large as Israel and you could pack in all the Jews from the whole world without trouble. But like all large countries, it has all kinds of terrain. There is desert that is good for nothing and there is fertile soil in which things grow like crazy. There are all kinds of places: virtual paradises and places where it is better never to go. But no one is forcing anyone to go where it is not good when you can go where it is good. Now all that remains is working out a contract with the Portugese government. If it will agree to all our conditions, all is well and good, and if not, that will be that. But no one is talking about not going ahead. What will Portugal do with such a large land and where will it ever get such a people like our Jews in the whole world?

So not long ago they convened a meeting of the biggest territorialists and they elected three delegates to go to Portugal to work out the contract. In the meantime, they will convene an even bigger conference of all the territorialists. They don't yet know where or when but I will probably be the first to know because I have to know—I have worked out, you understand, an entire project on how to settle this new land of Angola. This project took more than twenty pages to describe and I am about to make a clean copy. And as I have no time I will make this short. God willing, in my next letter I will write you everything at greater length. In the meantime, may God grant us all health and success. Kiss the children for me and send my best and most friendly regards to your mother, whom I honor, and to the whole family, each and every one.

From me your husband Menachem-Mendl

33. Sheyne-Sheyndl from Kasrilevka to Her Husband, Menachem-Mendl, in Warsaw

To my dear, honored, renowned, generous, and wise husband, Menachem-Mendl, may his light shine forever.

FIRST OF ALL, let me tell you that we are, thank God, in the best of health. Pray God we hear the same from you, never worse.

SECOND OF ALL, I am writing you, my dear husband, that because of you I am suffering shame and humiliation, I cannot walk down the street. Young smart alecks stop me: "What's this about your husband?" they ask me, "Why has he done an about-face and suddenly become a Mongolanik?" By that they mean the land you dug up for their benefit, God's knows where in Mongola, and are working up plans for it. These are Zionists and are disappointed because you don't prefer Israel. Israel is much better. Israel, they say, is ours, and Mongola is somewhere at the far end of the world! Because of you they have a problem. Since you were going to the Zionist Congress in Vienna anyhow, they were hoping to give you a letter to bring to the Congress. Now they have to send a representative of their own who would cost them money, which they don't have. You would have saved them the expense. As my mother says: "A kosher spoon matching a kosher pot . . ." But since you have been converted, they say, and you've become a Mongolanik, they are now without a cantor to lead their prayers.

Honestly, Mendl, why did you need this? I know I am just a woman and don't know as much about these things as you, but it seems to me, and my mother agrees, that "your own is not a stranger and a stranger is not your own . . ." But what good will my writing do? When you get some crazy idea in your head, whatever anyone else says, is wasted! No one can budge you. Were you ever in Mongola? Did you look it over? How can you praise it to the skies? You're listening to what brokers tell you? What does a broker know? A broker wants to make money. So long as there's business to be done, what else does he care about? Or maybe you have some idea of tricking me and the children and my mother into going there? I tell you straight out, my dear husband, knock it right out of your head. I'd rather die than go to Mongola! Let your rich folks go first, the ones you listed in your letter. Once they get there, settle in and suffer a little and then want to write us a letter that all is well and good, completely ready, then we can consider whether to go or not. But don't bank on it! Your rich folks would rather live here in prosperity and honor, comfort and luxury, this one in Yehupetz, that one in Warsaw, another in Baku, and it is us they will send off to suffer, God knows where! As my mother says: "With other people's hands it's good to rake hot coals . . . and on someone else's beard it's good to learn how to cut . . ."

But I'm afraid that from your Mongola and from their Israel it will end up the same as all your dreams and the world will stay the same as it always was. The rich folks in Yehupetz will continue to enjoy their wealth, may they be punished for it, and we here in Kasrilevka will still suffer as we have always suffered, living crowded together, suffocating to death and trying to mimic like monkeys what they do in Yehupetz, not only in styles and in speaking Russian, in everything. You can say for sure that there is not a thing in Yehupetz that we don't have exactly the same here in Kasrilevka. As my mother says: "It is written that whatever is in the bottle is soon in the glass . . ."

For this we have to thank our wealthy Shlomo-Velvel Charlatan, the one I wrote you about with the parrot and the police commissioner. Every week he travels to Yehupetz where he witnesses miracles and great wonders. And as money he has and a charlatan he is, he always brings back something new which, if I hadn't seen it in twenty years, I would never miss it. For instance, one time Shlomo-Velvel decided to bring back something that sings all kinds of tunes of the greatest cantors in the world by itself. When you stand from afar you imagine you are in a synagogue hearing the cantor chant and the choristers singing along with him. But when you go up close you see a funny-looking box, the devil with it! And how about a piano he brought back long ago, even before he bought the iron cupboard that ten peasants couldn't budge? The piano was bought for his daughters, those fine ladies, who dance in public with boys at all the weddings. One has already danced herself into a pickle, a curse on her! She ran off with Dodi Mezshiritshke's son, who has an even better family than Shlomo-Velvel Charlatan. They made her a fine bride—*mazel tov,* may a misfortune befall her. Perhaps you know why she had to run off when she could have gotten married like everyone else? "Getting married," my mother says, "is not like going bankrupt or a pogrom you have to hide from . . ." The reason is—it looks better that way. That's what it says in the magazines. First you run off, then you come back and get married. Gossips say it was for show, this running off. There would have been a marriage anyhow, but as a misfortune happened to them and the couple had to get married as soon as possible and they were afraid the town would find out, they created a distraction. But Kasrilevka is not so easily fooled. They re-member quite well when the wedding was and we'll see, God willing, my mother says, when the *bris* will be. Now this Shlom-Velvel has decided to do something else, just listen to what a charlatan can do!

There are, they say, in Yehupetz, "illusions," a kind of theater where they show guests live people on the wall, as well as animals, birds, horses, dogs, cats, whatever you want. The people on the wall move as if they were living and the horses gallop. It is really lively, a party! And all to cheat some money out of people. Then Shlomo-Velvl Charlatan gets this idea that if in Yehupetz you can drag money out of people, why not in Kasrilevka? It seems we have enough idlers here who have nothing to do but play cards. Better to let them go to the theeter and see the tricks that Shlomo-Velvel will show them. And you can't say he's altogether wrong. Rather than play cards, theeter is better. What does a man like Shlomo-Velvel do? He has his own courtyard and a large room, big enough to lose a dog in, he puts out benches in the room, sticks up red posters, sets up a box office at the door and stations two boys at the gate to pull in people by the coattails: "This way, Jews, illusions!" But they didn't have to pull them in. Boys and girls, young men and women poured in and filled the room like a cage full of chickens. What can I write you, my dear husband? It was a great success. He is taking in money day and night, may it all collapse around him! Since he opened the "illusion," he has a full house every day except *Shabbos.* He even wanted, that charlatan, to keep the "illusion" open on *Shabbos,* but they told him that if he dared do such a thing, they would destroy his room, his courtyard, and the house completely! He laughed it off and said he wasn't afraid of such threats. He was, he said, a friend of the authorities, in with the police. Still and all, the "illusion" was closed on *Shabbos.* What did he care? He had enough of a crowd all week. May he spend on doctors what he tricked out of me and the children and my mother and the whole family. If not for my mother, would I ever have set foot there? I would never have gone to see these "illusion" along with all the servant-girls, shoving and staring at his vulgar spectacle! But when the children came from school and began begging me to give them money to go to the "illusion," once and twice and three times, I gave them a piece of my mind. But my mother is a grandmother after all and couldn't bear to see the children begging, so she took pity on them and came to their defense: "What do you care if they go? Children," she said, "want to take a look, what can be so bad? True, it's trash, but it won't hurt anybody . . ." I began to tell her I was afraid to let the children go alone, the devil knows where and with whom. She said to me: "Go with them too. Why shouldn't you also see something different? Why are you being so old-fashioned? Do you have such a wonderful life with your chosen one who provides you with luxury and pleasure?" When my mother wants to say something, she knows how! And so she talked me into it. But I insisted on one condition, that she come along. Why should she stay home all alone? Let her also see this new wonder. Isn't she also entitled?

Finally we all gathered together, I and my mother and the children and my sisters and all their children. As my mother says: "A little family circle . . ." and all at my expense, suddenly I am the rich one in the family, and we were off to the theater. What can I tell you, my dear husband? I cannot possibly describe everything we saw! First of all it was pitch-black, you couldn't see a thing and so crowded you couldn't breathe. A woman in her ninth month almost suffocated. Luckily the police helped take her out, that's how loud she was screaming! Then there appeared on the wall a person and then a lot more people, riding on horses and without horses and all alive, all waving their arms, and all the horses are running and galloping with such speed that I don't know how they didn't break their necks! But the only thing is, you don't hear them talking. Otherwise you would think the people are real people and the horses are real horses. In the end it's all a dream, a make-believe, not real at all! My mother spat three times after we went out into the daylight. Still she said she was sad that my father had died. Would that he had lived to see this foolish dream rather than lie in the earth, his bones rotting. Everything reminds her of my father, of blessed memory, even though Uncle Avraham-Moishe claims she will remarry, may he live so long! I gave him a good talking to he will never forget. What an idea, my mother remarrying! I told him the naked truth. We women are not like you men. Before remaining a widower a man would prefer bringing the children a "gift" of a stepmother. But we would rather remain widows, as I wish you all good things and eternal happiness your truly faithful wife

Sheyne-Sheyndl

Do you think, Mendl, there aren't people here interested in getting together and opening another "illusion"? If in Yehupetz there are twenty "illusions" and in Warsaw forty, in Kasrilevka there can be two. They have simply become terribly envious of Shlomo-Velvel Charlatan because he is making such easy money. As my mother says: "It is written that the reason they put shards on a corpse's eyes is to remind us that when he was alive he desired everything he saw . . ."

34. Menachem-Mendl from Warsaw to His Wife, Sheyne-Sheyndl, in Kasrilevka

To my dear, wise, and modest wife, Sheyne-Sheyndl, may God grant her many years!

FIRST OF ALL, let me tell you that I am, blessed be His name, in good health and spirits, and may the Blessed One grant that we hear from one another only good news of comfort and salvation for us and for all of Israel—Amen!

SECOND OF ALL, let me tell you, my dear wife, that your Zionist Kasrilevkers are very wrong if they believe I have done an about face and am now a territorialist and no longer a Zionist. As a matter of fact, I never was either a Zionist or a territorialist. I was always a Jew and a Jew I will remain. And though I don't wear the Zionist stamp and there is no Star of David on my forehead, don't be afraid that I won't be going with all the Zionists to the Vienna congress. When I hear the word "Zion," or "Jerusalem," I am carried away. I feel a quickening and a longing for our ancient home and nation. My soul yearns, languishes, and aches for what is no more, so long as it is one's own, even one's own Jewish policeman, so long as he is one of ours. Oh, for a Jewish passport printed in Hebrew letters: "THIS IS THE PASSPORT THAT BELONGS TO Menachem-Mendl OF ISRAEL. Oy, how I long to see the day! But in truth, why should we fool ourselves? Let them give us thirteen Angolas and eighteen Galvestons and all of America, will we trade it for one tiny piece of Israeli earth? Such nonsense! What will we do, for instance, with the prayers that specifically name Jerusalem as the city where we will return? Or Zion, which we say three times a day in our prayers? What will we do with those prayers? Erase them? Throw them out? Some choice! No, my dear wife, there is nothing dearer to our hearts than Israel. Ah, you say I am knocking myself out for Angola? That's because Angola is being offered to us almost free and as of now I don't see any other land anywhere for Jews. There isn't one, even if you were ready to die for it! Little silly, if tomorrow they find another land for us, I will write in favor of that land, not ask which is better, which is worse, so long as *it is a land,* because *we are eager and ready, and if you are eager and ready, you take what you can get*—that's the way people are. To what can you compare it? You can compare it to someone you find lying almost dead in a field, not having eaten for three days and you ask him: "Tell us, what would you rather have, meat or dairy?" Don't ask him! Give him meat, give him dairy, even give him pareve—just don't let him die of hunger! I just wish there were enough money for the expense of sending emigrants to Israel, to America, to Angola or to any other land. But what about the problem that the handful of Jews are spread out among many different countries? That's an old curse—and yet that's better than living in eternally crowded conditions, eating ourselves up alive, as you say, or converting, as people are certainly doing here by the hundreds and thousands.

In short, let your Kasrilevker Zionists become more acquainted with my Angola project and my Israel project, and afterward let them say whether or not I have become a convert, as they call me, or whether I am a good true friend who has in him Jewish zeal combined with a businessman's know-how and foresight. I won't boast to you, as others do, and say I am the greatest diplomat. But I am a Jew who is steeped day and night in politics and sit, as they say, right at the source and meet with all kinds of people and glean from each whatever I can. Take a person like Khoskl Kotik. You can say whatever you want about him and your Kasrilevker sages can make fun of his Society, *"Haknesset Kalah,"* as much as their hearts desire, but I will tell you what our sages said in the chapter, "Who is wise? He who learns from everyone." I have learned much from this Jew that is worth a great deal—many thousands of things. He is invaluable! Then you will ask what exactly have I learned from him? I have learned from him that every project must be laid out on paper, divided into paragraphs, for each item a separate paragraph, everything well thought out, measured, calculated, weighed, and debated so that no questions remain. The Angola project has more than a hundred paragraphs and consists of two parts. The first part deals with organization, how to settle the land and how to conduct oneself there. The second part deals with money. To tell you, my dear wife, the whole plan is impossible! It covers more than twenty large sheets of paper on both sides. But the gist, if you will, I can tell you in brief so that you yourself will say it was cleverly thought out, nothing could be better.

First of all, I worked it out that the land would be divided into colonies. Not any old colonies, but according to a method calculated so that every colonist would own no more than two hundred hectares of land and each colony would consist of no more than fifty such colonists who would take up farming. All fifty colonists would be like one big family, each living in his own household. When he worked in the field, he would not work alone, but together with the other forty-nine colonists. You will probably ask why all together? It is necessary to explain. Farming, you must know, is really a demanding occupation. Besides needing to know *about it* you have to know how to *do it*. There's no getting around it—a Jew wasn't born for it. He is not equipped for hard labor.

That's a problem but here's a solution. The English have invented a machine to work the earth. Listen to what this machine can do. It doesn't need horses or oxen or people. Just one person sits on it, turns a wheel and the machine plows two hundred hectares of land for you before you can say, *"Sh'ma Yisroel"*! Plowed land must be harrowed. You take the same machine, remove the plow, put on a harrow, turn the wheel and it harrows all the plowed earth. Then you have to sow. You remove the harrow and put on a sower. When it's time to harvest and you have to mow, you put a mower on the machine and you mow. Then you have to thresh the grain and the machine becomes a threshing machine. Afterwards if you want to clear a wood or uproot trees, it will clear a wood and uproot trees for you. I tell you, it's a blessing from God!

A person just sits on the machine, reads a book, says some prayers or sings a few psalms and it does all the work for now. But there's one problem with this machine—it costs money—a lot! In our money it would come to ten thousand rubles. But it's worth it for fifty colonists. It would cost two hundred for each colonist and that's all—and not even in cash. The best machines nowadays can be paid out. And as with the big machine, so it is with the smaller machines, those that do the smaller jobs and can be used communally. For example, it's no longer necessary to milk cows by hand. One machine can milk fifty cows at a time. Or, for example, take brooding chickens. Once they used to set a hen on the eggs and she would sit and sit and would get used to sitting. Today they've come up with a kind of oven in which you put as many eggs as you want—a hundred dozen eggs, a thousand dozen eggs, and the high heat alone hatches the eggs into chicks. Isn't that a wonder? Usually, a farmer with two hundred hectares of land doesn't have the means to own all those machines, but for fifty farmers to go in together to buy these machines is a snap.

From this alone you can see that my project has been devised with a method in mind and with good sense, having seen to every detail, large and small. For example, I have laid it out so that each colony of fifty farming families has its own ritual slaughterer, ritual bath, synagogue, schools, even a market—everything outlined. Ten colonies, each of fifty families that do farming, should be enough to support one city. In the city thousands can live who undertake to do commerce, build factories, trains,

mills, plants, open shops, deal in grain, and speculate on the stock exchange, as is customary in a large city. All necessities like bread, milk,
cheese and butter, potatoes, onions, radishes, and vegetables will be sup-
plied by the ten colonies that take up farming.

The farming colonies are obliged to support the cities with money and
people. By money I mean the taxes that every person is obliged to pay, and
by people I mean soldiers. All twenty-one-year-olds will be sent to the city
(except only children) where they will become soldiers, something that
will also be important to the colonists in case of war or an attack, and serv-
ing also as police. With the taxes coming in, they will support high schools
and universities that will accept everyone, Jews and non-Jews, openly and
freely, without quotas or special requirements for outsiders. Finally, you
must know that in my project there do not appear the word "outsider" or
the word "privileges." To me there are no outsiders, no "one of our own."
Everyone has the same rights because to God Himself, who created
mankind, all people are equal, all the more so today, when a person should
be considered a person!

But all this I am writing you about is but an eighth of an eighth of my
project that contains everything in it, not leaving out so much as the least
detail. Now only one thing remains: MONEY! I have taken care of that too.
You will ask how? I don't know if you will understand it, because the plan
I am proposing is based on speculation, and you have always been, if I remember, against speculation. So I will try to give you the essence of this
speculation in brief. A bank issues shares. The shares are sold and the
money goes to the bank, which buys the land in its name including all the
machines, it builds houses, buys livestock and everything else you need,
and sells it to the colonists for a much higher price on time. The profit to the
bank is divided in half. One half goes to buying more shares and the more
shares, the more money. The second half goes for dividends, which the
bank pays out every year to its shareholders and the shareholders, besides
getting dividends, also earn on their shares proper because if the dividend
grows, the shares go up and up in price and then there are more interested
buyers of shares and the more shares, the more money, and the more
money, the more colonists, and the more colonists, the better for the country and if the country does good business, the shares go up and if the shares
go up, there are more buyers for shares and the more shares, the more
money and the more money, the more colonists—do you understand? It's a
wheel and it turns! Certainly there are many more details , but as I don't
have time I will make this short. God willing, in my next letter I will write
you everything at greater length. In the meantime, may God grant us all
health and success. Kiss the children for me and send my best and most

friendly regards to your mother, whom I honor, and to the whole family, each and every one.

From me your husband Menachem-Mendl

ALMOST FORGOT: This Angola has so addled my brain that I forgot about the Turk and his Adrianople. Let him stay there in good health. So long as he isn't bothering me, let him bang his head against the wall. I don't even want to get involved. And whoever was right—he or I—we will see later. Let us grow older by a week and let us find out what happens with the Bucharest peace and how Sezonov welcomes the representatives Adrianople sent recently to St. Petersburg. The delegation consists of six people. Among them, they say, are two of ours, Jews. It would be interesting to know if they gave any thought before they left to their residency permits or whether they relied on miracles?

As above.

35. Menachem-Mendl from Warsaw to His Wife, Sheyne-Sheyndl, in Kasrilevka

To my dear, wise, and modest wife, Sheyne-Sheyndl, may God grant her many years!

FIRST OF ALL, let me tell you that I am, blessed be His name, in good health and spirits, and may the Blessed One grant that we hear from one another only good news of comfort and salvation for us and for all of Israel—Amen!

SECOND OF ALL, let me tell you, my dear wife, that, God willing, I am not going to the Vienna Congress empty-handed. I am taking with me a complete, fully worked out plan for Israel, a much bigger and better plan than the one about Angola I sent you. Israel, understand, is not Angola. Angola is Angola and Israel is Israel. The name alone is enough to warm and stir the Jewish heart, to make it tremble with longing and burn with shame that all other people have a home and we have to hang around other people's celebrations, picking up the few crumbs from under the table granted us begrudgingly, until we are chased off by dogs and beaten with clubs—God have mercy on us!

Take the Bulgarians, the Serbs, even the Montenegrans. Who are they compared to us? Shepherds, coarse upstarts, savages, yet each is willing to sacrifice his life for his country, offering up the last child and pawning the last belonging. And we? The most ancient of peoples, the chosen of God, and show me what have we done until now, after two thousand years, for our land, for Israel? It's easy to say the word I-S-R-A-E-L! The land of Israel! Our *own* land where *our* ancestors lie buried, where we had *our* Temple in Jerusalem, *our* Priests and Levites, *our* Organ, *our* prophets, *our* kings, kings of the House of David—No! You can say what you will, no one, not even our worst enemies, can deny that we have a right to this land soaked in our sweat and our blood and our tears. Ah, you say, it now belongs to the Turk? That is for us the greatest advantage, little silly, because if it belonged to another country, God forbid, it might be much worse for us! You can ridicule the Turk in whatever way you wish, "Red yarmulke," "blue pants," "has a thousand wives," but he is, after all, one of ours, a distant cousin, and is descended from the same root as we, no shame to us, from Abraham our Father. The truth is, not from the same mother. Our mother was Sarah, his mother—Hagar, a servant and concubine. Isn't it obvious that it was fated that the land fall into the hands of our cousin Ishmael so that he could in time hand it over to us? You will ask an obvious question, how is this possible? We are not the same as others, we will not attack the Turk in broad daylight and take Israel away by force. The only thing we can do is—buy it. But first we have to ask the other party, maybe he doesn't want to sell. And second, even if he does say yes, what will the other nations say? *Everyone* has some power over the Turk. But let us say that even if there were no obstacle, you will ask a new question: where will we impoverished Kasrilevkers get so much money? I beg you, my dear wife, not to worry. Read this letter to the end and you will find an explanation for everything and you will admit that with God's help, I have worked it out in every way.

First, let us explore why buying isn't the answer. The Turk will certainly want to sell. It's as clear as day to me! And there never was a better time than now. You will ask, why now? You must understand what is happening in politics. Here's the situation: his taking over Adrianople and then not willing to withdraw has caused him great damage. He himself doesn't know how much because he doesn't allow the damage to be appraised. It has come to the point where the great powers are wracking their brains trying to figure out how to get him out of there, not with bloodshed but by the new means of boycotting that they learned from Poland. They will boycott him with money. The nations are of one mind not to lend him a groshen! It's likely "we" already informed him from St. Petersburg that he shouldn't count on "us" for a loan, that is, not "us," (where do we get money to lend when we ourselves borrow?) but "we" will work through our friends, the French. They will go along with "us" and won't discount so much as one Turkish promissory note and if the French refuse to discount you might as well take a sack and go begging. This we know from our own experience. May we have what "we" owe the French! Probably twenty million francs! That comes to eight million in our money. A fine sum of money, don't you think? Khoskl Kotik says that he figured out that if we had given Adam the eight million in single rubles and if Adam were still alive today, and had been counting rubles twenty-four hours a day without eating or drinking or sleeping he would still have a long, long, long time to go till he finished! Now do you understand?

As I see it, this is now an opportune moment, the best time to do business with the Turk. What then is the problem? It's simply impossible. How do Jews come by enough money to buy Israel from the Turk, even with the Rothschilds and the Schiffs and the Brodskys and the Polyakovs? That's the big problem! But I came up with a solution—and I think even you will say it is the best idea a person's mind could ever think up. What is it? I have worked out a plan for *leasing*. The Turk gives us back Israel on lease for, let us say, ninety-nine years. An outright sale gets you into politics, diplomacy, this one has a say, that one has a say. The English don't approve, the French are offended. But with a lease—whom would it bother? With a lease I can give away my house, my room, my bed, even my coat—whose business is it? Who can tell me what to do with my coat? Do you understand or not? We are not taking anything away from anybody, we are not buying anything from anybody, we are just renting the land of Israel from him for ninety-nine years and we are putting in writing that the land is still his land and he is still king, or sultan, as before, nothing changed so much as a hair. And as we are renters, we can introduce into our place our own customs, our own business practices, and act like proper householders. We would not only have our own language and our own synagogues, schools and universities but would be ruled by our own laws, have our own decrees, police force, governors and even our own ministers. All this is discussed at length in my Israel project. I even had the foresight to identify the appropriate people for all the highest positions and at the Vienna congress I will see who is available. For the time being I have marked the names of the most appropriate candidates.

The very first one, the president, has to be, according to my thinking, none other than Max Nordau. He is truly a man who can speechify, you understand me, a roaring lion. When he speaks, they say, the walls tremble and pearls pour forth from his mouth. And for vice-president we should choose Wolfson. David Wolfson is a Jew, you understand, who has a dignified appearance, resembles Doctor Herzl, of blessed memory, and is a fine leader as well no one's fool! When he speaks, he speaks like one of us, in ordinary Yiddish like me, like you, not like the other Germans for whom a

Yiddish word is *trayf* as pork. We don't have to worry about ministers either. We can't have a better minister of the interior than Usishkinn a man
with character! When he says something it must be so, even if the world
turns upside down! Even if it isn't so, it *must* be so. True, Doctor Tchlenov
would also not be a bad minister but he is too soft a person. He would be a
good diplomat. I would make him foreign minster if we didn't have
Sokolov. Sokolov is preferable. Sokolov is a linguist, speaks all languages
and Hebrew fluently. Doctor Levin, Shmaryahu Levin, is suited for minister of education. With nothing more than his own two hands he established
a polytechnic institute in Israel, he's been to America, earned money from
speaking and any other way he could! And for minister of transportation,
Goldberg is made to order, Isaak Goldberg from Vilna.

But all these ministries are nothing alongside the minister of finance!
As it is said, without food there is no Torah, if you get my meaning. But we
have a minister of finance, praise God, from whom all ministers of finance
can learn—Zlatopolsky. Believe me, my dear wife, even Witte, the great
Witte, can't reach to his boottops. The only fault he has is that he's a bit too
shrewd and is too sharp a speculator! But on the other hand, I believe this
fault is really his greatest virtue. Finances have to do with the stock exchange and the stock exchange lives by speculation, and speculation loves
a speculator. I myself once earned my bread that way so I know the taste.
But the people whom I listed for you are not the whole list. There are plenty
of other candidates. With people we have nothing to worry about. Praise
God, but we will not be embarrassed with our ministers and they will easily be the equal of the Turks' pashas and mashas, whose grandfathers not
too long ago were chasing pigs. Take even the great Mayoresky, who is
today in his glory, what is he? Certainly not a rabbi's grandson. His grandfather, if not his father, was a shepherd with a shepherd's crook in Rumania. What is there to talk about? When we send our delegates across the
world, to the peace conference in The Hague or to an arbitration, or some
issue requiring trustworthiness, or simply to London, Paris, Berlin, or
Moscow (if they let us in), they will be the people to take into account and
listen to. Then the world will see *who* we are and *what* we are, and they will
beat their breasts and feel remorse—mark my words! They will be sorry
that they treated us like the lowest of the low. It will be an honor to have us
as guests and they won't know what to do with us—after all, the delegates
from the new Jewish State, from Israel!

I am simply amazed that no one has thought of this till now. Where
were our brilliant minds? I refer to my plan of leasing Israel. The Zionists,
forgive me, always made a fuss up till now, either buy the land, get a char-
ter, or colonize it. Did anyone think of anything else? No! For that they

needed a businessman and your Menachem-Mendl is that businessman. I am not saying I am a genius or a Doctor Herzl. I am simply a businessman and have a feel for these things. This you will see from the second half of my plan. Leasing is well and good. Every Jew understands that. The question is: how do you arrange it, how do you work it out so it will be ten times more appealing to the Turk to lease the land than to sell it? That's one consideration. Second, and this is the most important, where do we get the cash? That question kept me up three nights, my dear wife, writing and writing and writing, and with God's help, I set up a procedure over which they will lick their fingers! But as I have no time—I have to run and get a foreign passport—I will make this short. God willing, in my next letter I will write you everything at greater length. In the meantime, may God grant us all health and success. Kiss the children for me and send my best and most friendly regards to your mother, whom I honor, and to the whole family, each and every one.

From me your husband Menachem-Mendl

ALMOST FORGOT: I hope, if God grants me life, on my way back from the congress, to visit you and the children, long life to them, and all the family in Kasrilevka, not for long, for a few days. I am a bought man. I won't be coming directly from Vienna. I must be in several big cities first, in Yehupetz, in Odessa, in Moscow, in Riga, and a few other places. They want me to give a lecture on my Angola and Israel projects. And not for free. On the contrary, they are promising me the sky. They will, they write, more than recompense me, including paying my expenses. It wouldn't be a bad idea if I could give this lecture in cities everywhere. If we count seventy-six provinces, at least ten cities in a province, we have seven hundred sixty cities besides small towns and villages, and each city should pay at least a hundred besides expenses, so we have a total of about seventy thousand rubles. That would not hurt me at all and would add a nice bonus to my writing income. How does that strike you?

As above.

36. Menachem-Mendl from Warsaw to His Wife, Sheyne-Sheyndl, in Kasrilevka

To my dear, wise, and modest wife, Sheyne-Sheyndl, may God grant her many years!

FIRST OF ALL, let me tell you that I am, blessed be His name, in good health and spirits, and may the Blessed One grant that we hear from one another only good news of comfort and salvation for us and for all of Israel—Amen!

SECOND OF ALL, let me tell you, my dear wife, that I now have an official government passport. Do you think it's so easy for a Jew to get a government passport? With God's help, I had to agree to return the following evening or at the latest, the next day. If there won't be any last minute problem, I am leaving immediately for the congress. I am already imagining what a hue and cry my plan to lease Israel will cause once the Zionists find about about it. Until now every Zionist thought that just by being a Zionist he was making the Jewish people happy. He contributes a shekel or buys a share and feels he has done enough, especially if someone goes to Israel and buys a piece of land. For that you can never be grateful enough! No matter how much you write about him in the newspapers, it's never enough. He thinks he deserves a gold medal. After all, a Jew sacrifices himself, leaves his homeland where they love him so much, where they coddle and pamper him and give him every privilege—doesn't he deserve a pinch on the cheek?

No, my dear wife, let my plan to lease Israel be accepted and you will see that every Jew will become a Zionist and will go to Israel, unless he is a real enemy of Israel or a cripple who cannot move from the spot, or a convert. Think about it, who would refuse such an opportunity? You're brought to your own country, to your own homeland, for God's sake! They settle you, build a dwelling for you, buy you cattle and machinery to pay out, the latest improvements, all yours! In return, please plant grain or put in a vineyard and they will say to you, "Reb Jew! Here you can enjoy three regular meals a day, start a farm, a dairy, or raise chickens, ducks, geese." No, you would have to be absolutely crazy to say you would rather die of hunger three times a day except for dinner so long as you can live in Kasrilevka!

Now one big hurdle remains: how to get the cat to cross the river? By that I mean how do you manage to get millions of Jews to move themselves with wives and children and all their household goods, Passover dishes of course included, to a new place? The smallest child would understand that you couldn't do it all at once. Odessa wasn't built in a day. You have to move people and settle them gradually, slowly, one at a time. First, of course, the well-to-do will go, our prominent people, the Brodskys, the Visotzkys, the Ginsburgs, the Polyakovs, the Halperns, the Zeitzevs and our other millionaires. Then you'll move the less rich but still wealthy people, then the middle-class Jews, next the more common Jews, artisans, clergy, and those fallen on hard times, finally just plain poor people. The world is a market and life is a fair. As at a market, you must offer all kinds of merchandise, and as at a fair, you must offer all kinds of commodities to buy and sell, so it is with building a community. In a country you must have everything. As long as there are very wealthy people and millionaires, you must also have poor people of all kinds because if you have no poor people, what do you need the rich ones for? Ah, you will say—we need them like a hole in the head. You don't have to convince me. You can believe me, I would not be opposed if they took all their millions and divided them up equally among all the poor so that everyone would have an equal share. The problem is you have to get the rich people to agree and they will never do it. On the contrary, the more millions a millionaire has the more he wants. If he could, he would swallow up whole all the millionaires and all the millions in the world! That's the way of the world from the very beginning. I have nothing but contempt for those who want to convince me with a thousand reasons offered by learned philosophers that a time will come when people will be brothers and there will be no more rich and no more poor. Idiots! They don't know that is what our prophet Isaiah said thousands of years ago. But he said it with a warning, "It will be at the end of days when the Messiah will come."

And so, we were talking about emigrating, with moving Jews to Israel, and it's almost as good as done. Now all that remains is the old problem: MONEY! Where on earth, you ask, will we get so much money? I must remind you, my dear wife, what I wrote you in a previous letter, that I have a remedy for that: stocks. You must know that one person alone, he may be the biggest millionaire, let us even say Rothschild, cannot start a business without partners or investers. The biggest deals Rothschild makes with nations are never made alone but with partners. If you want to talk business, you talk to Rothschild! You haggle over interest rates with him alone. But when it comes right down to counting the groshens, you go to Blechreder or Mendelsohn from Berlin and Reb Yankl Schiff and Vanderbilt and all the other money bags from the stock exchange and you hold a meeting in London, in Frankfurt, in Vienna, or Paris. Rothschild stands up and utters a few well-chosen words: "Friends! This or that nation must have a loan of several million on these and these terms and for this and this percent interest. If you are interested in investing, in becoming partners, I will take two and a half million for myself and the rest you can take. Is that a deal? And may it be blessed with good luck." And thus Rothschild ends his sermon.

If it sounds like the deal is a good one, one where you can make a profit over and above interest, Vanderbilt from America stands up and says to Rothschild: "Tell me, I beg you, what is it with you, Panye Rothschild? How come you're taking for yourself the biggest portion and are handing out the other half to all the rest of us poor beggars? You certainly are aware that I, Vanderbilt, can take the entire loan on my shoulders, all five million!" Rothschild replies politely, diplomatically: "I believe you, Herr Vanderbilt, and know that with your appetite you can swallow five times five million. But you mustn't forget that in our Torah it says: 'Live and let live.' " This offends the Christian Vanderbilt. Here a Jew, Rothschild, is teaching him how to conduct himself. Vanderbilt replies, also politely and diplomatically, that although he hasn't the honor to be a Jew like Rothschild, nevertheless he knows quite well what it says in the Jewish Torah, it's the same as in his Bible. And as for his appetite, he says, he believes the Rothschilds will soon catch up to the Vanderbilts. Not a bad comeback! But Rothschild can't let this dig go by. Rothschild is not accustomed to digs, and he wants to retaliate with an even bigger dig. But Reb Yankl Schiff from America, who is a Jew with a head on his shoulders and a sharp tongue, sits up and separates the two, one here, the other there, be quiet! He insists they divide the shares equally. But do you think that ends it, telling them to divide up the stocks, provide the money for the loan and good day? You are mistaken! They do provide the money for the loan, but they make it right back. How? Simple. Each of these moneybags goes home, lets out the word in the newspapers that he floated a loan to this and this nation, a real sweet deal, a jewel of a deal! He begins to praise that nation, saying it is a marvel among nations and that its finances are solid as a rock! The stock exchange begins cooking and they start grabbing up stocks like hot noodles. Stocks have the habit that no sooner do you ask about them, up they go! In that way the stocks are grabbed up and sweetened to the point where not a single one of Rothschild's stocks remains even if you are ready to die for it!

What do you think Rothschild does with the money? He looks to make a new loan, with another nation, not alone, God forbid, but through the diplomat brokers and with the same partners, the big moneybags from the stock exchange. And again they get together for a meeting and again buy stocks and again come home and sell the stocks to the public, taking a nice profit off the top.

It turns out that all these loans the nations are getting from Rothschild puts them in the same position as the rest of us, like you, like all of Israel and the whole world because anyone who has money, has a share of the loan. And even the one who doesn't have money also has a share. How is this possible? I will explain it in two words. You buy meat from the butcher and bread from the baker. The butcher and the baker buy their wives a dress and shoes for the children with your money. The shopowners and the shoemakers buy their merchandise from the factories and the factory owner gets rich and buys stocks. Doesn't that prove you have a share? Therefore, you understand, it will not come as a surprise when I tell you that there is no amount of money the world cannot provide. And no one need be afraid that the Turk will ask a high price for leasing Israel or will ask to be paid a premium several years in advance or wants a big deposit. Let's hope there will not be any snags and that we will sign a contract to lease according to the plan I worked out with God's help. And as you see we have come to the very point I wanted to bring out about the leasing plan. But as I have no time I will make this short. God willing, in my next letter I will write you everything at greater length. In the meantime, may God grant us all health and success. Kiss the children for me and send my best and most friendly regards to your mother, whom I honor, and to the whole family, each and every one.

From me your husband Menachem-Mendl

37. Menachem-Mendl from Warsaw to His Wife, Sheyne-Sheyndl, in Kasrilevka

To my dear, wise, and modest wife, Sheyne-Sheyndl, may God grant her many years!

FIRST OF ALL, let me tell you that I am, blessed be His name, in good health and spirits, and may the Blessed One grant that we hear from one another only good news of comfort and salvation for us and for all of Israel—Amen!

SECOND OF ALL, let me tell you, my dear wife, that I am on my way. I am really on my way at last! In a few hours the train will be departing for Vienna and I already have my ticket. I don't actually have it yet but it's as good as in my pocket. The editors promised to buy my ticket because I am traveling at their expense. Do you think I am the only one going? Not at all, several other writers from the editorial office are traveling with me, and like me, at the office's expense. We are traveling as a group. When you travel as a group it's different. You sit with people, you chat about this and that, you tell stories, reminisce, and all the while you are covering a good distance and the time flies.

We are going to the Vienna congress, or rather, we are preparing to go. We're packing for the trip, not I, but my colleagues who are taking with them their pens and notepads and their luggage. I, thank God, have long been ready. I don't need to pack, I don't have any luggage. I am just taking along my prayer shawl, *tefilln,* and pen—I have a pen that writes by itself—

how about that! The main thing I am taking with me is something that is more important than all their luggage and pens and notepads. I refer to my project for leasing Israel. I sewed it into a safe place so that I can travel with a clear mind. First of all, we are traveling by train and going to a German country, who knows what can happen. Second of all, I don't want the rest of the group to know I am bringing a proposal to the congress. They are big pranksters. They love to make fun of everything, not just of others, but of themselves as well. That's the way it is with our writers. We have among us a writer, one of the greats, the really greats. He's a fine fellow but a clown, and what a clown! He has a nickname for everyone. For instance, he crowns me with a new nickname every day: Bismarck, Biksenfeld, Vanderbilt, Kokovtzev, Lekhutchan, Witte. Since the excitement began over the congress, he calls me no other name but Theodore Mendl, or Menachem Herzl. Do you know why? Because of something that happened recently at the editorial office.

I came into the office one day and discovered a fine-looking man sitting at his ease wearing a gold watch, stroking his beard, perspiring, and speaking slowly and expansively in a hoarse voice like a cantor after the High Holy Days, and with a little smile on his lips. What does a Jew talk about? About his children, of course, about a son of his. He had one son, an only child but what a son—handsome, talented, extraordinarily brilliant, and a scholar from whom other scholars could learn. He was a writer too, putting all writers to shame, and a speaker with whom no other speaker could compete! Especially in Hebrew. Clearly this was a son beyond compare. If that weren't enough, he was a graduate urologist. Not just a graduate, the man said. There are as many graduates these days as there are stray dogs. What Jew doesn't have a son who is a graduate? But to the devil with all those other graduates! What do they know? What are they able to do? And who are they? Boors, shopkeepers and charlatans, uncultured, not speaking a Yiddish word, empty heads, idlers, sporting high collars, rolled-up trousers, with flat heads, shallow minds, pure idiots! To make a long story short, his brilliant son went crazy, may it not happen to you or to anyone. Poor soul! A man has one son, an only child, and such a brilliant son, and he goes mad!

What was his madness? Did he beat people? Did he run wild through the streets? God forbid! His madness was, he said, Zionism! Suddenly, out of the blue, no one knows how or why, he became a Zionist, and what a Zionist! He became obsessed with farming. He wanted to become a common laborer and nowhere else but in Israel! What can you do? He could not be talked out of it, not with kindness, not with anger. Did you ever hear of such a tragedy, he said? One son, an only child, strong, healthy, normal, handsome and a graduate besides, and he is willing to give it all up to go to

Israel and become a farm laborer, the ingrate! True, he said, here they wouldn't give him a position unless he converted first. So what? Is that a reason to run off someplace and become a farm laborer? And where but in Israel? A wild country! Savage Turks! Beggars! Vagabonds! He raged on and on, fire and brimstone!

This really made me angry. The nerve of a man taking out his anger on a nation for no reason! Had he at least said something intelligent or wise— but not at all! He simply didn't like Israel and that's that. Is it possible to remain silent? I sprang up and gave this man what for: "Aren't you ashamed of yourself? You should be burning with shame. Better be silent and let your enemies speak for you! What do you know about Israel? You are surely one of the rabble! Do you know when Jews like you will decide to go to Israel? When your children become converts and when your rich Jews become poor, then you'll remember that there is a land called Israel, but it will be too late."

In short, I really told him off, as he deserved! I myself don't know where all this indignation came from. The man heard me out and said to me with a smile and one eye closed: "Who are you?" I said: "Who am I? A Jew." He said: "That you're a Jew, not a Pole, I can see. But what's your name?" "Menachem-Mendl," I said. The man rose, didn't say another word, wiped his lips, buttoned his coat, turned around and said to all of us: "Good day!" And was gone. What can I tell you? It had a powerful effect! The staff congratulated me afterwards: "Bravo! We had no idea you were a Zionist, Reb Mendl, and such a fanatic Zionist at that. We all assumed you were a territorialist." I thanked them for the compliment and said to them, "Who told you that? Don't be so sure. I am neither a Zionist nor a territorialist, nor anything, I am simply a Jew . . ." That is how I dismissed them and went back to my work, to the Israel leasing project, and I quietly worked out the whole plan I will now summarize for you so you can see that your Menachem-Mendl doesn't busy himself with nonsense.

First of all, I propose that they send a deputation to the sultan, the very same candidates that I mentioned to you in one of my last letters. These will be educated men, you understand, men who know how to speak, men of note, not just anyone. When such men meet the sultan it will be a pleasure to behold! First they must introduce themselves, telling him *who* they are, *what* they are, *where* they are from, and *who* sent them, not sparing any words, not speaking at once, but one at a time and they must tell him the reason for their coming. They came first to congratulate him on his victory in driving out the enemy from Adrianople and Kirkeles. Then they will gradually move to the real purpose for which they came. Before anything, they must make it clear he should not be afraid and think they were coming to him with a claim that Israel once belonged to us, that it is our land from time immemorial, promised to us by God from Abraham's times. We know very well, they must tell him, that the land now belongs to him, even though it was once ours. But that's another story. It was all God's doing. You don't ask questions of God, and they will cite a commentary, a passage, it doesn't matter which, until they arrive at the main purpose for which they had come. They have come to make a deal, a deal that would be to the Turk's benefit. What was the deal? Now they would have to describe it, politely, not condescendingly, talking as good friends. The Turk was without doubt a big debtor, one could say that not even the hair on his head was his own. Although he was not altogether destitute, yet he still needed a great deal of money to exploit the victories he had won in the war over Adrianople and Kirkeles, and so on. He was having some difficulty obtaining new loans, not because he was, God forbid, unworthy, but on the contrary, on the contrary! It was because the great powers, for political reasons, were threatening him with a Polish-style boycott so he would return Adrianople and Kirkeles. And so the emissaries were offering not only a loan but to put him back on his feet again, to clear him of all his debts and promissory notes, to make him no longer a debtor, free and clear! How? Let him be so kind as to draw up a contract specifying that he would return Israel on lease, for ninety-nine years, on these and these conditions. Further, they must give him to understand that he would be assured of a premium by signing the contract. They could give him, if he wished, a sizable deposit. Besides the deposit they would throw in another sweetener worth more than anything, cash.

As the Turk was dealing with Jews, the biggest moneybags on the stock exchange, they would promise to see to it that their bankers would take over all his debts and promissory notes at the same rates he was paying others, maybe a percent less. In addition, they would offer a new loan if he needed more now. After all, he had just waged a war with Italy on one side and with the Balkans on the other. True, he did win, but it was costly, as all wars are! And it would probably cost more and more. With this very language they must speak to him, really convince him, not sparing any words. They should then immediately rush off to all the moneybags in London, Paris, Berlin and Vienna. First they must go to Rothschild with the plan for leasing and tell him the entire Jewish people calls on him, not begging for charity, no, but with a business deal for him, a deal that comes up once in two thousand years! The deal can bring in for him a substantial profit on his capital while giving work to twelve million Jews at a bitter time for Jews all over the world, especially here, where we have no rights, endless taxes, high interest, and persecution. People are fleeing wherever they can, converting whenever possible, and Mendl Beiliss, for God's sake, don't forget Mendl Beiliss! This brings them to tears. Aren't the Rothschilds also Jews with Jewish hearts, kosher kitchens, fasts on Yom Kippur, they say? In Frankfurt there is to this day a synagogue of theirs where poor Jews say the evening prayers every day.

Having finished with the Rothschilds, they must get to work on our own Jews so they won't think this is just a game and they can depend on miracles. First they must go, as usual, to our own wealthiest millionaires and tell them in clear language to make a choice: "If you are Jews, show your Jewishness. Join us, if you please, in our own land, with your capital. Don't worry, when it comes to money, you won't do any worse business there and maybe a lot better. What is the problem then? You don't want to do it? It isn't convenient for you or it won't be good for your children, the graduates? Perhaps you are worried about what your neighbors will think? Very nice! Stay here! But on one condition. Stop calling yourselves Jews! Let them stop persecuting us on account of you and let us stop suffering for your sins!"

At this point it would be appropriate to cite an example from the Kelmer Preacher, or a story from Motke Khabad. These rich people must not be spared because they are rich and the common man must also not be patted on the head. They mustn't think that because they are poor they are special, the chosen people of Israel, with no responsibility, who don't have to do anything anymore. They must forget everything that was until now and must begin from the beginning, as our forefathers did. As Abraham, Isaac, and Jacob saw fit to tend flocks of sheep, it should not be beneath them to cultivate the earth, plowing and sowing, mowing and threshing, raising poultry in Israel, geese and ducks and all things having to do with agriculture. It's alright, it will do them no harm. On the contrary, they will be elevated and exalted in the eyes of all the nations of the world. Believe me, I am not out of my mind. I am not saying that all twelve million Jews should go out in the field to work. There is enough to do in Israel besides farm work and besides tending vineyards. There is commerce, shipping, they can open stock exchanges, make the greatest speculations. God in heaven, there will be enough for everybody! And here I have a whole list of occupations, commercial enterprises, speculations, resorts, expositions, and more and more, each in a separate paragraph like Khoskl Kotik's by-laws. But as I have no time I will make this short. God willing, in my next letter I will write you everything in greater detail from Vienna. In the meantime, may God grant us all health and success. Kiss the children for me and send my best regards to your mother, whom I honor, and to the whole family, each and every one.

From me your husband Menachem-Mendl

ALMOST FORGOT: As I am going abroad and hope to be home for Succos, I would very much like to bring something home for you and for the children and my mother-in-law, something special for each one. With God's help, I was in America and came back in good health and got a job that earns me an honest living and with which I can do something beneficial for the world, so it is only right that you too should enjoy it. And so, my dear wife, write me in detail exactly what you want and what you need. Be sure to write me at the Vienna Zionist Congress—here is the address: D'lya Menachem-Mendl, Yiv Sobstvenye Ruki.

As above.

38. Menachem-Mendl from Vienna to His Wife, Sheyne-Sheyndl, in Kasrilevka

To my dear, wise, and modest wife, Sheyne-Sheyndl, may God grant her many years!

FIRST OF ALL, let me tell you that I am, blessed be His name, in good health and spirits, and may the Blessed One grant that we hear from one another only good news of comfort and salvation for us and for all of Israel—Amen!

SECOND OF ALL, let me tell you, my dear wife, that I am in Israel. That's just a way of saying I am still in Vienna, but I feel as happy as if I were in Israel. Imagine, Jews walk around freely and comfortably wearing Stars of David on their lapels, they speak Hebrew on the streets and kiss one another, myself included. When we arrived in Vienna, we went right downtown to our lodgings the Zionists had reserved for us. They had made sure to have our accomodations ready a few weeks ago, most certainly having put in much time to make sure everything was in order, where each delegate was to stay, this one here, that one there, all done just right, set down in detail in the German style. But no doubt on account of great urgency and rush—so many Jews arriving all at once, *kayn eyn horeh* —it turned out there was a bit of a mix-up and some of the delegates were sent to the wrong hotels! So we had some running around to do, as you can imagine. We sweated it out, lugging our bags from one hotel to the next because the hotels were full, until finally, with God's help, almost at night it was, we barely found a place with some German whose language *we* don't understand and who doesn't understand *our* language even though our language is almost half German, as everyone knows. But that isn't so bad. All right, the German doesn't understand us, so what! We don't have to do business with him and we won't be staying there forever. Sooner or later the congress will end and we will leave, God willing, may we be redeemed from the Diaspora as quickly. And in a pinch, if things get really bad, all you have to do is hold up a coin between your two fingers and the German understands you very well indeed!

It is bitter for our *own* language, for Yiddish, which is not allowed to be spoken here; one must speak Hebrew. What's to be done? Everyone speaks Hebrew. Usishkin, they say, gave out the word: Hebrew or Russian. And when Usishkin speaks, that's it. Ah, you will ask, what about those delegates who can't speak either Hebrew or Russian? What do you think? They sit in silence. It's really bad. What alternative do they have? Did I say they were really silent? How is that possible? A person is not an animal, and especially when one has come to a congress! They came up with a solution: they go off in a corner and speak quietly in Yiddish so Usushkin won't hear, but wait till you hear the rest! We're not finished yet.

The rule to speak Hebrew wouldn't have been such a problem if we could speak the way we do at home, but they decreed you must speak Hebrew, not as our Jews do, but as the Turks in Israel. It's called "Sephardic." That means all the "oh" sounds are pronounced "ah" and the "esses" are pronounced "t." Take the word for pants, plain pants that you wear. Why would it hurt them if they said, *"mikhnasoyim,"* the way we say it? But no. They say you it has to be pronounced, *"mikhnatayim."* Do you see what I mean? You know very well that I am not such an ignoramus, I once went to cheder, wasn't a bad student, yet I'm struggling to catch a word here and there! Still and all, when someone speaks Hebrew, it's a pleasure to hear. Even those who don't understand a word of it say it's like music to their ears, as if they were listening to the most beautiful melodies sung by the best cantor. So there you are. A girl stood up and gave a speech in Hebrew and it was the greatest pleasure. And you should hear, there's a delegate from Odessa, a dear man, wonderful, they call him Zhabotinsky, his first name is Vladimir. It's not a Jewish name but what a passionate Jew he is! Fire and flame and still a young man! When this Zhabotinsky, this Vladimir, stands up and starts speaking in Hebrew—what can I tell you? Exquisite! You forget all the best cantors in the world! You could sit and listen to him all day and night without getting tired! It doesn't matter that you don't understand Hebrew but you enjoy it so much you can't tear yourself away. That's the effect he has! And don't forget this is still before the congress starts. It's still the conference. You will ask, what is a conference? I'll explain. You already know what a congress is. When the delegates come to the congress and before the congress begins, they meet every day, several times a day, and every time in a different place and they dis-

cuss and they talk and they debate with one another and they come out
with a resolution in preparation for the congress—and that is called a conference. Now do you understand?

At the first conference there was a hairsplitting dispute over which language to speak at the conference so we could understand one another. On
the face of it, this hairsplitting was, according to my limited understanding,
entirely unnecessary. Remember, Jews are coming together and want to
meet and talk, let them talk however they can. And if you want to be fully
understood, it seems to me there is no easier way than with our simple Yiddish language, because what Jew does not understand Yiddish? But no!
There are such stubborn Jews here, especially our Russian Jews from St. Petersburg, from Odessa, and from Boslev, who are adamant that they do not
understand one Yiddish word, go chop off their heads! "We don't understand Yiddish!" And they complained and pleaded and looked so miserable that it was pity to look at them. Others insisted: "Either Hebrew or
Russian!" There followed a commotion and outcry, some arguing that three
languages should be spoken, Hebrew, Russian and Yiddish, while others
screamed: "No, two languages are enough, Hebrew and Russian, because
we don't understand Yiddish!" And then it would start all over again.

The presiding chairman, realizing it could go on till morning, hit upon
a solution and said: "Quiet, brothers! Let us have a show of hands. Whoever agrees to have two languages, Hebrew and Russian, raise your right
hand high!" Hands went up. Of course, my hand never moved an inch. Do
you think I would renounce my Yiddish? In short, it appeared that by a bare
majority it was voted that one may also speak Yiddish. But one delegate
from Yehupetz, a teacher, a fanatic Hebraist, raised *both* hands, and pointed
out that Yiddish was not kosher, it was *trayf!* It overturned the vote and that
is how our poor language was buried alive, and on account of one hand!

Certainly that broke my heart. Why were we being punished? So
many Jews speaking Yiddish for so many years and it seems to have come
to nothing. No one has ever died of speaking Yiddish. And suddenly—
here's a ruling: no more Yiddish! I was feeling a bit melancholy about it. I
was thinking, God in heaven! aren't these Zionists destroying themselves
by shutting our mouths so we cannot speak a word to the people, not
about Zionism, not about anything? What should we do in that case?
Speak Hebrew to a Jew or speak Russian when I cannot speak it and he
cannot understand it? I felt like jumping up and shouting: "God in heaven,
Jews, what are you doing? You're killing yourselves! You are passing a
death sentence on yourselves! Think of your millions of brothers who
speak only Yiddish, who know no other language!' But then I remembered
what is written in the Mishneh, "Fools have seven attributes. First, fools

rush in . . ." But who am I to judge them? Aren't they Jews too? Or are they Zionists who want to drown all of Zionism in a teaspoon of Hebrew? Could it be their brains have dried up and can't see what danger lies ahead?

When this Vladimir Zhabotinsky I told you about rose and began speaking in Hebrew, all my anger and disappointment vanished and I had to agree with him that he was right in wanting all Jews to speak Hebrew. He says that a Zionist who cannot speak Hebrew has no excuse—let him learn how! They have time till the next congress two years from now. Right he is! In two years you can even teach a bear how to dance. Why shouldn't we all be able to speak Hebrew? They say Vladimir Zhabotinsky himself didn't know Hebrew two years ago, and today, may all Jews speak as he does! I am determined when I get back home to Warsaw to hire without fail someone who will spend an hour, two hours, three hours a day with me, the more the better, and when I master it, I will speak no other language but Hebrew in the office and where I live and everywhere!

You can imagine how carried away I was when afterward I became good friends with that delegate from Yehupetz who had raised both hands and murdered Yiddish. He came over to me, introduced himself, and in Hebrew complimented me, sang my praises and said he loved my work. How do you answer that? So I responded by telling him what I thought of the two hands he had raised up and let him know that I knew what he was up to. Do you think he was hurt by what I said? Not at all! When he heard those words, he complimented me further. In short, we embraced and from then on we were inseparable. We always go around together and talk, he with quotes in Hebrew, I in Russian. I would love to describe our conversations word for word but as I have no time—Zionists are always running to a new conference, I among them—I will make this short. God willing, in my next letter I will write you everything in greater length. In the meantime, may God grant us all health and success. Kiss the children for me and send my best and most friendly regards to your mother, whom I honor, and to the whole family, each and every one.

From me your husband Menachem-Mendl

ALMOST FORGOT: I knew it would be like this. Did you think they would disparage our language and everybody would be silent? The response was swift. The first bomb came from Smorgon who was strongly protesting the twenty-seven hands that were raised against our Yiddish! After her, the Boslev delegation stepped forward, protesting loudly, and it appears they were a bit upset, "If our delegate's hand was among the twenty seven, may it wither. But that's no proof that all of Boslev and the whole world has suddenly gone crazy and stopped speaking Yiddish"! Then I received a letter from Oshmyane. They write me that though we aren't well-acquainted, we are, after all, distant relatives through a Shmuel Mateses who now lives in Baku. They were asking my advice as a good friend. What should they do? Their children don't understand Hebrew. Russian their fathers don't understand. Should they speak in sign language? Then I received a sharply written protest from our Kasrilevka, scolding me in their empty-headed way, "After all, where were you? Why were you silent? Why this and why that? You'll be sorry! If you dare come to Kasrilevka, you'll see what will happen!" The letter was unsigned except for two words: "Real Jews!"

And from that great Yehupetz aristocracy (last but not least) I also received a fine written protest, signed by the richest sugar refinery owners and millionaires: "You know very well, Reb Menachem-Mendl," their protest began, "that we Yehupetz millionaires are not such enthusiastic adherents of your Yiddish and no great readers of your Yiddish books, newspapers, and so on. First of all, who has the time? It's enough that we scan a Russian paper, telegrams, stock market quotations, and so forth. Should we be expected to read your Yiddish newspapers too? And second of all, it is beneath us, as the French say:'*Zablesse oblage.*' (What this means I don't know, they probably mean you mustn't let a Jew get away with anything.) But you know very well—you were once one of our Yehupetzers, that we like, we *love* when someone tells us a Jewish joke in Yiddish, a really spicy joke and especially right after eating. Try to tell that same joke in Hebrew, who will understand it? Or in Russian—what tang will it have? Why are they wasting their time, your Zionists?"

That is how they registered their protest and it was signed by all the greats—the Brodskys, the Halperins, the Zeitzevs, Baron Ginsburg and Polyakov. Then were listed the lesser millionaires and movers and shakers: Robinerzon, Balakhovsky, Hefner—the others were impossible to make out.

As above.

39. Menachem-Mendl from Vienna to His Wife, Sheyne-Sheyndl, in Kasrilevka

To my dear, wise, and modest wife, Sheyne-Sheyndl, may God grant her many years!

FIRST OF ALL, let me tell you that I am, blessed be His name, in good health and spirits, and may the Blessed One grant that we hear from one another only good news of comfort and salvation for us and for all of Israel—Amen!

SECOND OF ALL, let me tell you, my dear wife, that all hell has broken loose, the world is turning upside down. People are running, talking, applauding, shouting bravo, going out of their minds, I among them. Now the conferences are over and the real congress begins! It cannot be described what this congress is like! You have to be here to see it! Imagine a hall larger than our entire marketplace in Kasrilevka, if not larger, and packed, not an inch to spare, with delegates, correspondents, and guests from all over the world, so many you can't count them! People are crushed together, pushing and shoving each other in this awful stifling heat! That's inside. Outside is another mob who cannot get in because there is not a hall in the world large enough to hold so many people. The organizers came up with a solution (trust a German to come up with a solution!) and foresaw how many people would attend. They counted the seats in the hall and printed invitations—as many invitations as seats. Understand? They distributed the invitations free, first to the Zionist delegates, then to the newspaper correspondents, and the rest they sold to guests, those coming just to observe the congress. And that was very clever. If you are not a Zionist and are just coming to observe, then you must pay! But as a thousand times as many guests arrived than there were invitations, there weren't enough invitations and people started grabbing them and paying the highest prices for them, up to twenty crowns, fifty crowns, a hundred crowns for an invitation. People were willing to pay any amount to have one! Seeing that it was getting bad, the Germans came up with the idea of selling seats. But whose seats did they sell? The free ones for the newspaper correspondents, of course, so that many of the correspondents had to remain outside, I among them.

There was a loud hullabaloo and protest, loudest of all from the Yehupetz delegate, the one I wrote you who had raised both hands and killed our Yiddish at the conference. He is also a correspondent, a writer like myself, but from a Hebrew-language newspaper. He raised such a hue and cry against the Germans that they will never forget. "Germans!" he screamed, not in Hebrew but in Yiddish, "Robbers! Bandits! We'll wreck your congress!" he ranted and raved. Good, good, he really gave it to them! And how do you think it ended? They let us in! What else could they do? Writers are respected everywhere, little silly, especially if they raise their voices and speak out! True, when we were let in, they got even with us. We found there were no seats and had to stand, but who cared? So long as we were inside and could see everything and hear everything like the rest and could applaud like everyone else. That's what happens at a congress. Whoever mounts the stage is applauded. When he begins to speak there is more applause. And when he finishes speaking they really applaud him, for several minutes! You can imagine what goes on when a crowd of perhaps ten thousand people all start applauding at once.

More than anyone they applauded Sokolov it seems almost every five minutes. But when Sokolove began talking about Mendl Beiliss and how the poor man was suffering though he was innocent as a lamb, and what they were accusing him of, there was so much clapping that the walls almost collapsed! A pity Mendl Beiliss himself wasn't there. If he had been there, he would have heard the shouting from ten thousand throats who kept insisting, "It's a lie! It's a libel! Utter falsehood!" As I say, if he had seen and heard all this, he would have been very proud and it would have been easier for him to endure the agony he is suffering in prison! Oy, Beiliss, Beiliss! When I think of that Jew, my heart aches and a thought flies through my mind: how do you repay such a man, an innocent sacrifice for all of Israel, once he is cleared, with God's help, and released from prison? There is not enough money in the world. But I have a scheme on his behalf and may it happen right now, this very minute! Meanwhile, let's return to the congress.

What can I tell you, my dear wife? I don't have enough words to describe what a great congress this is! To see before me thousands of Jews, all dressed as for a holiday and all with one thought, with one idea in mind—Zion, is enough to put one in a holiday mood! Just to know there are still countries in the world where Jews can come together freely and openly and speak out loud what each is thinking in his heart! You should have been here when they read the telegram we sent blessing the old Emperor Franz Josef, and congratulating him for having the congress, wishing him many long years for his commitment to the Jews and then not long after, receiving his response.

And you should also have seen the sea of people that flooded the streets of Vienna when we went en masse to pay homage at Herzl's grave and shed a tear. The unexpected hush at the graveside! You yourself would have said that this congress was like an ingathering of the exiles, a holy pilgrimage, as in the days of the Temple when Jews used to gather together from all over Israel for a holy pilgrimage to Jerusalem. May I not be blaspheming, but I believe the Divine Presence now resides in Vienna. I tell you, the Jew who has not been to a congress at least once is not worth the ground he stands on! In all my life I have never felt as much among Jews as I have here at this congress. I feel new-born, as if I had sprouted wings and I am flying, flying! It's just a shame the congress will not last longer than one week. What is a week?

I am almost afraid to say it, may the devil not hear me, but I am thinking, Lord in heaven, when will You favor me? When will You shine Your countenance upon me and the blessed hour come when I can step forward publicly with *my* project? Everyone wants to go up on the stage, everyone wants to speak, to say something and everyone has something to say. But all the speaking slots are allotted, who will speak at what time and for how many minutes—here a ten-minute slot is a great deal! No, I don't foresee my turn coming up so quickly. Maybe, with God's help, I will grab a few minutes here and there. If there's still time before the last session, I will "ask for the floor," as they say here. You have to apply to speak. You will surely want to know what that means? I'll explain.

Say you want to go up on the stage and speak. You can't just stride up there and start talking. Not at all. They won't let you. What then? You must first sign up indicating you have something to say and they will put you on a long list. But as there are plenty of people eager to speak on and on and time is short, it's impossible that all those who have asked for the floor will actually get to speak even if you were to sit for days and nights without eating, drinking, or sleeping. That's the problem. But there is a solution— trust a German to have a solution for everything! When all those who ask for the floor see so many speakers before them, they choose from among themselves a general, one who will speak for all of them. But there's a new problem: if they choose me as general, that's well and good. If not, I will hand my project over to the elected general, let him read it, let them applaud him. Never mind the kudos, never mind the applause. The main thing is the good that can come out of this for the Jewish people. And as I have no time—there is still plenty of work to be done, there's a bank and a national fund that must be secured—this isn't small change but real money, nine million! Worth quite a bit! They must form an executive committee, choose a president and officers, when will we ever be finished with all that? So I will make this short. God willing, in my next letter I will write you everything at greater length. In the meantime, may God grant us all health and success. Kiss the children for me and send my best and most friendly regards to your mother, whom I honor, and to the whole family, each and every one.

From me your husband Menachem-Mendl

ALMOST FORGOT: Do you think the sky has fallen and not one person has had the courage to come to the defense of our Yiddish? There was such a person, not one, but two. Do you want to know who they were? One was an engineer from Yehupetz and the other a lawyer from Warsaw—both young men, smart as whips! If you get into a debate with them, God help you! Oh, did they settle the score with the opponents of Yiddish! Oh, did they spout words! Fire and flame! They cut them to ribbons! It's just a shame that when they so selflessly stuck up for our Yiddish, they didn't say it in Yiddish. If they had said the same thing in Yiddish, everyone would have understood them. But the way it is, there is still hope that our Yiddish may yet be saved, so what more do you need? It's likely that Vladimir Zhabotinsky will announce that for the Twelfth Congress he himself will speak in Yiddish and just try and stop him! That, you see, would really be something! But best of all, let God perform a miracle—and if God wants to, He can!—and let Usishkin come out unwittingly with a Yiddish word. Don't think he doesn't know Yiddish. He knows it very well but he won't speak it—out of spite! If he would let a Yiddish word creep in, then all the Jews could speak Yiddish openly, no more Exile! For everything there is a time . . .

As above.

40. Menachem-Mendl from Vienna to His Wife, Sheyne-Sheyndl, in Kasrilevka

To my dear, wise, and modest wife, Sheyne-Sheyndl, may God grant her many years!

FIRST OF ALL, let me tell you that I am, blessed be His name, in good health and spirits, and may the Blessed One grant that we hear from one another only good news of comfort and salvation for us and for all of Israel—Amen!

SECOND OF ALL, let me tell you, my dear wife, that we are almost at the end. Tonight the congress will close, and I am still waiting to present my project. And that's no surprise. There is so little time, so much to do, that I can't imagine how we will finish all the work we started. Or will we still be in the middle of things when we have to end? Dear God, when will we choose an executive committee? And what about a president? A president must be chosen for two years! I keep looking on the platform where our officers are seated and wonder which of them we will choose as president. There are, God bless them, so many outstanding candidates and all of them extraordinary and not a one would refuse. No one questions the ability of the Germans. Every German is a born president. Their appearance, their demeanor, the way their dress sparkles and shines and sings! They also know how to push people around when they have to, make no mistake! They know how to bang the table with the gavel so the hall shakes. And take their language. You have to have the right language, no laughing matter. Why fool ourselves? I try to picture what would happen if I were president and began to speak in our Yiddish langauge: "Hear me out, gentlemen, the story is like this . . ." True, they would all understand what I was saying and what I *wanted* to say, but what kind of impression would that make? Too ordinary! It would sound much better in Hebrew, but the problem is the *Sephardit* pronunciation! *Rabotai!* (Gentlemen!) *Hakongret* (the congress) *b'odet* (in Odessa), and so forth. It's actually nice-sounding, but who will understand it? How can you compare it to German? When a German stands up, clasps his hands behind him, and begins to intone: *"Meine damen und herren!"* or *"Ge-her-ter Kongres!"* it rings out like a bell!

No, say whatever you will, we don't have as many good candidates as the Germans. When you look at the sitting president, David Wolfson, you can clearly see that God Himself created him to be a president. The way he sits, the way he stands, his manner of speaking, his sincere smile, his gaze, the gesture of his hand—an emperor! And what is Bodenheimer then? A bad president? And Warburg? And Handke? And Simon? And John Fischer from Antwerp? I am not now speaking of the Germans, I am now speaking of our own Russians. Take our Sokolove—what a president he would make! Or how about Doctor Tshlenov? Or Usishkin? Doesn't he look like a president when he sits up there on the platform? Or Doctor Shmaryahu Levine? And why not Doctor Weitzmann? Or Mezah from Moscow, or Tiomkin from Yelizovetgrad? Wouldn't it suit them to be president? Vladimir Zhabotinsky, though he's a bit young, would also do well. I would be happy with Doctor Pasmanik too, if he weren't one of the loudest "positioniks" who is always criticizing and whom nothing pleases. They have but one aim, those "positioniks": finding fault with everyone and pointing out what is wrong with everything. That's how it is in all parliaments and that's the way it is with us at our congress. If someone goes up on the stage and begins to say something, or to propose something, we keep our eyes on the "positioniks," and especially on Doctor Pasmanik, to see what he will say. It seems the speaker is saying good things in a persuasive way, pearls of wisdom, but most likely it won't suit Pasmanik. And sure enough, that's what happens. Before the speaker has so much as begun to speak—aha, Doctor Pasmanik is writing a note, preparing to ask for the floor! No sooner has the speaker finished, the audience is still applauding, he hasn't even had a chance to catch his breath, to wipe the sweat from his brow and already he is being thoroughly savaged, torn to shreds, dismembered—a bloody corpse! Doctor Pasmanik has finished him off. He has a mouth—God help us!

Here at the congress, if you can imagine it, there are several more

loud-mouths like him. There is a David Tritsh from Kaprisin and a Doctor
Cohn from The Hague. But I am not as afraid of anyone as I am of Doctor
Pasmanik, I am terrified of him! I know beforehand that he will demolish
my Israel project, turn it into a heap of ashes! But I don't care. Just let me get
my turn and it will go well. What do I care about the loudmouthed critics
when the public, the people are with me! How do I know this? From my
new good friend from Yehupetz, the one who killed Yiddish at the conference. You have no idea what a dear man he is and what a close relationship
we have developed. One soul! We go everywhere together. At the groups
we attend with all the delegates we stand next to one another. For one portrait we are standing with our arms on each other's shoulders. I am sending it to you with his inscription underneath in Hebrew: "Those who truly
love one another can only be separated by death." He doesn't go anywhere
without me or I without him.

And there are plenty of places to go, praise God. We have here our own
Yiddish theater with Hebrew plays. We even have our own Yiddish movie
house where for half a crown or twenty kopeks, you can see all of Israel
and Judea and the Wailing Wall, where it all sweeps before your very eyes
and as real as life itself. You should have seen the tears we both shed looking at those scenes! My friend was right when he said to me, in Hebrew of
course, that had we come to Vienna for this alone—it would have been suf-
ficient, *dayeynu* ! I don't know why but I have become very attached to this
man. Shabbos we went together to the German Synagogue. But as neither
of us had top hats, they wouldn't allow us in. To the Germans the top hat is
more important than the prayer shawl. If they see a Jew in synagogue without a top hat, they fly off the handle. We then had to find a Yiddish synagogue and since Vienna is fairly large, we had to walk quite a long
distance. Along the way I told him of my plan for Israel and it so pleased
him that he almost went out of his mind! It's just too bad, he said, that I
worked it out in Yiddish and not in Hebrew. In Hebrew it would have an
altogether different flavor. But he said I needn't worry. He will undertake
to translate it into Hebrew before the next day without fail, and free of
charge. He wants me to dictate it to him in Yiddish and he will translate it
word for word. It is as easy for him, he said, as smoking a cigarette, even
easier, because first you have to obtain a cigarette whereas writing is nothing—you dip the pen in ink and write, especially Hebrew, which is his
mother tongue.

We would have gotten to work right then and there but there was no
time, not a minute! We had to establish a university in Jerusalem, no easy
task! But we've almost succeeded. Money is pouring in—fifty thousand,
seventy thousand, a hundred thousand. No one even pays attention if it's a

mere three thousand, five thousand, or ten thousand. The heart swells and the soul rejoices when one sees the wealthy members tossing off their big donations—hundreds of thousands are just like nothing to them! With such benefactors it will be no surprise that we soon have all we need. We almost do have all we need. We have our own gymnasium in Jaffa. We have our own polytechnic institute in Haifa and now our own university in Jerusalem. What else is left? All that remains is to move our few Jews there and we are completely finished. I have already taken care of that with my plan and for that they will have to come to me. They will not, with God's help, be able to do without me. In the meantime we must run off to the hall of the congress. With any luck, it's the day I have my turn to present my ideas. And as I have no time I will make this short. God willing, in my next letter I will write you everything at greater length. In the meantime, may God grant us all health and success. Kiss the children for me and send my best and most friendly regards to your mother, whom I honor, and to the whole family, each and every one.

From me your husband Menachem-Mendl

ALMOST FORGOT: I kept this letter in my pocket all day thinking that any minute now my turn would come and I would present my project, and then I could write you about that too. In the end it turned out it was too late, the congress was at an end and I was left holding my project in my hand! I held it till the very last hour. What was I to do? I thought that as the congress was coming to a close, I would not wait to be called on but would go up on the stage, slap the table and say: "Hear me out, gentlemen, this is the story. You kept this crowd here for eight days and nights and thank God, you accomplished many great things, but one thing, gentlemen, you forgot—Israel! What I mean is, how will we get to Israel? To answer that, I have for you a fully worked-out plan." And I would take out my packet of writings and read to them the entire project from beginning to end. That was what I was planning. But man proposes and God disposes. At the very moment I rose and hastened to the platform, the president, David Wolfson, stood up, banged the gavel on the table and announced: *"Meine damen und herren!* I hereby declare that the congress adjourned and we will meet next time in Jerusalem!" There was great applause and the audience as one person broke into the *"Hatikvah,"* I among them. What can I tell you, my dear wife? Whoever did not hear that singing missed something truly beautiful! And whoever did not witness how people parted with such emotion and with such kissing and embracing, missed a beautiful sight! Everyone was making his farewells, I among them.

Now I must begin to give some thought to how I can get the fare for my return trip. The Germans have managed to relieve us of our last bit of money. But don't worry, I'll think of something—the editors won't leave me stranded. But what will others do? I'm not going to noise it around, but take the plight of my new friend from Yehupetz. He is silent about it, but I understand his pockets aren't too terribly full and he will not have enough money to get himself back to Yehupetz. But he boasts he has strong legs . . . "To a congress, it's all right to go by foot," he says, laughing. A strange Jew! He laughs while I fume. With so many rich men at the congress, really wealthy, all self-satisfied Jews with fat bellies, do you think they would so much as give a thought that someone might not have enough money, might need something? Feh, a nasty world, do you hear? A rotten world!

For instance, take me and my project. It seems everyone knew quite well that I wasn't coming to the congress empty-handed. Shouldn't it have occurred to someone to come up to me and say: "Reb Menachem-Mendl, come show us what you have"? No, everyone had only *himself* in mind. Everyone came with *his* issues and wanted everyone to hear *him* out! But then again, maybe that's as it should be. I have to travel about the world anyway and will be giving lectures to the public on this project and all my other projects—there will be time enough. One needn't rush, one needn't ask for the floor or be afraid of Doctor Pasmanik. I know I will make a hit with the public, especially when I come out with my newest project that has been brewing in my head, a new plan, a brand new scheme, actually about Russia, but a scheme—I tell you—a gem among gems! With that prospect in mind, I can truly say, "May it be for the best."

As above.

41. Menachem-Mendl from Vienna to His Wife, Sheyne-Sheyndl, in Kasrilevka

To my dear, wise, and modest wife, Sheyne-Sheyndl, may God grant her many years!

FIRST OF ALL, let me tell you that I am, blessed be His name, in good health and spirits, and may the Blessed One grant that we hear from one another only good news of comfort and salvation for us and for all of Israel—Amen!

SECOND OF ALL, let me tell you, my dear wife, that I am still here in Vienna. All the delegates and guests left right after the congress adjourned but many correspondents and writers, I among them, are remaining on for a few days, not to carouse, you can be sure, but for a very necessary and quite practical matter. We realized that everything at the congress had been accomplished, thank God. We chose a very fine executive committee, two presidents—Professor Warburg and Doctor Tshlenov, we have our own bank, a university too, and we are speaking Hebrew. We have taken care of everything. Why shouldn't we take care of ourselves too? Why shouldn't we writers give some thought to our own concerns? Why shouldn't we have our own pension fund? Writers the world over have pension funds but we Jewish writers haven't so much as a kopek set aside! How are we any worse than other workers? Tailors, shoemakers, furriers have pension funds and not we? You will probably ask what exactly is a pension fund and why we need it? I must clarify it for you and also tell you a story about how we came to think about a pension fund. The story goes like this.

There is this famous writer with the name of Mordekhai ben Hillel Hakohane—Mordekhai the son of Hillel and a *kohane* to boot. This Kohane lives happily by himself in Israel, they say, but he still cares about us, his friends, the Jewish writers living outside of Israel. He decided to send the congress a plan that would make provision for us Jewish writers in our old age, or in case one of us were to become ill or die, in which case there would be a fund that would take care of him, his wife, and his children. You will ask: where will the money come from? There will be enough money, more than enough, don't worry. First of all, from what the writers themselves would contribute, each according to his ability. Kohane makes the point that every writer must be a member and he who is not a member is not a writer, meaning he is a writer but not a member. Second of all, there will be money from the lectures writers give in all the cities and towns in the Diaspora. That will bring in thousands! What about donations, pledges, bequests? How can we not find one wealthy man among us who will not think of his mortality and will leave us a sizable bequest for a pension fund for Jewish writers? Also the collection plates placed in the synagogues the evening before *Yom Kippur* can bring in quite a good bit. I was the one who came up with that scheme. So many collection plates are placed in synagogues at Yom Kippur, let there be one more. It's no tragedy, Jews won't be impoverished by it! What about weddings, circumcisions, and the redeeming of the first-born son as well? Someone has a fine funeral—that's the best time to collect money. When you remind a Jew of the Angel of Death, he reaches for his wallet and gives money! Not a lot, he scratches out the smallest coin, but he gives! In short, everything was thought through and worked out carefully and intelligently ahead of time so that there would be no worries about money. The main thing is unity. We among ourselves must agree to dedicate ourselves to this cause with trust and friendship, because it is in our own best interest, no doubt about that, especially since we writers are not tailors or shoemakers! When we writers speak of unity and peace and take it upon ourselves to reprove the public for lacking them, if we don't have one voice, one soul, it would really mean the end of the world was near!

And that was what happened, no sooner said than done. As soon as the congress adjourned, all the writers, I among them, were invited to attend a meeting to hear that famous writer in Israel's project for a pension fund and to work out the by-laws, with all the paragraphs, according to Khoskl Kotik (a pity Khoskl Kotik wasn't there—he would have been very proud!). We were invited to the meeting very officially by letter in which it said everyone was invited who writes from right to left. It didn't matter whether it was in Yiddish or Hebrew! The letter wasn't signed by just anyone but by none other than Kh. N. Bialik himself! Not that Bialik from Yehupetz who deals in lumber, but the famous, the great Bialik who writes songs, gives lectures in Hebrew, and publishes books that astonish the world!

Well, we gathered together, those who write from right to left, all the noted writers, each in his own speciality, in all almost thirty men. The first order of business was to choose a chairman. A bit of a controversy broke out. The Hebraists wanted to seat one of their own, and the Yiddishists protested, saying they were afraid the fund would be dominated by the Sephardic speakers. So they came up with the idea of choosing someone who would be acceptable to both sides—Reuben Breinin by name. This Reuben Breinin is a famous Hebrew scholar and a great advocate of Hebrew who took on himself the task of disseminating Hebrew in America. But while there he became an editor of a Yiddish newspaper, probably to make a living, what other reason could there be? As it says in the Gemorrah: "Help yourself," or as your mother would say: "The goy is *trayf*, the groshen is kosher . . ."

They could not have chosen a better chairman. The meeting began and everything was going nicely, smooth as silk. What does God do? Up springs this little runt of a writer, one of the young Hebrew fanatics, one of those who had raised such a fuss at the conference. He flares up, saying, " We don't want to speak Yiddish! Our mother tongue is the language of the country we live in, Russia. He would not sit next to a Yiddish-speaking person, would not even stand next to one. He would not give you, he said, one Pole, forgive the comparison, for ten thousand Jews who speak Yiddish! What do you say to a man like that!

After him one after another came forward saying Yiddish should be totally forgotten and never used again! Yiddish was more *trayf* than swine, than pork sausage and ham, and on and on! Don't you know they managed to insert a paragraph saying the fund was created only for those who write in Hebrew! Yiddishists protested loudly, shouting and arguing, I among them. What an outrage, that one Jew should ostracize another because he speaks Yiddish, as if they were the real Jews and we were Karaites, rejecters of the Talmud, converts, or impious louts! Peace-loving people intervened, most of all the chairman, Reuben Breinin, that famous Hebraist who edits a Yiddish paper in America. And they worked out a compromise (long may they live!) Even though we write in Yiddish, we are also Jews, the equal of any Jew. But since there was a sharp difference of opinion—some who don't recognize us because of our language, they proposed to take a vote by a show hands, as the Germans did at the congress. Almost thirty hands went up. Fifteen were for Hebrew and fourteen were for Yiddish. An even louder outcry ensued and an even greater racket. People almost came to blows! In fact people did, but for another reason.

But you must surely want to know how the story ended? The end was that we left with nothing! The Hebraists and we went our separate ways. It remained for us Yiddishists to create our own pension fund and the same with the Hebraists. May they live to be a hundred and twenty, we will manage without their favors, with God's help, with no complaints against them! One of ours, Nomberg is his name, said: "Let any one of them come to us with a request to join us to receive support from our pension fund and we will honor it! We will not remind him of how he once threw us out and made outcasts of us!" That's the kind of person Nomberg is and that's the kind of people we all are, and that's how we Yiddishists act! We are of the opinion that when God created the world there was no Hebrew and no Yiddish, and God, blessed be His name, is a better judge of people than we are. He isn't particular in which language you speak to Him. If a woman comes to Him who doesn't speak Hebrew and cries her heart out in a plain Yiddish prayer, doesn't He listen to her? Didn't the Shpoler grandfather speak to him in Polish? Didn't Reb Yitzkhak Levi, the Berdichever rabbi, bare his soul in Russian to the Lord of the Universe every *Yom Kippur* at *Kol Nidrei?* And even if we keep our different lineage straight and pure—what difference will it make a hundred years from now once we are all dead? Will the world hold us in greater esteem? Not a chance! All of us, the Hebraists and the Yiddishists alike will be laid deep, deep in the earth, so why make so much over our differences?

I said this very thing to one of them, a famous writer who is also a deep thinker and the publisher of a newspaper. His name is Klausner and he calls himself Doctor Klausner. He heard me out thoughtfully, considered what I had said, smiled, and admitted that my ideas had been spoken before by a great, a really great philosopher, whose name he mentioned but which I have forgotten. When the time came to say our farewells, he proferred two fingers and said he knew I sometimes wrote in Hebrew too but he hoped there would come a time when I would reconsider and come over entirely to them, the Hebraists. We parted the best of friends!

I parted good friends with everyone, embraced everyone before leaving. That's my way, thank God—I don't fight with anyone. You know I hate quarrels. Jews don't need to fight, there's no reason for it. Meanwhile I am preparing to leave Vienna, I have train fare sent by the editors and my mind is already filled with schemes and more schemes about how our pension fund can get more money because the more money a fund has the better it is for both the fund and its members. And as I have no time, I will make this short. God willing, in my next letter I will write you everything at greater length. In the meantime, may God grant us all health and success. Kiss the children for me and send my best and most friendly regards to your mother, whom I honor, and to the whole family, each and every one.

From me your husband Menachem-Mendl

42. Sheyne-Sheyndl from Kasrilevka to Her Husband, Menachem-Mendl, in Warsaw

To my dear, honored, renowned, and wise husband, Menachem-Mendl, may his light shine forever.

FIRST OF ALL, let me tell you that we are, thank God, in the best of health. Pray God we hear the same from you, never worse.

SECOND OF ALL, I am writing you, my dear husband, that we, I and my mother, long life to her, have just came from the cemetery with swollen eyes and aching hearts. We both cried our eyes out at my father's grave and drank deep of our troubles. As my mother says, "You have to have the heart of a Tartar to withstand what is going on at our Holy Place on the first day of the month of *Elul* when people come in droves to honor the graves of their relatives." People come from everywhere, mostly women, countless women, as many as stars in the sky! It's as busy as a town, I tell you! After the pogrom and after the cholera, may it never happen again, and after Jews were driven from the villages, the cemetery is growing in the length and the breadth. It has grown so quickly that there will soon be no place to bury anyone. We'll have to buy more fields or we'll need, as my mother says: "to beg God to die sooner . . ." Picture it, behind my father's grave, of blessed memory, are three rows of fresh graves, among them more than half as yet not marked with gravestones. You have to have the mind of a cabinet minister or of a Yekhiel, the cemetery warden, to find who is buried where! That Yekhiel must be made of iron to put up with all the women who practically tear him limb from limb: "Reb Yekhiel, show me where my husband is!" "Reb Yekhiel, show me where my father is!" "Show us where our mother is!" He remembers every one by heart, knows where every dead person lies. You should see Yoel, the cantor! If they don't tear him to bits at *Rosh Khodesh Elul*, it's a miracle! I don't know how it is every year—this is the first year we visited my father's grave—but the wailing and the weeping and the keening of the women was so loud that my enemies should have as many years as we were able to hear the cantor sing the memorial prayer. All you could see was a Jew weaving back and forth in prayer and when he was finished, he stuck out his hand to be paid—that was the most important thing for him. As my mother says: "It is written that rabbis and cantors were created by God to take from the dead and from the living . . ." What do they care about someone's else's pain or tears?

It seems to me a stone would melt watching a woman like Khyena, the widow, throwing herself from one grave to another. One minute, it seems, she was lying on one grave, wailing hysterically, and then there she was on another grave weeping in another key, and before you turned around— aha, she was crawling onto a fresh grave and her cries were reaching the very heavens! She owns an entire estate of graves, that Khyena! But where does a woman get so many tears and so many complaints? You should hear her complaining to the dead—you have to be made of iron! But this is still better compared to what is going on on the other side of the cemetery! I am talking about the poor people who tug at your sleeves, tear coins from your hands, make you black and blue begging for a little handout. *Rosh Khodesh Elul,* my mother says, is *their* time, the poor people. "If poor people," she says, "didn't have *Rosh Khodesh Elul,* they would be utterly destitute . . .'

Why am I telling you all this? So that by reading about these days of mourning you will remind yourself that you have a home somewhere and a wife, till a hundred and twenty years, and children, may they be well, and if you remind yourself, you will arrange to make your travels shorter so you can come home sooner. We are all so looking forward to seeing you. Almost the whole town! But there is something that doesn't sound right to me, do you hear, Mendl? So you suddenly decide to come home? I won't be surprised if along the way you don't run into seventeen *shlimazels* who will turn your head eighteen times with their dreams and schemes, "*L'kho Dodi*" books, crazy deals, air-headed plans and so on? You can say about me, Mendl, that I am a small-town woman and whatever else you want, but I don't have enough room in my head for your miracles and harebrained schemes, like renting Israel, which you put off from one day to the other. Make up your mind—if you have something to say, say it! Why do you have to wait to be recognized? That's one thing.

And the second thing has to do with all your fine experts, the Zenists who led you by the nose at the congress. I must tell you the truth, I can't believe they are as eager to go to Israel as you say. It's common sense—if you love Israel, you go to Israel, not to Vienna. As my mother says: "If you want to start the Sabbath meal, you don't start with the Sabbath songs, and if you sing the Sabbath songs, it's a sign you're finished . . ." They would have done better to make the congress here in Kasrilevka. At least that way the few rubles you spent there would have stayed here. You did a good deed for the Germans, who are not worth my old shoes rolling around the attic! You wasted money there while here poor Jews don't have enough for the holidays. At least at Passover the poor are provided with matzo and wine but at the High Holy Days there is not even that! If your Zenists would give it one moment's thought they would bury themselves alive with shame!

But what are my words to you now that you are in your glory with such great people who are above speaking Yiddish with a Jew? I would just like to know who this Shishkin is who you say won't let anyone speak a word of Yiddish? How, tell me, does a Jew have so much gall? It seems to me that even the goyim, forgive the comparison, wouldn't issue such an evil decree forbidding us to speak to one another in our own language! And who is this Pismenik whom you're so afraid of? Blessed be the hands of God if He were to put enough sense into Pismenik's head to convince all of you to stop handing out honors like at Simkhas Torah, stop making each other president and better have in mind that Jews are without work and are being persecuted everywhere. It's a terrible thing when I am now considered rich, not only in the family but in the town itself. They don't let me breathe, they propose business deals to me, and more than anyone, Uncle Avraham-Moishe is free with his advice about what to do with the little bit of money I've saved up over the summer because I hardly spent anything. I share an apartment with my mother and I don't care about clothes. Only food and tuition for the children cost me any money. You should come and hear what they've learned. I am such an ignorant person, I don't even know which *cheder* is better for them. And by the way, if you were here, we would decide together what to do with the money. It's a shame. We could do something with it, though my mother gives me the best advice. She says I should hide the money where no one would know, not even you. She says: "It's wiser for the housewife if the cat doesn't know that there's sour cream in the house . . ." But never mind, let us live to see you soon in good health and to see what your face looks like, if you still look respectable, as I wish you all good things and eternal happiness your true faithful wife

Sheyne-Sheyndl

43. Sheyne-Sheyndl from Kasrilevka to Her Husband in Vienna

To my dear, honored, renowned, and wise husband, Menachem-Mendl, may his light shine forever.

FIRST OF ALL, let me tell you that we are, thank God, in the best of health. Pray God we hear the same from you, never worse.

SECOND OF ALL, let me tell you, my dear husband, that this is the second letter I am writing without having any idea where in the world you are, what you're up to, where you are traveling from or where you're traveling to or where, with all this traveling, you will end up. As my mother says: "The cloud doesn't know where the wind will take it . . ." Out of curiosity, I wrote your editor asking where you were, but he must have swallowed his tongue—not a word in return! I guess it's beneath his dignity to answer Menachem-Mendl's wife! I was not about to write a third time. That would be begging. As my mother says: "Whoever doesn't want to come to me, doesn't have to come . . ." When my mother comes out with a saying, you have to understand it. The poor woman is so distraught now during the High Holy Days it's a pity to look at her. It's awful to see how the woman hasn't stopped crying since the beginning of *Rosh Khodesh Elul.* It's been over a month that her eyes have not been dry. As if it weren't enough that we cried our eyes out at the cemetery when we visited my father's grave, Yoelik, the cantor made it even worse with his chanting the *slikhos* prayers that would move a corpse, and then with his *shakhris* and *musav* prayers both days of Rosh Hashanah. He himself was awash in tears as was the congregation. Our Yoelik was always known as a weeper. When he starts to cry you can't stop him. As my mother says: "This Jew was born on a rainy day . . ."

And maybe Yoelik isn't as much at fault as Mendl Beiliss, the one who is jailed in your great Yehupetz awaiting the day when they decide to tell him what they will do with him. That Yehupetz should either burn down altogether or sink into the earth like Sodom. What do they want from this poor Jew? As if we didn't have enough of our own troubles—the usual nice stories one hears about Jews everywhere being driven out, starved, persecuted, and then all those other good things you brag about in your letters, the new salvation and consolation from your congress, God has sent us another affliction! Whenever someone comes from Yehupetz they bring news about this Mendl Beiliss. They never tire of it! Wherever you go, all you hear is Mendl Beiliss and only Mendl Beiliss. In the synagogue and in the market and even in the bathhouse, forgive my mentioning it—everywhere. You go to the butcher shop and ask the butcher for a better cut of meat and he says: "Mendl Beiliss would be happy with that piece . . ." You go to Ezriel the fishmonger and complain about the fish. It's not fish, it's good for bait. He will tear the fish out of your hands angrily and say: "Bait? Mendl Beiliss doesn't even have that!" And the rich people, may nothing good happen to them as long as they live, all they need is an excuse. You ask them for an extra ruble for the poor who haven't enough for the holiday and they come back at you with a groan: "Mendl Beiliss would gladly give up his holiday if he could be free." What can you say to that?

There is this Yoneh Krepel who just came into some money. He really said something worth remembering to my mother the evening before *Rosh Hashanah*. She went to ask him for a donation for a homeless family, describing to him their poverty and pain. Yoneh didn't want to hear about it and replied that Mendl Beiliss had it a lot worse! My mother ran into him as he was hastening to the synagogue the evening of *Rosh Hashanah*. She stopped him and said quite familiarly, even though he is now rich: "Yoneh, go back." He looked at her, "What do you mean?" "Your prayers will be wasted." "Why will my prayers be wasted?" "Because it is written that prayer without charity is a petition to God without an official stamp—it isn't accepted." Yoneh Krepel didn't respond to her at all but he understood her very well. If you could get to him at this very minute, you could drag out of that miser the largest contribution.

Everyone here is so fixed on the terrible stories they tell about Mendl Beiliss that when the cantor began chanting the prayer describing the Day of Judgment, the congregation started wailing and weeping, the men as well as the women. And when it came to the words, "You judge and punish and know everything and are a witness. . . ," all understood this meant the trial that Mendl Beiliss has to suffer, and all felt a chill passing over their bodies. And later, at the words, "And You open the Book of Remembrances . . . ," it was as if the heavens opened! Women were fainting and had to be carried out one after another, one after another! My mother is right when she says: "If our tears don't wrest this Jew out of prison, it is a sign that all the doors of heaven have been locked . . ."

I would just like to know one thing, Mendl, you are a man of the world and have to do with great people, what exactly is going on with this blood libel against Mendl Beiliss? From what I hear people say, I cannot figure it out. I beg God that we get through the *Yom Kippur* fast in good health and that we can welcome the dear holiday of *Succos* and the beloved *Simkhas Torah*. I pray the One Above will be merciful and you will finally come home as you promised for the last days of the holiday, but it is the ten days of penance and one must tell the truth,—I cannot really believe that just like that Menachem-Mendl will pick himself up and come home! As my mother says: "No *Succos* passes but is followed by joyous *Simkhas Torah* . . ." Well then, Mendl, I would like to see it, but may God grant you enough sense not to travel, God forbid, the final days of *Succos!* Do you think I'll do something to you? I won't do anything to you, but you'll know what kind of God we have and you will regret it the rest of your life, the ten days of penance notwithstanding! As I wish you all good things and eternal happiness your truly faithful wife

Sheyne-Sheyndl

44. Menachem-Mendl from Yehupetz to His Wife, Sheyne-Sheyndl, in Kasrilevka

To my dear, wise, and modest wife, Sheyne-Sheyndl, may God grant her many years!

FIRST OF ALL, let me tell you that I am, blessed be His name, in good health and spirits, and may the Blessed One grant that we hear from one another only good news of comfort and salvation for us and for all of Israel—Amen!

SECOND OF ALL, let me tell you, my dear wife, that I am in Yehupetz! That is, not in Yehupetz itself, but near Yehupetz, on the other side of Yehupetz, on the Slobodka, which is in Tschernigover province. You will surely ask what I am doing here. It's because of Beiliss! Writers from all over the world have gathered here on account of Beiliss, I among them, and you hear nothing but Beiliss, Beiliss, Beiliss. What price fame! I never dreamed I would turn up in Yehupetz. I would much rather, believe me, be visiting in Kasrilevka at home with you, my dear wife, and with the children, may they be well, and with the whole family—it's been such a long time since we've seen each other! I am as guilty in this as Beiliss is guilty. Let me tell you how it happened.

A half minute before leaving Vienna and the congress, all packed for the journey, I received an urgent telegram from the editors, saying: "URGENT. GO IMMEDIATELY YEHUPETZ. BEILISS CASE."

Receiving this bomb, I was struck dumb. First of all, why would they need me in Yehupetz and what do I have to do with Beiliss? And second of all, how can I show my face in Yehupetz—I don't have a permit? I immediately sent off a telegram to the editors, also urgent: "URGENT. HOW FIRST GET PERMIT?"

A furious reply arrived—my editor is an angry man: "DON'T WORRY, MENACHEM-MENDL—DON'T ASK FOOLISH QUESTIONS—GO IMMEDIATELY YEHUPETZ!"

You can't be ungrateful so I had to go to Yehupetz! Ay, but how would I get a permit? Well, it's the same old story, as your mother says: "Whatever will be with all Jews will be with Reb Jew . . ." And in truth, quite a few Jews travel every day to Yehupetz without any permit—and what happens to them? Are they killed? And so I went. I arrived in Yehupetz toward evening. It was already pitch-dark outside, damp and cold, but I was actually happy it was dark. Why do I need anyone to see me? Not because I am afraid, what do I have to be afraid of? Did I steal something? Or murder someone? It's just that I hate to have anything to do with the police. I hired a coachman and told him, "Go!" and he asked me: "Where to?" I said to him again, "Go!" The stupid goy, you tell him to drive and it's not enough for him!

To make a long story short, we were driving along and I was thinking: what shall I do? Where shall I go? They'll kick me out even before I set one foot down. I remember that time, that terrible time when I lived here and knew the taste of being an illegal resident, when I wasn't allowed to spend the night, when I trembled like a thief, lay freezing in misery in an attic all night or curled up like a dog in a cellar. There were plenty of other such memories compared with which the suffering of a sinner in his grave is nothing, and I had a thought: what if I had the driver go back to the station, bought a ticket and went straight home to Kasrilevka to celebrate the holidays? But then again, I thought: what about my job? If the editors order you to go, there's no excuse, I could wind up without a job! Bad—what to do? Then I remembered. Wait! I had a good friend who lived here whom I met recently in Vienna at the congress and with whom I became close! That was the teacher, the Hebraist, the one who with his raised hand almost murdered our Yiddish and who became a soul mate of mine afterwards.

I had written down his address. He lived somewhere on the Podol, on the Nizhne Rampart. He's a good man, I thought, he will help me out when I need him. He's not terribly rich? That's no tragedy. On the contrary, it's easier to get a favor from a poor man than a rich one—may I have a rich man's blessings! Without thinking about it too long, I called out to my driver: "Go to Podol, on the Nizhne Rampart!"

Hearing the words, "Podol," and "Nizhne Rampart," the driver, a goy, turned his head to look me over and decided I must be a Jew, not otherwise, because all the Jews live on the Podol. I was thinking: "What do I care if you look me over? Look me over till your eyes bug out of your head! So long as nothing worse comes from your looking me over. I glanced right and left—plenty of people walking around, thank God, and some soldiers also, armed and on horseback like during a pogrom, may it never happen again. I have become an expert on these matters and have a sixth sense. I suddenly felt very melancholy and my soul was heavy but I didn't want to let on to my driver. I took heart and called out to him in a loud voice: "Aha, knock wood, there are lots of people here, I see!" He turned and looked at me with one eye, let the horse slow down some and said: "They are trying your brother." I felt a pang in my heart but I played dumb. "Who is that?" The goy replied: "Beiliss!" I pretended not to know anything about Beiliss and didn't look at him. "Why are they trying him? Is he a horse thief or something?" He didn't answer, but whipped the horse and looked into my eyes with such cunning that my innards turned to ice. But let him know it? To the devil with him! Then I ordered him sternly: "Drive faster and you'll get your tip for vodka. (May you have a stroke for scaring me for no reason . . .)"

I arrived safely at the Nizhne Rampart, paid the driver and tried to figure out where in the world I was. It was pitch black. No street lights, you could be killed right then and there and not a rooster would crow. I felt along the walls, scrambled up slippery steps, and finally located my friend's place. True, not a fancy palace—Brodsky, I imagine, lives much better—but when my friend saw me, well, what can I tell you, just as if he had seen his father returned from the Other World! He put down his work and embraced me warmly as if we had not seen one another for ages! *Sholom aleikhem! Aleikhem sholom!* Welcome to my guest! What are you doing here? How is Menachem-Mendl? And you? Fine, fine. Not great but so-so. So it went, we talked and talked, and of course, in plain Yiddish, without ceremony, without any song and dance. And I asked him how come he had discarded his Hebrew, to which he responded with a wave of the hand:

"Eh, who can think of that? Now there is nothing else for us but Beiliss, only Beiliss!"

In short, I heard from him accounts and more accounts all about Beiliss, stories that would make your hair stand on end! We didn't stop talking and we repeated all the developments to date of the blood libel litigation. And we asked one another: God Almighty, how could this have happened? Can it be possible? Where are we? What times are we living in?

Meanwhile time was not standing still, it was well into the night and we were having our fill of sorrows. "You cannot forget your body," he said, "you have to put something in your mouth. Go wash up, Reb Menachem-Mendl." We washed, sat down and had a bite to eat—not a fancy meal, I imagine they eat better at Brodsky's—and we again began talking Beiliss and again blood libel. It was beginning to make the head spin and the eyes glaze over. "We have to give a thought, Reb Menachem-Mendl, to sleeping, don't you think?" he said. "Why not?" I said. Well, it's fine to say sleep, if

there's a place to do it but all my friend possessed was his own little sofa with one little pillow. He offered me the sofa and the pillow and said to me: "Here's the sofa, get undressed, Reb Menachem-Mendl, lie down and sleep." "And you?" I said. "Don't worry about me," he said, "I'll find a place for my head." I said, "No, you lie down on the sofa and I'll find a place for my head." Back and forth it went, I on the sofa, he on the sofa, when suddenly from the apartment next door we heard a noise, a familiar noise to me which sounded like trouble. I am, thank God, very experienced in these matters and have a keen sense of hearing. I said to him, "I think it's a house search." He said, "I think so too." I said, "What shall we do? We need to hide." He said, "I think so too." He was terrified and we spoke very quietly so as not to be heard. "Where can we hide?" I said. "That's not a problem. I have an attic and a cellar," he said. "Which do you prefer?" I said, "It's all the same to me, so long as we don't have to march to Kasrilevka in a prison-gang the night before the holiday, God forbid." "Do you know what?" he said, "Why should we both risk our lives in the same place? Let's do what it says in the chapter about Jacob in the Bible: If they catch one of us in the attic, at least the other one in the cellar will be safe. Or the other way around. How do you like that idea?" "The idea," I said, "is a good one, but I think we had better make tracks."

To make a long story short, we spent the whole night in fear and terror, may such a night never return! We finally lived to see daylight and as soon as it was light enough, I grabbed my belongings and prepared to leave, but my friend wouldn't let me, saying in Hebrew:

"What's your hurry? Don't worry, it's nothing. I've been living here almost half a year and on this street there have been no more than three or four of these searches. Believe me, we make more of a fuss over it than it is worth. It's just bad when a search happens at night, one is frightened, you think who knows what, but in the morning, when you come through it in one piece, you feel a little ashamed of yourself!" That's the way he spoke to me, wishing to convince me to stay. But I refused. I was adamant and stated that if he were to give me a roomful of gold, I would not spend another night there!

So we parted and I went as fast as I could to the Slobodka that is part of Tschernigover province where Jews can live freely wherever they wish, except in the villages. I managed to rent a room with board and sat down to write you a letter, and as soon as I finish it, I'll go to Yehupetz. During the day they allow you to be there and do what you wish. I'll try to meet with the people from the newspaper. Almost all the editors are in Yehupetz. And as I have no time, everyone here is busy with Beiliss, I among them, I will make this short. God willing, in my next letter I will write you everything at greater length. In the meantime, may God grant us all health and success. Kiss the children for me and send my best and most friendly regards to your mother, whom I honor, and to the whole family, each and every one.

From me your husband Menachem-Mendl

45. Menachem-Mendl from Yehupetz to His Wife, Sheyne-Sheyndl, in Kasrilevka

To my dear, wise, and modest wife, Sheyne-Sheyndl, may God grant her many years!

FIRST OF ALL, let me tell you that I am, blessed be His name, in good health and spirits, and may the Blessed One grant that we hear from one another only good news of comfort and salvation for us and for all of Israel—Amen!

SECOND OF ALL, let me tell you, my dear wife, that I am now a Vasilkover. You will ask what drew me to Vasilkov? I must tell you I didn't have any great longing for it, but if there is no other choice, it's as your mother says: "If you can't go over, you must go under . . ." Just listen to what can happen to a person! After the house search on the Podol that first night with my good friend, the Hebrew scholar, I had more than my share of terror in Yehupetz. I was already on the Slobodka and Slobodka is in Tschernigover province and I should no longer need to worry about a residency permit, house searches, and humiliations, I could spend days in Yehupetz and nights in Slobodka—pretty clever, no? What does God do? He says no! You can't be a smart aleck! If the prophet Jonah was fated to have problems, he found them on a ship in the middle of the ocean. That's how it was with me too.

Keep in mind, I hadn't even spent one night on the Slobodka, hadn't had time to look around and—aha, we have a pogrom! Not a real pogrom, they didn't let it get that far, but it was almost a pogrom. They say a few students got drunk in Yehupetz, headed for the Slobodka, and began threatening the Slobodka Jews! "Your Beiliss! We'll show you!" And they made for the Jewish shops and Jewish homes, almost, almost a pogrom. But God performed a miracle. The police arrived from Yehupetz, dispersed the crowd, arrested two or three of the gang, and it was quiet again. It was so frightening that people were afraid to undress and go to sleep. I thought it over: true, Beiliss is important, but why risk your life, Menachem-Mendl? Will it benefit Beiliss in Yehupetz if Menachem-Mendl from Kas-rilevka receives a stone in the head on the Slobodka?

I waited for morning to leave for Yehupetz, staying clear of anyone on the way and went right to the train station where I bought a ticket for Vasilkov. Vasilkov is not far from Yehupetz, the same distance as Slobodka, maybe an hour further. If the train is already going, what difference does it make if it goes another hour, it's already on the way? As luck would have it, I missed my connecting train because I first stopped off in the Kresht-shatik. I wandered around the Yehupetz station and figured I would be in Vasilkov by supper time and would stay there till the Beiliss trial was fin-ished. Once the trial ended, I would ask the editors for a week off so I could go home to you, my dear wife, and to the children, may they be well, and see everyone and relate everything with pride and joy. In the mean-time I am upset, I haven't accomplished anything, haven't even met with my colleagues from the newspaper. Where could I have met with them when they all are at the Beiliss trial and I am having problems with my documents, am looking for a place to stay and can't find one? With God's help, I will become a Vasilkover, I will stay in Vasilkov and I will get to work. Meanwhile my head is brewing with schemes and schemes and more schemes! And the best scheme is the one I have in mind for Beiliss, for after the trial, God willing. First, you understand, I hope that poor Beiliss will receive at least some compensation for the almost two and a half years he has spent in prison and for the pain and suffering he is un-dergoing even now while sitting in the prisoner's dock. Second, let the world see this "murderer" who provides Jews everywhere with blood for Passover.

In short, my plan is that immediately after the trial ends, Beiliss should not dilly-dally, should spend maybe two or three days at home with his wife and children, catch his breath and forthwith pick himself up and travel all over the world and first of all, to America. There he will make a fortune! In America there are, God bless them, about two million Jews, and I know American Jews. An American Jew won't begrudge a quarter (a quarter is like a half of our ruble) to take a look at Beiliss, just to take a look at him and no more. If we figure only half of the two million Jews will pay to look at him, you have a million quarters, which adds up to half a million rubles in our money. But even if you take off another half and deduct the fare to America, the cost of renting a hall, music, buffet, salads—everything costs money—I had all these figures in mind before and calculated it all— even after all these expenses I can guarantee two hundred thousand! But there is one thing—you need the first little bit of money for the fare. That's not a problem! Donors will turn up who will be willing to lay out the money. For such a cause there will be ten donors for every one needed.

With God's help may we see Beiliss freed! That is now our only thought. You hear nothing these days but that. People talk of nothing else but Beiliss. I went past the stock exchange on the Kreshtshatik, stepped in to Semadeni, where I once spent my days, better to forget them. I had some coffee, looked around and didn't recognize the place! What stock exchange? What Semadeni? A ruin! I saw a few familiar faces, sad-looking, miserable brokers. You didn't see them sitting down together at a table to chat, as in the good old days. You didn't hear them laughing. Apparently there was nothing to laugh about. They just kept grabbing a page of the newspaper, going off in a corner and sticking their noses in the page to read about Beiliss and the trial. What more do you need to know?

I went up to a policeman, one of those who stands on the Kreshtshatik and keeps an eye on Jews so not too many of them will congregate around the banks and offices. He was also reading a newspaper. I snuck up behind him to see what might a policeman be reading. Was he reading about our trial also? About our Beiliss? Sure enough. I stuck my nose in and read a headline in large letters: BEILISS TRIAL! But this little adventure almost cost me. The policeman froze me to the spot with a look! What if he were to grab me and ask for my passport? But I was smarter than he. I quickly stepped into the Volzheski-Komski Bank, got change for a ten-ruble note at the cashier, sat a while (in a bank every customer can sit as long as he likes), then I took off from the bank like an arrow. I hailed a carriage—"Take me to the train station!" Now I could do as I pleased. At the station I am a passenger like any passenger, I can walk around, I can drink tea, if I wish I can sit down and write a letter,—no one can stop me! Right now I am writing you this letter. Soon, without anyone bothering to notice, I board the train and I am off to Vasilkov. And as I have no time—I hear them ringing the bell to board—I will make this short. God willing, in my next letter I will write you everything at greater length. In the meantime may God grant us all health and success. Kiss the children for me and send my best regards to your mother, whom I honor, and to the whole family, each and every one.

From me your husband Menachem-Mendl

ALMOST FORGOT: In addition to my Beiliss plan another plan is brewing in my head. Since Beiliss is a simple person and shy, has never been to America, maybe I should go along with him, do you understand? He will appear before the public, tell of the miracles and wonders he experienced, and I will be the . . . the . . . there it's called "manager" in their American language. Ay, what if the editors won't let me go? Why shouldn't they? What difference would it make to them if I write them from there in detail how Beiliss was received, what he spoke about and what they said about him and what I said.

As above.

Glossary

Bar mitzvah: confirmation ceremony of a male reaching his thirteenth birthday, when a boy comes of age and assumes religious responsibility.

Bourjhuke: nickname for a person who works on the Bourse, or Stock Exchange.

Bris: circumcision ceremony of eight-day-old baby boys according to the covenant between God and Abraham.

Broit: bread.

Cheder: room in the rebbi's house where children were taught Hebrew, prayers, and the Bible.

Dayeynu: "It would be enough." Sung from the Haggadah at the Passover seder to refer to all the great deeds God performed for the Jews, any one of which would have been enough.

Eretz Yisroel: the land of Israel.

Fleish: meat.

Ganev, gonif: thief, robber.

Gehennum: Hell, inferno.

Gut Shabbos: Good Sabbath.

Haknesset Kalah: Bridal Society

Hatikvah: "The Hope," the Zionist and Israeli national anthem.

Kayn eyn horeh: literally, no Evil Eye; the equivalent of knocking on wood for fear of retribution for being presumptuous, for excessive praise, or when one hopes there is truth in one's words.

Kohane: member of the ancient priesthood.

Korakh: Hebrew equivalent of King Croesus, meaning very rich.

L'khayim: "To life!" Said as a toast.

Mazel tov: good luck, congratulations.

Megillah: the Book of Esther, the story of Purim, written on a scroll and read aloud, but has the colloquial meaning of any long, drawn out story.

Mentsh: human being, responsible, mature, decent person.

Milkh: milk.

Momzer: bastard.

Musaf: extension of the morning prayer, recited on the Sabbath and on holidays.

Nebish: unfortunate, helpless, no personality.

Pareve: neither dairy nor meat.

Rebbetzin: the rabbi's wife.

B&T # 983442
5/23/01

BALDWIN PUBLIC LIBRARY

3 1115 00490 9429

NO LONGER THE PROPERTY OF
BALDWIN PUBLIC LIBRARY

26.95

SS
Sholem
Aleichem

Sholem Aleichem,
  1859-1916.

The further
  adventures of
  Menachem-Mendl.

DATE			

BALDWIN PUBLIC LIBRARY
2385 GRAND AVE
BALDWIN, NY 11510—3289
(516) 223—6228

BAKER & TAYLOR